INTRODUCTION

A Living Doll by Cathy Marie Ha...
Widow Rosemary Fulton delivers a...
church nursery. Paul Kincaid sees l...
him the way to rescue children from...
inside Rosemary's innocent rag dolls buys precious lives. . .but when
Rosemary suspects he's smuggling, does he dare trust her with his
secret? When ordinary people serve the Lord, extraordinary things
happen—sometimes unexpected things, too—like love.

Filled with Joy by Kelly Eileen Hake
With the world at war, Valerie Fulton throws herself into selling
war bonds and helping make dolls to save orphans from the
Nazis—but deep inside, she aches from the loss of her fiancé.
Roy Benson must rebuild his life after being injured. As a ser-
viceman, he's invited to stay with the Fultons for the holidays.
The charming soldier manages to prove himself worthy of their
trust—but can he also win Valerie's heart?

A Thread of Trust by Sally Laity
Soon after her arrival in Copenhagen, Annelise Christiansen's
adventurous brother, Axel, plunges her into Danish underground activities. Then, to enable two tiny Jewish refugees to
escape Nazi tyranny—and help Annelise avoid the unwelcome
attentions of an infatuated German officer—Axel orchestrates
her engagement to charming American forger Erik Nielsen, a
man she barely knows. *It's for the children,* Axel avows. *After all, a
fake wedding won't change her life. . .or will it?*

A Stitch of Faith by Dianna Crawford
Lucky could've been Axel Christiansen's middle name. He inherited not only a thriving business, but more than his share of
dash and daring. Even when the Germans invaded Denmark, he
charmed their high command while brilliantly spying for the
Danish underground. Then one night the Nazis recognize him
when he stops to help Sorena Bruhn, a young woman desperate
to save a Jewish boy from the Gestapo. From that fateful moment,
the three are in a run for their very lives.

The
STUFF OF LOVE

© 2004 *A Living Doll* by Cathy Marie Hake
© 2004 *Filled with Joy* by Kelly Eileen Hake
© 2004 *A Thread of Trust* by Sally Laity
© 2004 *A Stitch of Faith* by Dianna Crawford

ISBN 1-59310-258-5

Scripture quotations are taken from the King James Version of the Bible.

Cover image © Corbis

Illustrations by Mari Goering

This book is a work of fiction. Names, characters, places, and incidents are either products of the author's imagination or used fictitiously. Any similarity to actual people, organizations, and/or events is purely coincidental.

Published by Barbour Publishing, Inc., P.O. Box 719, Uhrichsville, Ohio 44683, www.barbourbooks.com

Our mission is to publish and distribute inspirational products offering exceptional value and biblical encouragement to the masses.

Member of the
Evangelical Christian
Publishers Association

Printed in the United States of America.
5 4 3 2 1

The STUFF OF LOVE

*Joined by Love for Orphans
Four Couples Find Romance
During World War II*

DIANNA CRAWFORD

CATHY MARIE HAKE

KELLY EILEEN HAKE

SALLY LAITY

BARBOUR
PUBLISHING

A Living Doll

by Cathy Marie Hake

Chapter 1

Virginia—January 1941

Paul Kincaid paused outside the sanctuary as the bells pealed an invitation to worship. "Mrs. Ainsley, you've been busy." He smoothly robbed the old woman of the blue-and-lavender-striped afghan she carried and used his other hand to brace her elbow.

She grinned up at him. "Knittin' for Britain."

"This is nice and warm. Someone will be glad to receive it." He patiently helped her up each of the shallow marble steps. Last night's rain had left them slick, and he didn't want her to take a tumble.

"It breaks my heart," she murmured, "thinking of those poor folks over in England, doing without."

Beneath his fingers, her coat was threadbare. The contrast between her thin, old coat and the thick, soft afghan bothered him. She'd spent money she could ill afford on yarn. "I can't knit, Mrs. Ainsley. What if I donate some yarn?"

"Why, that's a generous idea!"

"I'll need specifics—or better yet, why don't you tell Abel

Nannington what you'd like?" Paul opened the church's heavy oak door and helped her across the threshold. "He can deliver it with your groceries this week."

"Yes, yes, we could do that."

Paul escorted her over to the donation box. The women of Gethsemane Chapel had been busy; dozens of multicolored afghans spilled over the brim. *Mrs. Ainsley ought to have the joy of adding hers on top,* Paul thought. He handed the afghan to her, glanced up, and did a double take.

Rosemary Fulton walked by. This time it wasn't her stunning Nordic blond hair or serene smile that captured his attention. The basket on her arm did. In that moment, Paul felt a bolt of sheer relief. *God, is that Your answer to the problem?*

He slid into a pew and tried to still his thoughts and prepare his heart for the message. As the congregation worshiped, the Lord seemed to be speaking directly to him. They sang "A Charge to Keep I Have," and Rosemary Fulton's grown daughter sang the solo "Children of the Heavenly Father."

Pastor Smith took his place at the pulpit. "Today's scripture begins in Exodus two, beginning at verse six. 'And when she had opened it, she saw the child: and, behold, the babe wept. And she had compassion on him, and said, This is one of the Hebrews' children.'"

Carefully, precisely, Paul moved the black silk ribbon marker in his Bible to that page. God's will was clear to him.

"Mr. Kincaid. What a surprise." Rosemary wiped her hands on the hem of her apron and wondered why Paul Kincaid had come calling. They'd exchanged social pleasantries at church;

stood side by side in the kitchen, serving the church Thanksgiving meal; and occasionally bumped into each other around town, but here he stood on her doorstep, hat in hand as a show of respect. The chilly breeze ruffled his thick, tawny hair. "Please, come in."

"Thank you. I'll only be a minute."

She inched back as he stepped across the threshold. Though her daughter often had friends from the youth department come over, it had been years since a mature man had crossed the threshold. Between Mr. Kincaid's impressive height and the spicy scent of his aftershave, she felt engulfed by his masculinity.

"I came to ask about the dolls you had this morning at church."

"Mom," Valerie called, "the chicken!"

"Oh!" Rosemary cast Mr. Kincaid an apologetic look.

"I didn't mean to impose."

"Forgive me." She waved toward the gleaming brass hooks on the wall as she started toward the kitchen. "Please, take off your coat. You're welcome to stay for supper."

A moment later, she turned the golden brown pieces in the frying pan. *These didn't burn. Thank You, Lord!*

No footsteps sounded, but Mr. Kincaid appeared in the kitchen doorway. His Windsor double-breasted, charcoal wool suit accentuated his height and the width of his shoulders. "Something smells wonderful."

"Mom's chicken. It's the best." Valerie sat at the table, mashing potatoes.

"There's plenty." Rosemary turned down the heat. "You're more than welcome to join us."

11

"Yeah." Valerie bobbed her head. "Have a seat."

He smiled at Valerie. "I enjoyed your solo this morning—your voice is very expressive."

"Thanks."

As he reached to pull out a chair, Rosemary hastily suggested, "How about if you take the chair next to that one? Valerie's ankle—"

"It's just a sprain. I was clumsy," Valerie confessed wryly as Paul's brows raised at the sight of the ice bag on her ankle.

"I'm sure Mr. Kincaid has had his share of sprains, too." Rosemary stirred the green beans, then set another place at the table. "I hope you don't mind. We prefer to eat in here."

He looked around the kitchen, taking in the cheery yellow gingham curtains and white cabinets. His brow lifted as he spied the white ceramic canisters she'd brought from Denmark when she had come here as a bride.

"Your kitchen's cozy. I like it. Do you really keep barley and oatmeal in those?"

The deep green lettering across the front proclaimed what each piece held. *Mel, Sukker, Kaffe, Te, Salt*—he could have guessed those. The other two should have been a mystery. "You speak Danish?"

"Enough to get by." A whimsical smile made him look years younger. "When I was growing up, our housekeeper kept treats in those two canisters."

Rosemary waved her tongs at the canister with *Havregryn* painted on it. "I do keep oatmeal in there."

He pointed toward *Byg*. "And the barley?"

"Cookies." Valerie laughed. "But you're out of luck. I ate the last one yesterday."

He chuckled. "I've been unforgivably rude to pry. Had they been English, I wouldn't have asked. For a moment, I became a boy again."

"It's understandable." Rosemary turned a chicken wing as the pan sizzled. "I keep only mint tea in the tea canister because the fragrance reminds me of my grandmother's house."

When Valerie awkwardly tried to scrape the side of the bowl, he lifted it away from her. "You're at a distinct disadvantage, trying to do this while seated." He proceeded to continue mashing the potatoes, went to the icebox and added a splash of milk, and whipped them to a satisfying texture.

"You know how to make potatoes?" Valerie's voice held the surprise Rosemary felt.

A grin lit his face. "My first father was Swedish and insisted Mom hire a top-notch cook. By staying in the kitchen, I got treats. While I was there, she put me to work."

Rosemary grimaced. "That's a handsome suit. You don't want to get food on it."

"It wouldn't be the first or last time."

Five minutes later, the meal sat on the table. Rosemary didn't know what to think. Paul Kincaid managed to act as if he were part of the family. It boggled her mind how he stepped in, decided what needed to be done, and set to work. After finishing the mashed potatoes, he'd sliced half a loaf of bread. Rosemary couldn't recall the last time a man had asked the blessing at their table, and she gladly accepted his offer to say grace.

Once they started eating, Paul looked at her intently. "Had I known you could cook this well, I might have come asking for dolls months ago!"

She smiled. "Thank you. So you're looking to buy a doll?"

"I'd like several. I'd also like another slice of bread. I haven't had homemade bread for nine years."

"Nine years!" Valerie hurriedly passed the basket to him.

As he helped himself to a slice, he said, "Widowers don't bother to bake. We buy those convenient, already-sliced loaves and make fools of ourselves over fond memories of cookies."

Rosemary shook her head. "I found your memory charming."

Paul pensively spread butter on the bread. "Your dolls are charming."

Rosemary figured he didn't want to discuss having lost his spouse and the odd ways little things could trigger the memories and make the loss feel new all over again. How often had she felt that same way? She took his cue and asked, "Do you have a preference as to the size or hair coloring?"

He shrugged. "A variety—blond, brunette, black-haired. More dark-haired ones, though. The size you had at church today looked perfect."

"Little girls tend to like dollies that look like them. Do you need plaits or short curls?"

He chewed slowly, appreciatively, then swallowed. "A variety. It'll allow me to be flexible."

"Oh. I just assumed they were for a niece or—"

"Well, I do have two nieces; however, they're close to Valerie's age. I have several business associates, and I thought the dolls would be suitable gifts for their children. I'm willing to pay whatever you feel is fair."

"That's very generous of you." Rosemary dabbed the corner of her mouth with her napkin. "I'm more than happy to make them, but if you're in a hurry, girls seem to love Raggedy Ann dolls."

"No, no. I want these all to be homemade. That personal touch is what makes them special. Each should be unique."

"When would you like them, and how many do you need?" He turned to Valerie. "Will you help your mom?"

Valerie burst out laughing. "Me? Sew? Oh, I'm sorry, Mr. Kincaid, but I'm hopeless if you put a needle in my hands."

"But you can sing. You can't be good at everything." He turned back to Rosemary. "I don't want to pressure you, but I'd love a bunch of them as soon as is reasonable."

"How about a week and a half? I'll have some done, and when you come get them, if you still want more, you can tell me. I'll need to figure out what the cost is since I just used scraps to make the ones for the church nursery." She picked up the platter and passed it to him. "Help yourself to more chicken."

"Thank you, I will." He accepted the plate and forked a crispy thigh onto his plate. Paul said he traveled extensively, acquiring art for museums and private collectors.

"How do you manage to travel now?" Rosemary couldn't fathom how he got around.

"We're not at war, Mom," Valerie said. "We probably won't be, either. The America First group is strong enough to hold us back."

"Even if we aren't, Roosevelt declared us the 'Arsenal of Democracy.' " Rosemary frowned at Paul. "Hasn't that angered Hitler?"

"America's isolationist stance is crumbling." He grimaced. "Entering Nazi-held countries is forbidden now."

Rosemary and Valerie exchanged a baffled look. "Then how do you manage?"

"Sweden is neutral, and Germany needs its iron, so Swedes are the exception. My legal name is actually Lindhagen. Though my stepfather had me informally assume his last name, my citizenship was never altered."

Valerie tilted her head to the side. "So do I call you Mr. Kincaid or Mr. Lindhagen?"

He smiled. "There's less confusion if I go by Kincaid here in the States."

"How often do you go over there?" Valerie's questions echoed what Rosemary wondered. At times, she'd rued Valerie's curiosity and spunk. Today, those qualities were a blessing.

"Quite frequently now. Many private collectors are discreetly selling off things in neutral countries because the Germans are claiming art as war bounty."

"I read it was bad in France." Rosemary's fingers tightened around her cup.

"Hitler has a special task force called the *Einsatzstab*. They're crating up everything they can get their hands on. The Rothschild family alone lost over five thousand works." He paused. "It saddens me to buy family treasures, but on the other hand, I'd rather allow the owners to receive the money and have the artwork end up in a reputable museum."

He cleared his throat. "My apologies. I didn't intend to spoil a pleasant meal with ugly politics."

"Not at all." Rosemary lifted the bowl of potatoes and passed them his way. "Do you favor any particular style of art?"

He set aside the bowl without taking more. "Though the Oriental art has been well received, I lean more toward the European works. Oils, watercolors, sketches, bronzes, icons—" He held both hands wide. "I like it all. Speaking of art, I noticed the picture in your living room as I came in."

Rosemary smiled. "The one of the little girl?"

He nodded.

"Mom loves that picture. Dad bought it for her when they went to Copenhagen," Valerie said.

Paul's eyes lit up. "So it's an original Aigens?"

"Yes. You're welcome to take a closer look."

He let out a throaty laugh. "Now there's a quandary I don't mind: having to choose between the company of two lovely ladies and a tasty meal, or gazing at a fine piece of art." He winked at Valerie. "I'll stay put. The painting will still be there after lunch."

To Rosemary's delight, Valerie laughed. It was a rare sound these days. Her fiancé had gone to Canada, enlisted, and been killed in action. Grief still held Valerie in its grip, so moments like this when she found happiness were particularly precious.

They spent the remainder of the meal in pleasant conversation, then Paul admired the painting before he left. As Rosemary washed the dishes, Valerie eased back into her chair. "It's not fair."

"What's not fair?" Rosemary looked over her shoulder at her daughter.

"He makes better mashed potatoes than I do."

Rosemary moaned dramatically. "And you used my recipe!"

Paul slipped behind the wheel of his Duesenberg and set his hat on the gray mohair seat next to him. He'd hoped to catch Rosemary Fulton right after church, but by the time he arranged a delivery of things to Mrs. Ainsley with Abel Nannington,

Mrs. Fulton was gone. A sense of urgency drove him to the door of her stately old home. He hadn't planned to go inside, but her warm smile and the mouthwatering aroma of fried chicken drew him in.

Now he'd return to get the dolls. Last Sunday, Mrs. Fulton had seen him at church and invited him to come for supper on Friday. He'd promptly agreed.

Mrs. Fulton was a widow, but with her daughter at home, there was nothing shady about a gentleman stopping by. He curled his hands around the steering wheel and started down the street.

Truth of the matter was, he'd been watching Rosemary since June. Her nephew, Axel Christiansen, was one of Paul's contacts in Denmark, and he'd requested the favor of knowing if his aunt and cousin were faring well on their own. Even if Axel hadn't asked, Paul would have paid attention to Rosemary. The first time he met her, attraction sparked.

Most women wore stylish full sleeves and French cuffs, but Rosemary wore a white silk blouse with a lace collar. Rich waves rippled her platinum blond hair, framing Delft blue eyes. He thought she looked like an Old Master's painting come to life. Had he not been slated for a mission, he would have asked her to the church's July Fourth picnic.

Other than being home during the holidays, he'd been gone on "business" more often than not. Courting a woman under those circumstances rated impossible. Nonetheless, he'd jockeyed to be next to her to serve turkey at the church's Thanksgiving dinner. He'd learned right away that she was blessed with the gift of works—Rosemary didn't sing solos or chair committees. She was the woman who cooked meals for the new mothers of the congregation, weeded the church rose garden, and replaced the felt in the bottom of the offering plates when it looked worn. Her quiet grace and servant's heart appealed to him.

Only he'd just stepped onto a tightrope. He wanted to get to know her better—much better—but he couldn't be completely honest with her. At least not yet. He hoped she'd forgive him when the time came for him to tell her the full truth.

Chapter 2

I sn't she a charmer?"

Rosemary smiled as Mr. Kincaid pulled the first doll from the wicker basket. "I'm glad you think so."

His large hand dwarfed the doll, and muslin legs flopped on either side of his wrist. He fingered the looping, dark brown yarn curls and grinned. "Some little girl is going to be lucky to get her."

"I made a dozen." She watched as he fiddled with the ruffled apron and reached for another doll. "I didn't know how many—"

"At least one hundred."

His quick answer had her laughing. "I'm glad you like them, but seriously, Mr. Kincaid—"

"It's Paul, and I am serious."

Rosemary sank onto the brown-and-beige-striped chesterfield and blinked. "You really are sincere, aren't you?"

He pulled a few more dolls from the basket and stuck them on his forearm as if they were riding a toboggan. All of them leaned into his chest, but he added yet another. "I'll break hearts if I don't have enough."

"But one hundred?"

He gave her a patient smile.

"I never thought there were that many art dealers."

"There aren't. It is a small circle, but as such, it's good form for me to know about my associates' families. It would be novel for me to give gifts for their daughters and granddaughters. A doting grandfather, seeing all of his granddaughters playing with the dolls I gave them, is more likely to think of me when a work of art becomes available. Surely you can see it's good business."

"So you've given gifts before?"

"You'd be amazed at some of the things I've given as gifts." He flashed her a smile. "A couple of years ago, I had a collector strike a bargain with me, and the thing that motivated him was the Monopoly game he learned I was giving to my associates."

Laughter bubbled out of her.

"Duncan yo-yos are great, too. They take up very little space in my attaché case."

"You can't mean to carry dolls in your attaché case!"

"Why not?" He rubbed his thumb over a mop of yarn hair. "Most will be in a crate, but I'll keep a few with me. No one will think anything of it. Art dealers put a single etching inside a huge container. I've carried containers the size of your wood box that held a carving smaller than my hand. In their own way, your dolls are each a work of art."

"That's quite a compliment."

"An honest one." He studied them. "No two are alike."

"You said you wanted them to be unique. I used four different patterns."

He slid the dolls onto the coffee table and added the last few. Tilting his head to the side, he pursed his lips. "This one—" He lifted the one with inky braids that had been her favorite of the bunch. White eyelet pantalets peeped from beneath a pink-and-white-striped seersucker dress. "Was she hard to make?"

"Actually, she's the easiest pattern of them all. The one in the blue plissé was the hardest."

His mouth twisted wryly. "Plissé?"

"The light blue on your left." Rosemary winced at the memory of having to restitch the seam at the top to catch all of the hair. She'd taken it out three times before it was right. "If you truly want lots of them, that model will slow me down. Of course, I can ask a few women to help me."

"No." His chin came up. "I want them all by you. These are special, and I can give them with the assurance that you'll make each one so she'll hold together. I know they'll be cherished, so they have to be well made."

"I suppose since your contacts are accustomed to quality art, they'll be particular." She looked at the rag babies. "I used everyday fabrics—organdy, gingham, calico. Should I be using silk or rayon?"

"I've never had children, but it seems to me if a doll is dressed in silk, she'll sit on a shelf instead of being played with. The endearing part of your dolls is they are made to be cuddled and dragged around."

"Valerie had one of those." She smoothed her skirt and confessed, "As did I. Mine was dressed just like the one you chose."

"Do you want to keep her for yourself?"

Shaking her head, Rosemary stood up. "I had my fun making her. Let some little girl enjoy her. Pardon me. I need to go check on supper."

He'd come to his feet the moment she rose. Paul's impeccable manners made her feel special.

"I'd like to help. What can I do?"

"Nothing, really. I have a roast in the oven. I'll just make some gravy."

He followed her into the kitchen and grabbed the hot pan holders from her, then opened the oven. "Is your brown gravy as good as that chicken gravy you made the last time I was here?"

"Better," Valerie said as she finished setting the table. "Would you like coffee or tea with your supper, Mr. Kincaid?"

As meals went, it was plentiful, but that was all Rosemary remembered about the food. Seven years of widowhood had left her accustomed to living without a man, but she still felt the loss of masculine presence, strength, and support. Paul Kincaid filled her home with all of those qualities, and she couldn't shake the sense of rightness and balance.

He entertained them with tales about some of his travels. Humor and intelligence sparkled in his stories. Just as important, he proved to be an apt listener. Rich, deep laughter rolled out of him when Valerie told them about the crazy customer she'd had at the bank that afternoon.

After taking a final sip of his after-dinner coffee, Paul methodically rolled up his sleeves, baring strong forearms. "I'll wash the dishes."

"Oh, no." Rosemary gasped. "That's not necessary at all. Valerie and I—"

"Valerie needs to rest her ankle. She's been on her feet all day."

"Actually, I was sitting." Valerie propped her elbow on the table and rested her chin in her palm. She looked thoroughly entertained by this turn of events.

"Good. We want her to heal completely, don't we?" Paul started running water in the sink and added Palmolive. As the bubbles started to pile up, he asked, "What time is it?"

Rosemary glanced at the clock. "Just after seven."

"Great. The Tommy Dorsey Orchestra comes on now. How about if Valerie tunes in some music for us?"

Valerie fiddled with the dials on the Zenith console. After a Nature's Remedy ad, strains of Frank Sinatra singing "I'll Never Smile Again" filled the air. Paul scrubbed dishes in time to the music and occasionally whistled a few bars.

Rosemary rinsed and dried the dishes. Each time she stepped from the cupboard back to the sink, confusion crackled through her. Even when her husband was living, he'd not done dishes. The coziness of sharing such a mundane task was unmistakable but wholly innocent. It felt so good to have Paul there—in their kitchen, by her side. He just seemed to fit.

Lord, don't let me make a fool of myself. Occasional company for a business dealing—that's what this is. Help me to guard my heart and tongue.

His soapy hand brushed hers as he plunged the roasting pan into the rinse water. She shivered.

"Chilly?" He swiped the dish towel from her. "Grab a sweater. We're done in here, and we still need to firm up a schedule and costs."

Rosemary didn't argue. She needed a moment to gather her wits.

"I've been thinking," Paul said as they walked into the living room after she donned her sweater. "The doll that was hard to make—forget making more of her. In fact, you can just stick to the one pattern that you said was the easiest if you'd like."

"I can still dress them differently and embroider different expressions on them."

"Great." He stood in front of the Aigens painting again. "I've seen several of his paintings. He's particularly good with children's portraits. Do you have any idea who the little girl is?"

"None at all." Rosemary smiled. "There's just something so sweet about the way she's nestled into that window seat, looking at the bluebird."

"It's unusual for him to paint a portrait in profile. It adds to the allure of the piece." He turned around. "What kind of sewing machine do you have?"

The change of topic took Rosemary by surprise. She stammered, "Singer."

"Is it a new electric one, or one of the old treadle ones?"

"I have both."

He nodded. "I couldn't imagine you making so many dolls with an old one. You'd wear yourself out. I'm assuming you've calculated the cost of material. What's a fair price for the dolls?"

She crossed the richly colored Aubusson carpet and opened the drop desk front of the antique oak secretary. Handing him the slip of paper, she said, "I made a list of the yardage and costs. I can get two dolls from a yard of muslin, so that's four cents apiece. It depends on which fabrics you want for the clothing."

"I know what gingham is, but the rest of this. . ." He hitched his shoulder. "Plissé didn't make sense to me, and neither do challis, batiste, or percale." Studying the page, he mused, "It's all in a similar range. A few pennies here or there don't make much difference when you can get this many outfits per yard."

"Gingham is sixteen cents—the other is far less."

"Nine to eleven cents?" He chuckled. "I'm not going to quibble about a penny per doll, Mrs. Fulton. Put together whatever fabrics you think a little girl would like."

She'd carefully put everything on the ledger—the embroidery floss, yarn, thread, and cotton stuffing. It would cost about seven cents per doll.

"You don't have a figure here for your labor." He looked at her expectantly.

"I don't know how to do that." She lifted her hands in a gesture of helplessness. "I enjoy sewing. As a banker, my late husband provided well for us. Valerie and I live quite comfortably."

"How long does it take to make one doll?"

"I'm not sure. I cut them out and sewed them like a Ford production line."

His dark eyes glimmered. "The average man earns about two thousand dollars a year. I'll pay you. . .fifty dollars a week."

"Mr. Kincaid! Minimum wage is thirty cents an hour for a man. That's far too much, and I'm not sure I want to be chained to my sewing machine."

"You won't be chained to your sewing machine. I'd want you to feel free to have luncheons with your friends and help out at the church and such. As for pay—you're working as an artisan, so that's worth more."

"I always heard artists were supposed to be starving."

He swept up an armload of her dolls. "But those artists don't know me!"

Paul adjusted the light and carefully wrapped the glittering ruby in a section of a handkerchief he'd torn off. He'd bought a dozen handkerchiefs Thursday at Nannington's with the grand hope of needing to buy many, many more. Nannington had been busy relating how pleased old Mrs. Ainsley had been when she'd found the coat Paul bought for her at the bottom of the basket of yarn, but Paul wouldn't chance buying more handkerchiefs there. No detail was too small to ignore.

Tucking the wrapped gem into the doll's head wasn't all that easy, considering how small he'd made the opening and how wide his fingers were. Still, if he opened the seam any farther, it would mess up her yarn hair and draw attention to the stitching. After poking in a tiny wad of cotton batting over the gem, Paul pinched together the gaping inch and painstakingly sewed it back together.

This was the last one. He'd been up all night finishing the task. Every poke of the needle felt awkward. Perhaps he could have Rosemary show him how to sew. . .maybe if he took a shirt that needed mending, that would provide a good excuse to spend more time with her. He'd been coming up with all sorts of reasons he should drop by. The initial attraction he'd felt for her had grown each time they were together.

"Ouch." Jerking back, he glowered at the drop of blood on his fingertip and knew he needed to concentrate on finishing with this batch without bleeding all over it. As he wiped away the blood, he couldn't take his mind off of Rosemary. She'd worked hard to get the dolls done just in time.

He'd set sail at noon today to obtain an Abildgaard oil for a private gallery. That provided his cover for the trip. Once done with that, as a Swede on business, Paul Lindhagen would slip over to Denmark.

It was there Paul would drop off the dolls.

He'd served in the navy and knew his knots. A figure-eight knot seemed to work well, but the thin thread might still slip through the weave of the fabric, so he repeated another figure eight, then snipped the thread.

He picked her up and examined his handiwork. "Ah, sweetheart, I have big plans for you."

Chapter 3

The voyage to Sweden was uneventful, and the small case of dolls didn't raise any eyebrows. The same customs official examined Paul's belongings on the next trip three weeks later. He opened the much larger crate of dolls and commented, "Someone must have liked your samples last time."

Paul accepted his stamped passport and nodded. "I'd like to see them do well. A widow makes the dolls."

He smiled as he thought of Rosemary. There hadn't been any reason for him to see her other than to pick up the dolls, but he'd been drawn to her serenity and warmth. His working world was full of darkness; Rosemary was a beacon of light. During his time in Virginia, he found himself making excuses to go see her. He'd bought yarn and delivered some to old Mrs. Ainsley and dropped off the rest for Rosemary's rag dolls. Twice, he went over for Sunday supper.

Rosemary couldn't bear to just sit at her table and allow him to fix the second meal. They'd enjoyed puttering around in the kitchen together and took a refreshing walk after cleaning up. They'd spoken about all sorts of things—surviving the loss of a beloved mate, current events, her antics of having learned to drive her husband's old Pierce-Arrow. He took that opening and invited her to drive them both to a small art exhibit that weekend. Their date went smoothly. She happened to mention she hadn't read *Grapes of Wrath*, so he used that as justification to stop by later in the week to lend her his copy.

"Ahh," the customs official drew out the sound and waggled his brow. "So the widow—she is pretty?"

"Beautiful." Paul shoved his papers into a coat pocket. "I'd like to take her a gift. Is there a jeweler you recommend?"

Early the next morning with his Swedish passport that identified him as Herr Lindhagen, Paul boarded a small Swedish vessel bound for Denmark. Danish fishing vessels were out, but the Germans made their presence felt. Paul minded his own business and exchanged a few desultory comments with a *Wehrmacht* officer just before they reached shore. *Lord, thank You for Your mercy and protection. Bless this trip, Father. Let it be successful so we can rescue innocents in Your name.*

Not long thereafter, Paul delivered the crate to Axel, just as he had the first. They stood in the back room of Christiansen Enterprises in Copenhagen and exchanged all but ten of the dolls for a watercolor and two antique miniatures. Those miniatures would provide Paul's *raison d'être* for being in Holland. The Germans had invaded and were starting to round up Dutch Jews. Greedy Nazi officials looted each country of art. Surely these pieces would allow Paul access to the "right" people.

He already had contacts in Germany, Holland, and France—some because of his previous trips, but others courtesy of his friend "Wild Bill" Donovan. If Bill weren't so incredibly patriotic and bright, he'd be downright unnerving. He'd approved the concept of the dolls, though. In fact, he'd managed to slip Paul several *reichsmarks* and loose gems to put inside them.

A small, highly secret cell of people had formed and resolved to do their utmost to ransom the Jewish children. Paul played a pivotal role. The booming gray market in fine art provided an ideal cover.

If Germans looked at his papers and searched his luggage, they were welcome to confiscate the art pieces he would be dealing. The dolls would hide in plain sight.

Axel boxed his share of the dolls into two smaller crates. "I'll make a receipt for these just as I did the last time. That way, it'll be on a manifest so you can deliver more in person or have them shipped with us. We've already showed the import was established, and I'll be able to point out that with the effort going toward agriculture and munitions, the poor children won't receive toys if my business doesn't import them."

"Good." Paul glanced around and asked softly in Swedish, "How many children do you think your network can smuggle?"

"Several families in our church have already taken in children. Can you bring film?"

"Here." Paul pulled three rolls from his suitcase. He'd brought them with the expectation that they'd be used in forging identity papers. Denmark was starting to form an underground and would require far more than those three rolls as time passed. "Next trip, I'll bring more. Anything else you need?"

"I want my sister to go back to America. She refuses and says her place is here with me and our grandmother. Could you talk sense into both of them? Aunt Rosemary has more than enough room to put them up."

Someone entered the warehouse. Paul hadn't heard any

31

footsteps, but the hairs on the back of his neck prickled. He stuck out his hand. "It's a pleasure, Mr. Christiansen. I'd be happy to see those watercolors."

Axel shook his hand. "It's very exciting news." He turned and gave an excellent imitation of surprise. "Herr Torwald! What can I do for you this fine day?"

The pinch-faced man approached. He lowered his voice, "I saw the American come here. I came to beg a favor."

"I'm afraid you're mistaken," Paul said in flawless Swedish. "But I won't take offense that you mistook me for one of them. I couldn't resist buying a new overcoat the last time I went to New York."

Herr Torwald grabbed the sleeve of Paul's suit. "I have a nephew. He's eight."

"You must be proud." Paul shrugged away and pretended not to understand the request to smuggle the boy out of Denmark. He sensed this was a trap. "But I am confused by your request. I don't paint portraits—I am an art dealer."

"Mr. Lindhagen knows my Aunt Rosemary in America. She told him about the watercolors in my grandmother's home." Axel beamed. "He's going to come examine them."

Paul held up a hand. "Now don't get too excited, Mr. Christiansen. They might not be anything at all. I wouldn't want you to be disappointed."

"Oh, but they're from the same set." Axel bobbed his head. "Aunt Rosemary has the winter field. My mother had the summer scene, and when she came back, my sister brought it along. Spring and autumn were still on the wall, and Grams hung summer back between them."

"America's National Gallery of Art is due to open in March.

It would be quite a feather in my cap to buy—"

"Americans," Herr Torwald spat. "They think they can buy anything. And you Swedes—you're growing fat, living off both sides of this war." He glowered, then slowly shuffled off.

Axel cleared his throat. "My apologies, Herr Lindhagen. Desperation leads people to grasp at straws. Shall we go? You must stay to supper. Grams is a wonderful cook."

"I'd be honored."

They walked out of the warehouse, and Axel locked the doors. "I'm able to offer you a ride. The Germans allow me to keep a vehicle since my business helps provide well for the region." He got into the car and muttered under his breath, "I want my sister out of here. This place is overrun with spies."

"You threw him off with the talk about the pictures. If you have watercolors and paper, I'll do a quick set to back up your story."

Axel cast him a sly smile. "I was telling the truth. You're about to stumble onto a treasure."

Paul shook his head in disbelief and chuckled. He took a deep breath. "Actually, I already found a treasure. I wanted to tell you: I've started courting your aunt and intend to marry her."

ز

"There you are." Rosemary walked into the living room and waved toward the basket. A sense of sadness swamped her. How quickly she'd come to anticipate Paul's visits! His intelligent conversation, witty insights, and warmth lingered after his visits. She didn't want this to be the end of their times together, but nothing was more pathetic than a lonely widow chasing after a man. She pasted on a perky smile. "That's the last of the dolls."

Paul let out a crack of a laugh, but it died quickly. "I hope that was an April Fool's joke."

"You said you wanted one hundred dolls." Slowly sitting by the basket, she lifted one and smoothed its sunny yellow skirt.

"That was just the first order." Paul sat down and gave her a patient look. "Those little rag babies are the rage. If anything, I need more, faster."

"Surely you can't have that many associates!"

"I have a special associate." He leaned forward. "Axel Christiansen."

"Axel!" Rosemary nearly dropped the doll. "You know my nephew?"

"I do." Paul patted the striped cushion of the chesterfield in silent invitation.

Rosemary hastened to his side and pled as she took a seat, "How do you know him? I can't believe this!"

"Since he's in the import-export business, he's been of help to me at times in following proper protocol. I've found him to be well informed about all of the increasingly stringent rules."

"Yes, that sounds like Axel. How is he? Is he well? I haven't seen him in almost five years! Letters—they don't come through well anymore."

"Yes, he's well. I have letters for you from him, from your niece, and one from your mother." He drew an envelope from the inside pocket of his suit coat.

"Oh, Paul! You can't know how much this means to me!"

He slipped the crinkled envelope into her hands. "Please don't wait to read them. Axel told me how he and his sister lived with you."

She bobbed her head and tore the envelope in her haste.

"Yes. They're such good children." She let out a nervous laugh. "I guess they're not children anymore. Axel went back to take care of the family business after my papa died. . . ."

Her voice died out as she unfolded the pages and began to read. Tears misted her eyes as she saw her mother's handwriting. Paul slid his arm around her shoulder and drew her into his sheltering strength. His other hand pressed a crisp, white handkerchief into her lap.

Rosemary hungrily read each letter, then reread them. "They sound okay. Are they really safe?" She looked up at Paul.

"Axel looks strong and well fed. He wants more of your dolls to sell."

"I'll make as many as he wants. Can I send letters back with you when you deliver them?"

"Absolutely. Rosemary, even if he didn't want another doll, I'd still like to spend time with you." He tenderly cupped her cheek. "You're becoming very special to me."

Chapter 4

Rosemary looked into Paul's face. "I care for you, too." Here she'd thought this was the last time he would come to her home, and now he wanted to pursue more than a business association—he wanted to pursue *her!* The very thought made her breathless.

The corners of his eyes crinkled. "I'm out of practice with courting. I've been a widower for a long time."

"I've been a widow for almost as long. Even then—" She laughed. "My first courtship was just two visits and several letters. I'm afraid I'm not just out of practice—I never had much to begin with!"

"We'll just do things our way. How does that sound?"

She smiled. "I'd like that."

"Then it's not bad form for me to ask about how you married someone you barely knew? You led me to believe it was a happy marriage."

Rosemary rested her head on his shoulder. "I was a schoolgirl and thought I knew Lief well. Our families did business together, and we seemed well suited. Now that I look back, I can't imagine what I was thinking. After he made two visits and we exchanged letters for nine months, I came to the States and we married. God looks out for fools and children—and in that instance, I think I was both. Yet it was a good marriage."

"I was in my last year of college. I was so poor, all we did was ice-skate or take walks." He chuckled. "It's a marvel Elsie looked at me twice."

"Not at all. Simple pleasures are the best. That time together let her see how smart and fun you are."

"If you keep complimenting me like that," he said, his voice deepening, "I'll be tempted to kiss you."

Rosemary gasped—as much from her reaction as from his comment. She wanted him to kiss her!

"I know," he sighed. "It's far too soon. You'll have to forgive me for forgetting to bring flowers."

"You brought me something much better."

"The letters?"

They crinkled in her hand. "I forgot about them. I was just glad you came home. I worried about your safety while you were gone."

"Mom!"

Rosemary jumped and looked up. Valerie stood in the doorway, eyes wide with shock. At that moment, Rosemary realized just how close she'd managed to cuddle into Paul's side.

"Mom—" Valerie stared at the wet handkerchief. "You've been crying?"

Rosemary let out a watery laugh. "I'm happy, honey."

Valerie crossed the floor and shot a wary look at Paul.

Paul didn't seem bothered in the least. To Rosemary's surprise, he curled his arm a bit more. "Valerie, I'd like to speak with you for a moment, too."

Valerie perched on the edge of the overstuffed armchair. "What is it?"

"Being away made me realize how much I enjoy your mother's company. We're adults and can make our own decisions, and I've prayed about it. I feel the Lord has brought us together, but I'd also like to ask your blessing as we court."

"It's about time." Valerie grinned at them.

Rosemary felt as if a weight had lifted from her shoulders. Even though Valerie was nursing a broken heart, she was generous enough to wish them well. "Thank you, honey."

Paul let out a relieved sigh. "Good."

"So why were you crying?"

"Oh! I forgot!" Rosemary held out the pages. "You'll never guess who Paul knows—Axel! He brought letters!"

"Wow!" Valerie hopped up and grabbed them. She promptly plopped back down sideways in the chair, with her legs dangling over the arm.

Rosemary winced at the sight.

Paul dipped his head and whispered, "Don't. I'm glad she's that comfortable with me around."

A few minutes later, Valerie looked up. "It sounds like they're okay and Annelise is finally over that guy. Thanks for bringing the letters, Mr. Kincaid."

"You're welcome. So now that I'm courting your mom, do you think you could stop calling me Mr. Kincaid like I'm some old grandpa?"

"Just how old are you?"

"Valerie!" Rosemary couldn't believe her daughter's nerve.

Paul chuckled. "I'm forty." He squeezed Rosemary. "It was a reasonable question."

"Since you don't mind questions. . ."

Unsure what her daughter would ask next, Rosemary cringed.

"Yes?" Paul sounded downright blasé.

"What did you do to the mashed potatoes? Mom and I are dying to know."

"It's an old family secret." He pressed a kiss against Rosemary's temple. "Someday, I might have to share it."

Paul shuffled across the linoleum floor along with the beat of "Chattanooga Choo Choo," which played on the Zenith. Washing his hands at Rosemary's kitchen sink, he said, "You're low on oil, and the tires look a bit worn."

Rosemary set down her shears and frowned. "I just bought those tires last year."

"It's not bad at all. They could last awhile yet." He opened the *Byg* canister and helped himself to an oatmeal cookie. That momentary delay allowed him to weigh his words carefully. "I think it would be wise to buy a set now."

"Surely you don't think there'll be a shortage of rubber?" Rosemary picked up her shears again and started cutting more doll parts from the muslin spread across the kitchen table.

"I'd feel better knowing you and Valerie had them in reserve. The rest of the world is suffering from shortages of several things. I don't advocate stockpiling, but since we know you'll need the tires, it's smart to anticipate. I'll pick them up tomorrow."

"If it makes you feel better."

"It does."

"Father McCoughlin was speaking on the radio. He said Roosevelt is wrong and we have no business getting drawn into Europe's war. Even Charles Lindbergh is part of the America First movement. With so many opposed, how do you think America could come to the point of being so involved with what's going on over there that we'd find it difficult to get basic supplies here?"

"With Roosevelt passing the Lend-Lease Act, we're using resources differently, sweetheart. We're bound to see some changes."

"Not like Europe, though. The news said Holland is rationing milk! Can you believe it? Those poor children."

Paul didn't want to tell her it would get much worse. From what he'd seen on his last trip, the Nazi war machine was systematically stripping the countries of their resources. Instead, he reached over and picked up a thin strip of material that ended with a mitt shape. *The arm.* "You're doing something for the children, Rosemary."

"It feels like precious little. Paul, I want to show you something." She left the kitchen and returned with a magazine. "What do you think?"

The words "Jewish Crisis" jumped out at him as he accepted the magazine. The profile of a mother and little boy on the cover made his heart twist.

"It's from 1938." Rosemary's voice shook. "And it talks about the persecution of the Jews in Germany. It says we need to worry that it'll cross the Atlantic."

"I've read similar things. The stories of what's happening over there are true, sweetheart. It's not just Germany. Poland, Bulgaria, France, Holland, Romania—nearly every country the Reich invades develops a policy of mistreating the Jews."

"So it's not just a bunch of lies to try to rope us into the war?"

He said very quietly, "It's the truth."

Tears filled her eyes. She swiped the material into a heap on the table. "What good is this?"

Paul reached across and tilted her face to his. If only he could tell her the truth about how her dolls would save little children—but he couldn't. It wasn't safe. "Sweetheart, children over there don't have toys. Having something to cuddle matters a lot to those little girls."

The door opened, and Valerie swirled in with the spring wind. "I'm back! Mrs. Ainsley said—whoops!" She halted abruptly and shot her mother a guilty look.

Paul regretted only telling a thin slice of the truth, and he was relieved the conversation had been interrupted. He broke contact with Rosemary and folded his arms across his chest. "What did Mrs. Ainsley say?"

Valerie blushed. "It was nothing."

Rosemary laughed. "It's okay, honey." She turned to Paul. "We gave Mrs. Ainsley a kitten to keep her company, so Valerie takes fish to her a couple times a week."

"Fish for Mrs. Ainsley, or fish for the cat?" Paul was sure of the answer, but he wanted Rosemary to know he was on to her.

"You have no room to grin, Paul Kincaid!" Valerie's chin tilted at a challenging level. "Mom and I both know who bought her that nice coat she's been wearing."

Paul pretended not to hear her. "Mrs. Ainsley's not very spry. I don't suppose you'd know who planted all those bulbs that are sprouting in her garden."

Rosemary laughed, and Valerie's cheeks went pinker. She

couldn't meet his eyes and suddenly exclaimed, "Oh, I smell something wonderful!"

"Paul's cooking Swedish beef stew." Rosemary played along with the change in subject and wrinkled her nose. "I don't remember the name. It sounded like *Cyclops.*"

Paul chortled. *"Kalops."*

"Whew. I was afraid you were going to feed me eyeball soup." Valerie finessed the radio dial. Bebop filled the air. "Much better."

"Dizzy Gillespie." Paul nodded. "Great jazz player."

"I like Thelonious Monk better." Just then, the music stopped and an update came across the air about the Canadians pulling American planes across the border that had been provided through the Lend-Lease arrangement. Valerie's smile faded. She turned off the radio, then pointed at the magazine on the table. "No matter where I go, I can't get away from that war."

"Honey. . ."

Valerie held up a hand. "Don't tell me you're sorry. I'm tired of everyone giving me sympathy. Words won't bring back Frank. We're all sending Bundles for Britain and acting as if all they're getting from us is soap, medicine, and blankets. The truth is, lots of American boys like Frank are going over there and joining their army, and Britain doesn't even bundle them back to us for a decent burial! All those mothers from America First went and knelt in prayer by the Capitol building. Instead of old women, maybe it should have been girls like me. Then maybe everyone would see what wars really cost—bridegrooms, young husbands, and babies' fathers!" She ran from the room.

A door slammed shut, but it couldn't completely muffle her sobs. Rosemary buried her face in her hands. "We're only making it worse, you know."

Paul pulled her from her chair and enveloped her in his arms. "You and I understand grief. She's right—no matter where she turns, she's surrounded by reminders. We'll just love her through the sorrow."

Rosemary wound her arms around his waist and rested her cheek on his lapel. "She really does like you."

"Yeah, I'm pretty crazy about her. You. . .well, you, I'm wild about." He threaded his hands through her silky hair. "I never thought I'd fall in love again, but I have. I'll just pray God will bless her as generously as He's blessed me."

Chapter 5

osemary let out a small, disappointed sigh as she looked in the butcher's case. "Better just make it the roast closest to the back."

Mr. Twisselman bobbed his bald head in understanding as he pulled out a tiny one and thumped it onto his scale. "Two pounds even. If Mr. Kincaid were in town, you would have gotten one twice this size."

Rosemary let out a small laugh. Her courtship had become cause for comment around town. The butcher's observation was right, and she enjoyed the fact that Paul shared supper with her and Valerie more often than not when he was in town. Because she tended to shun the limelight, the attention others cast on her on such occasions left her feeling a bit self-conscious. Having Paul in her life more than made up for such fleeting moments.

Mr. Twisselman's mustache twitched as he wrapped the roast in white, waxed butcher paper. "Mr. Kincaid seems like a nice man. He can pick out a good cut of meat, too. Not often you find a man who can do that."

Understanding that was high praise, Rosemary nodded.

"He makes a great stew. The bacon looks nice and lean. I'd like a half pound, please."

"As much Spam as is being sent in Bundles for Britain," he said as he took a handful of rashers and flipped them onto the scale, "you'd think there wouldn't be an ounce of pork left in these United States!"

"I saw those striped quilts Nelly and Wanda made for the bundles. They reminded me of Joseph's coat of many colors." Rosemary watched as he added two more rashers.

My life is like one of those colorful quilts. I thought all I had left were worn scraps, but God brought color and texture back by bringing Paul into my life. There's so much more warmth and purpose.

"Yeah, Bundles for Britain keeps my girls busy," Mr. Twisselman said, oblivious to Rosemary's musings. "Today Wanda's making a baby blanket, though. Marcy Heath had her baby."

"I hadn't heard the news!"

"A boy." He puffed up as if the baby were his own. "Tipped the scale at eight pounds."

"Eight!"

"Yep. Hospital-born, no less!"

"Well then, I won't buy a chicken to roast for them until next Wednesday. The hospital will keep her for a week, you know." She decided she'd go home, gather flowers from her garden, and pay the new mother and baby a visit this afternoon, though. Paul had helped her cultivate the soil for her flower and vegetable gardens. They'd gotten dirty as could be that day. On the days he was so far away, she still found comfort in walking barefoot where he'd worked.

"Anything else today? Ground beef's on sale."

"Oh." She snapped out of that fleeting memory. "What

kind of fish do you have?"

"Mrs. Ainsley was just in." He winked. "She bought some snapper for the cat already."

Rosemary sighed. "Then I don't need anything else today."

"Paul Kincaid better get back soon." The butcher wedged himself behind the register. "Seems to me a certain lady gets mighty lonesome when he's gone."

"The cure for loneliness is hard work. This woman needs to occupy herself instead of mooning around. Nothing's more useless than a lady who sits and pines for a man." She glanced out the window, then sighed again. "But I'm antsy. Since Paul left, the Germans sank the *Robin Moore.*"

"Roosevelt declared a state of emergency. Ships are being careful, and the navy's on alert. Don't worry. Paul will make it home in one piece."

"That's my prayer," she said softly.

"That's $1.59." Mr. Twisselman accepted her money and grinned. "Absence makes the heart grow fonder, Rosemary. A little pining's not bad."

She nodded and left. Truth be told, she kept her hands busy. . .but Paul kept her heart and mind tied up in knots.

Paul spied the Nazi officer and continued to walk through the door of Christiansen Enterprises. As Paul Lindhagen, he had every reason to come here. Balking at the sight of a German would ruin his cover. Instead, he cleared his throat. "Mr. Christiansen, if this is an inopportune time, I can return."

"No, not at all." Axel motioned urbanely toward the Nazi. "May I introduce Captain von Rundstedt. Captain, this is

Herr Lindhagen, an art dealer."

"Herr Lindhagen." The captain nodded his head curtly and studied Paul closely. "What business does an art dealer have with an import-export enterprise?"

Paul made a vague gesture. "You know how it is. Times change. We all adapt as necessary. Of course, the fact that a pretty widow makes dolls I can import is good motive."

"Dolls?"

Axel chuckled. "Yes. I'll have to show them to you. The fact is, the lady in question is my aunt."

"Ahh, I see."

"Speaking of her, your aunt sent you a gift." By openly setting out the bulky package, it made everything look perfectly innocent. Had Paul waffled or tried to hide the package, the officer would have become suspicious.

"A gift? How thoughtful of her." Axel smoothly set the package aside.

"Do not let our presence hold you back." The Nazi motioned toward the bundle. "By all means, open it."

"Thank you." Axel promptly tore through the brown paper. "A camera and film—oh, my!" He shuffled through a half dozen photographs with notable glee. "Pictures of Aunt Rosemary and my cousin Valerie."

"*Sehr schon,*" the captain said.

Axel chuckled. "The gift is very beautiful, or my aunt and cousin?"

"The ladies are both very beautiful. The Aryan ancestry is much evident in the coloring and features. Why do they not live here, with you?"

"Rosemary met her husband in Sweden."

Paul patted himself on the chest. "And if things continue to go well between us, her next husband is Swedish, too."

Axel straightened his shoulders and extended his hand. "Congratulations. Rosemary is a wonderful woman. I approve."

"Thank you." Paul shook Axel's hand.

"So the camera is Swedish, *ja?*" The captain picked up the camera and read the label. "Hessco Model B. The camera is known to me. I personally prefer my Swiss-made Jaeger. It is clever because it can take both glass plates and rolls of film."

Paul nodded. "In my travels, I'll be passing through Switzerland. If you have need of plates or film, I'd be happy to keep an eye out for some."

"So you are a *resourceful* fellow."

Paul shrugged. "It is a small matter. Axel, your aunt expects pictures of you and your family in return. Don't forget. She'll be upset if I go home without them."

"We'll take pictures tomorrow morning. I can just send the film back with you then. You must come to supper and tell Grams the good news. Captain, would you care to join us?"

For a moment, it looked as if the captain planned to agree. Then he shook his head. "I have other obligations."

"Perhaps some other time."

"Yes, another time. Herr Christiansen, Herr Lindhagen. Heil Hitler." He marched toward the office door.

Axel pulled out a ledger book. "Let me find that account here. . . . How many dolls did you bring this time?"

"Fifty. I plan to take a few with me as gifts for my clients, though."

The captain turned around. "I should like to see these dolls."

Chapter 6

Paul pried the lid off the crate as Captain von Rundstedt leafed through the paperwork. The captain set the sheaf of pages off to the side with a decisive shove. "The stamps on the forms are in order."

"Naturally." Paul pulled out several dolls. "Here we are."

The captain pulled two from his arms and tossed them back into the crate. "Dark hair does not appeal to me."

"How many would you like?" Axel's voice took on the schmoozing tone of a businessman.

"One. I have a niece."

Paul didn't so much as blink an eye. The whole rescue operation would be destroyed if this went poorly. He'd planned for such an eventuality, though. A few dolls of each shipment didn't have gold or a gem inside them. He purposefully chose blond, blue-eyed dolls and exchanged their clothing so they wore red, white, and black—the colors of the Third Reich. Those dolls would serve as bribes for any German who got too nosy.

"The flowered dress—it is something a girl would like." The captain started to stuff the bribe doll back into the crate.

"I agree." Paul moved to throw the last two in his arm into

the crate as well. "This pale blue—that color doesn't catch the eye, even if her face is sweet. There is something cheerful about this one, though."

Axel chuckled. "She reminds me of Annelise playing Little Red Riding Hood. All she needs is a cape."

"That story is in a book I bought for my niece." The captain took the doll. He nodded decisively. "*Ja.* She is the one."

"Take her as a gift." Axel smiled.

The captain left, and Axel tugged out a few dolls. "How many do you need to take?"

"Make it a half dozen. Give me another red dress. The Red Riding Hood angle was great."

"I have no idea what made me say that."

"God gave you the words. The minute I saw that Nazi, I prayed for protection. How did we do on the first shipment?"

Axel grinned. "The underground distributed all of the dolls. We were able to forge documents for twelve children. Four are with families here in Denmark—ostensibly they are orphans who came to live with distant relatives. The other eight were taken to safety in Sweden. The second shipment: I don't have all of the information yet. So far, I know two dozen children have gone to safety carrying a rag doll from that group."

"God be praised," Paul said softly as he closed the lid on the crate. "May there be hundreds more."

"Turn down the radio, honey." Rosemary dashed for the phone as Bing Crosby crooned "Only Forever." Breathlessly, she said, "Hello?" into the receiver.

"Hi, sweetheart!"

"Paul! Are you home?"

"Yes. I've been trying to call you all afternoon. The line's always busy."

Rosemary sighed. Most of the families on their party line were considerate, but Myrtle Louis seemed to live on the phone. "It's a problem. I'm sorry."

"It's not your fault. I—"

The line clicked, and Paul stopped speaking. "Hello? Paul?"

"I'm still here. I think we have company."

"I need to use the phone." Myrtle's voice radiated with petulance.

"We just got connected." Rosemary tried to squelch her irritation. "I'm sure you heard the call come through—long and two short rings, which is my signal. You couldn't have mistaken it for your single short ring."

"Well, it's only Paul." Myrtle tsked. "He's at your house all the time anyway."

Paul cleared his throat. "Ma'am, I'm sure Mrs. Fulton's more than considerate of you when you're on the line."

"Well, I never!" Myrtle slammed down her receiver.

"Never?" Paul snorted. "I have a hard time believing she's never on the phone."

Rosemary sang along with Bing Crosby on the radio as her response, "Only Forever."

A deep, rich chortle came over the line. "I must be crazy to travel. The only thing that makes it worthwhile is coming back to you. Go put on a pretty dress. I'm taking you out to supper tonight."

"We can just eat here, Paul. I'm sure you're tired."

"Nope. I'll be there in an hour." He made a smooching sound and hung up.

"I know that smile," Valerie teased. "It's the Paul's-home-and-I'm-thrilled look."

"He's taking us out to supper."

"Not me. You. Mom, it's a date, not a family meeting! Besides, I have plans." She rubbed her hands together. "So what are you wearing?"

"What about my Easter dress?"

Just shy of an hour later, Rosemary heard Paul's Duesenberg come to a halt outside her house. Whistling Jimmy Dorsey's "Green Eyes," Paul came up the walk.

Rosemary hurriedly latched her pearls and patted them in place. She hoped he'd like her dress. Made of pale green silk, it nipped in at her waist and swirled just an inch and a half below her knees. She'd gotten it for Easter, but he'd been away on business that week. This was only the second time she'd worn it.

As he knocked at the door, Rosemary's heart beat twice as fast. She wanted to run down the stairs and fling herself into his arms like a starstruck teenager. *It's his fault. He makes me feel like a young girl again.* As Valerie greeted him, Rosemary dabbed on a little Evening in Paris perfume. The silk of her dress and stockings whispered as she descended the stairs.

Paul waited at the foot of the stairs. Aware their reunion wasn't private, he pulled Rosemary close and brushed a kiss on her cheek. "You look beautiful, sweetheart."

"Thank you." She straightened his tie. "You look very handsome."

"Mom, I'm going to Angela's."

Rosemary frowned at her daughter. "Not until you change, young lady."

"We're not going anywhere, Mom. This isn't the olden days. There's nothing wrong with wearing slacks."

Paul cleared his throat. "I'm not meaning to horn in here, but even if you don't go anywhere, plenty of people might show up."

"Angela wouldn't do that." Valerie shook her head.

"She wouldn't, but her parents might." Paul slipped his arm around Rosemary, and she nestled into his side. "I happened to overhear Mr. Zilde this afternoon. He was grousing about his wife throwing a surprise birthday party for Angela tonight."

"Swell!" She ran up the stairs yelling, "It's a good thing I already bought her that record she wanted!"

Paul's breath stirred Rosemary's hair as he confessed, "I had a bracelet in my car, just in case."

"Did you really?" She smiled up at him.

"Yes, but I'm just as glad. I'd rather give it to Valerie."

His warmth and generosity never ceased to surprise her. She gave him a hug. "I'm sure she'll treasure it."

"Speaking of treasures. . ." He reached over and took a bag from the corner of one of the steps and handed it to her.

Rosemary squeezed the bag. "What is it?"

He started whistling "Green Eyes" again and waggled his brows at the bag.

Laughing, Rosemary opened it and peered inside. "Buttons?"

He reached in and pulled out a fistful. As he let them spill back into the bag, he gloated, "Green eyes. And blue. And brown. I was watching you embroider doll faces the last night I was here. It occurred to me that if you show me how, I could sew on buttons for eyes. Wouldn't that be faster?"

"But these aren't just ordinary buttons." She held one of the bright notions. "These are darling!"

He grinned. "I hoped you'd like 'em. I found them in Switzerland. Look. Black centers, just like a pupil. Black thread won't even show."

"But these are glass. They must've been expensive, Paul."

"You're not fretting over the cost of a bag of buttons, are you?"

Valerie pattered back down the stairs. "Boy, am I glad I read that mix-and-match article in the magazine!"

"You look snazzy," Paul said. "I wish I could match my ties and suits that easily."

"Why should you? Dad couldn't. The pastor doesn't." Valerie gave him a silly smile. "I don't think there's a man alive who isn't color blind."

"Oh, yeah?" He grabbed several of the buttons and jabbed the blunt end of his forefinger at them one at a time. "Look. This one is blue. This one is green. Blue. Brown. Red."

Rosemary and Valerie burst into laughter. He'd purposefully misnamed every last color. "Red?"

"Bloodshot." He flipped it over his shoulder. "Can't use it. Poor kid will think her doll is drunk!"

"Oh, you! Mom, he's impossible!" Valerie opened the door and scampered out. "Good-bye!"

Shutting the door, Rosemary nodded. "What am I to do with you? Each time you come, you bring gifts. You can come to visit with empty hands, Paul. Just having you here fills up my heart."

"Just being with you fills up my heart, too." He tugged her

into the living room, grabbed the bag from her hands, and poured the buttons into her lap. "But there's one more gift in here. . . ."

He knelt by her side, pretended to search through the buttons, and muttered to himself, "Where is it?"

She dipped her head closer to his and stirred through the bright buttons that filled her silk skirt. "What?"

"I remember now." He pulled something from a pocket and held it out to her—a ring. It shone as brightly as the love in his eyes. "Rosemary, I love you. I was going to ask you at the restaurant tonight, but I'm acting like a kid who can't wait. Marry me, sweetheart."

"Oh, Paul!" Rosemary looked at him through tear-misted eyes. The man she'd grown to love had taken her by complete surprise. In quiet moments alone, she'd dared to dream their courtship might blossom into marriage, but after years of widowhood, they'd seemed just that—dreams. Only he was here, making her dreams come true. "I'd be honored to become your wife."

Chapter 7

W e'll check with the church calendar," Paul said two days later as his fingers laced with Rosemary's. He'd invited some friends over for a barbecue so he could introduce his future wife to some of his associates. "I'm hoping for August."

"Congratulations." Bill flipped hamburgers on the grill and winked at Rosemary. "As for you, I suppose someone ought to warn you that Paul snores something fierce. Last summer when he left the bedroom window open at night—"

Rosemary gave Paul a questioning look.

"Bill, you're not supposed to lie and scare the bride-to-be." Paul squeezed her hand. "I should have warned you about Bill. He's known for his lousy sense of humor, but he's been a fair friend."

"Yeah, well, you could have introduced me to Rosemary instead of keeping her for yourself."

"Not a chance. She's mine."

Rosemary smiled up at Paul, and he could see love and joy sparkling in her eyes.

Paul released Rosemary's hand and slipped a plate to her.

He set two hamburger buns side by side on the plate and motioned Bill to serve up a pair of sizzling patties. "I heard you might be interested in renting my house. Rosemary's place will be better suited to us."

"Why?"

"My place is too small." He cast her a smile.

"You're not going to have kids, are you?" Bill blurted out the question, then cleared his throat. "Sorry. That's none of my business."

The color in Rosemary's cheeks tickled Paul. He shrugged. "No telling what God has in store for the future."

Later, as Rosemary carried the condiments into Paul's house after the last of the guests had left, she asked, "Do you want children, Paul?"

"We have Valerie." He took the mustard from her and stuffed it into the icebox. "It seems like a mighty late start for us, but I'm willing to tackle whatever God sends our way. What do you think?"

"We'd hoped to have other children, but Valerie was our only one. I don't know that I could carry another child." Tears filled her eyes. "I should have said something. I'm sorry. With Valerie this old, it never occurred to me—"

"Shhh." Paul wrapped his arms around her. "If anything, I'd be worried sick about you the whole nine months. Thirty-nine isn't ancient, but I know it's more dangerous for a woman to carry a child at your age."

She snuggled closer.

"How would you feel about adopting? I think it would be a great option."

"Could we?" Her face shone with hope.

"Sweetheart, God's given us an incredible love for one another. If He has little ones out there He wants us to rear, He'll fill our hearts with love for them, too."

"So maybe someday I'll be sewing a doll for our little girl?"

He laughed. "Who are you kidding? You'll have a whole family of dolls for her, and they'll be the best-dressed rag dolls the world ever saw!"

As she laughed, he held her tight. He trusted her implicitly, and Wild Bill had come to the cookout just to check her out. He'd let Paul know that Rosemary had his resounding endorsement. Paul would have married her regardless, but with Bill Donovan's approval, he could occasionally "socialize" and continue to conduct business on the sly.

Rosemary probably would never know that most of his trips carried a clandestine purpose. It was the only way he could protect her—both from danger and worry.

Brakes squealed outside. "Hey, Mom!"

Rosemary wheeled around. "What does Valerie think she's doing, driving like that?"

"Mom!" Valerie sprinted through the wide-open door. "Mrs. Ainsley fell."

❦

"Thank you, Valerie," Mrs. Ainsley said. "You're such a good girl."

Rosemary smiled as Valerie carried the breakfast tray out of the downstairs guest bedroom. Thankfully, the old woman hadn't broken any bones, but she'd been badly rattled and bruised by her fall. Rosemary insisted on having her stay with them for a week or so until she recovered.

As Valerie left for work a short while later, she raised her voice and called from the front door, "Mom, don't forget to make those dolls for Paul."

"Dolls?" Mrs. Ainsley perked up.

Rosemary knew Paul didn't want the doll business to be general knowledge. She understood why, too. Many of the folks in the community and especially in their church had been hard-hit by the Great Depression. They'd welcome the opportunity to make dolls and earn money, but Paul's reputation rested on the quality of the dolls. She didn't want to lie, though.

"Paul takes rag dolls to Sweden."

"Well, that makes sense." Mrs. Ainsley fussed with the edge of her sheet. "If they don't have blankets and soap, those little girls over there won't have toys, either. What can I do to help?"

"Would you like to embroider a face or two?"

"I'd love to! Back when my girls were little, I always used the scraps from their dresses to make tiny clothes for their dollies. It brings back such fond memories."

That first morning, Mrs. Ainsley sat propped against the walnut headboard in the blue-and-white bedroom and embroidered three faces. She threaded red floss through her needle, then glanced at Rosemary, who was tying tiny bows on the ends of flaxen yarn braids. "You go ahead and cut more. It won't hurt for us to make a couple extra for your nice young man to take on his next trip."

"He is nice, isn't he?" Rosemary smiled.

Mrs. Ainsley let out a cackle and waggled her finger. "I knew it! You didn't argue about him being yours."

"He's asked me to marry him."

"Well, glory! Now isn't God good to give you love again? I

remember when you lost your husband. Now, here you are, alight with that special glow only love gives. And I thought I saw a new ring on your finger."

"God is good." Rosemary handed Mrs. Ainsley a glass of water. "Dr. Harwell wanted you to rest. Why don't you take a nap?"

"Only if you promise to let me do more dolls when I wake up."

Rosemary laughed.

"Oh! And if you give me my crochet hook and some yarn, I can make a few blankets and dresses!"

"You're a prize." She gave the old woman a kiss and left her to take a nap. During the next week, Rosemary sewed in the mornings as Valerie kept Mrs. Ainsley company before going to the bank. She also sewed up a storm in the hours Mrs. Ainsley napped. Even then, it wasn't possible to make as many dolls as usual.

Each evening, Paul would come over and escort Mrs. Ainsley to the table for supper, then to the living room where they'd all chat, listen to the radio, and play Monopoly or Sorry! Valerie sat at the piano and played, or Rosemary would accompany her so Valerie could practice the solo she'd promised to do the next week at church. Amid the chatter, crocheting, and cooking, the new balance of having a man there felt so good, so right. Hearing Paul's deep, resonant voice, watching his gentleness with Mrs. Ainsley, and relishing the warmth and strength in his good-night hugs made Rosemary glad they'd set a date for their wedding.

Friday night, Paul came for supper. His step dragged a bit, and his smile seemed forced when she met him at the door.

"What's wrong?" She brushed the roguish lock of hair back from his forehead.

"I got a telegram. Some art's coming available that a client wants. I need to leave as soon as possible. I've booked passage on a ship that sets sail tomorrow."

"Oh." Disappointment flooded her. "You haven't been home long at all—only nine days."

"I know." He came on into the house. "Good evening, Mrs. Ainsley, Valerie."

"I didn't mean to eavesdrop, but I heard you. I'll be going home in the morning. Perhaps Rosemary can drive you to the port."

"You're welcome to stay here, Mrs. Ainsley." Rosemary turned to him. "But I'd love to drive you."

"How about if I come here and pick you up for lunch? We could spend a few hours together. My ship sets sail at four."

"I'd like that."

ৡ

Paul dialed again and drummed his fingers as he waited for the call to go through. He'd been trying to reach Rosemary all morning. Bad enough he was making another trip this soon, but if he stood her up for lunch, then left—well, he didn't want to think of that.

Lord, please help me get ahold of her.

All morning long, the phone had been busy. He had several uncharitable thoughts about Myrtle what's-her-name being such a phone hog. The one time he got through, the phone rang and rang. Rosemary was probably taking Mrs. Ainsley home.

She's got to be home by now.

The phone rang.

Lord, thank You—now please let her be home.

"Hello?"

"Rosemary! Listen, sweetheart. I've gotten tied up in a meeting and have to go to the museum, then the bank. I'm afraid I'll have to cancel lunch."

"Oh."

"I know. I'm disappointed, too. I wanted to spend more time together before I had to leave."

"I guess I'd better get used to you popping in and out. It's part of your job."

He could hear the sadness in her voice, but Paul admired how she wasn't kicking up a big fuss. Rosemary's serenity was one of her best traits. "There are supposed to be a few big lots for me to cull through. If I find the right pieces, I might be able to satisfy my stateside clients for a while."

"I'll be thinking of you and praying for you. Do you need me to go to your place and pack for you?"

"No. Not at all." He kept his voice level, but alarms inside jangled. He'd left home in a hurry after receiving an emergency call from Bill. If anyone else saw what was on his desk, it wouldn't be a big deal; if Rosemary did, he'd have a huge problem on his hands. "I packed last night. I'm an old hat at it."

"I suppose as often as you travel, you have to be."

He forced a laugh. "Actually, Valerie's probably right. I might not have things matched up."

She laughed, too—a slightly thin sound. "I'd love it if you didn't have to go back for a little while after this trip. I noticed your blue suit's getting a little shiny. When you come home, we'll go to the tailor."

"And you'll help me pick out ties that don't all look the same?"

"I like your ties. You just don't put them with the right suits."

"That's proof that I'm in desperate need of a wife. Want the job?"

"More than anything in the world!"

They clung to the phone and spent every last second of the time his nickel bought. She told him she loved him half a dozen times in as many ways. He assured her of his devotion and love, too. He promised to pray for her, and she committed to praying for him. One last "I love you," and the phone clicked.

The empty sound echoed in his heart and mind. He already missed her.

☙

Rosemary's Pierce-Arrow purred to a stop in Paul's driveway. She couldn't bear to think of him leaving without them saying good-bye. Besides, after he'd left last evening and she'd tucked Mrs. Ainsley into bed, Rosemary and Valerie had stayed up most of the night, making more dolls. They'd worked like crazy and made six more. Added to the ones they hadn't been able to sneak out to his car, that would be twenty-two—maybe not a lot but certainly better than what he'd expected to take.

A whirlwind trip through her garden yielded lettuce and tomatoes for BLTs. She packed a picnic lunch including his favorite oatmeal cookies and tossed the dolls in the car.

Paul would come home to a surprise.

Thrilled, Rosemary slipped out of the car and headed toward the house with the wicker laundry basket full of dolls.

No one ever locked the door in this neighborhood. She knew she could slip in, put the dolls in his study, and come back outside to spread the red plaid blanket in a shady spot beneath the tree. It was a perfect day to eat outside, and it was also a wise move. They weren't married, and avoiding temptation and preventing gossip were important for their witness.

The wooden floor echoed with her footsteps, then the Persian rug in his study muffled the sound. He'd mentioned this was where he usually kept the crate of dolls, so it seemed like the natural destination for her now.

She liked his study. Shelves of books lined two walls, and a solid-looking desk commanded the wall by the mullioned window. A large oil painting of Christ kneeling at Gethsemane hung on a wall. When she'd first seen it, she gasped and Paul wrapped his arm around her. "I prize it. It's not by anyone famous, but of all the works I've ever seen, it speaks to me the most. It makes me reflect on the cost of my salvation and the depth of His love."

As soon as she set down the basket of dolls, she'd spend a few moments admiring that painting again. Paul was right—it did make her reflect on God's infinite love. But Rosemary didn't get that far. She stopped cold when she saw what was on the desk.

A needle with a length of tangled thread had been jammed into a sponge—which was odd enough—but alongside it were two of her dolls. The seam along the head had been carefully snipped open.

Chapter 8

The wicker basket made a squeaky creak as Rosemary set it down. Actually, it tumbled to the side and dolls spilled across the floor. She didn't pick them up. She couldn't stop staring at the table. Surely she was mistaken.

Maybe a seam had come loose.

No, it couldn't have. I'm careful, so careful. And even if a seam did come loose, it would be on one doll—not two.

She picked up the first doll. A pair of manicure scissors lay on the desk blotter beneath where it had lain.

He did it. He cut her open. Why? What kind of stupid question is that? The answer is obvious. He's smuggling something.

Pain speared her heart.

Smuggling. *But what? Why?* She could barely breathe. *What has he gotten me into as well? I've been making these!* The next thought made her knees go weak. *Lord, help me. Oh, please, God help me. Valerie has made them, too. And we're sending them to Axel.*

Wildly, she looked around the room. Everything looked so ordinary, so orderly. Tears made her focus waver as she stared at the picture of Christ. Was that just part of Paul's ruse? How deep did his deception run? Had he merely bought a religious painting to use as a prop in his home?

"You never really know a man." Her sister's bitter words echoed through her memory. Elsa was a loving wife, a good housekeeper, a fine mother to Axel and Annelise, yet her husband, Frederick, had abandoned the family and run off with another woman. Years of trust had been shattered in a single night.

Do I really know Paul?

Rosemary carefully set down the doll. The gaping seam taunted her.

He's not the man I thought he was. How could I have let him sweep me off my feet? Is it love or loneliness that made me promise to marry him? How did I ever think I knew him well enough?

As she pivoted, her toe nudged one of the rag dolls on the floor. She stooped and picked them up one at a time. With each doll she placed into the wicker basket, her heart tightened more.

Lord, I thought this was Your will. I thought I was doing something to help all of those poor, frightened children. I thought I was helping my man with his business. It was all so clear, so simple. I've been such a fool! Show me what to do. Help me. . .

Tears slipped down her cheeks as she held the last doll to her aching heart.

☙

Paul glanced down at his watch. If he grabbed his luggage and took the shortcut, he'd still be able to squeeze in almost an hour-long visit at Rosemary's. He refused to leave without seeing her once more. He turned the corner onto his street. Her car was parked at the curb.

The flash of joy dissolved at once. *She's inside. What if she found the dolls?*

Paul parked and immediately headed for his home, for Rosemary. He didn't know what to expect from her. An oppressive silence filled the house. He went from room to room, looking for her. Then he saw the wicker basket full of dolls right by his desk. One of the dolls on his desk had been moved, and the scissors lay in plain view.

She knows.

Everything inside rebelled. What would this revelation cost? Their love, their future? Would she understand? Would she forgive him for keeping such a secret? If she told anyone, lives hung in the balance. He had to find her.

As he stepped into the hallway, Paul felt a draft. The kitchen door was ajar. He walked through it to the backyard and spotted her sitting on a blanket. Rosemary tensed, and he knew she'd heard him, but she didn't look up. Each step he took, he prayed. *Lord, I love her. Make this right. Father, please. . .*

No one in the neighborhood had fences, and Mrs. Sawyer was out at her clothesline, taking down her laundry as J.J.'s kids scrambled in and out of their tree house. They were out of earshot, but he couldn't be sure what Rosemary would do.

Paul disciplined himself to stroll over to her instead of yielding to the temptation to sprint. He halted at the edge of the blanket and cleared his throat. "I planned to whiz over to see you before I left. Why don't we go for a drive?"

She tilted her face up to his. Her red-rimmed eyes made his heart lurch. "Rosemary—"

"I'd like to speak first." She gestured toward the picnic

blanket. Anyone who cared to look would see a casual invitation. Paul saw how her hand shook—from fear, or from anger?

He nodded. He owed her the right to speak her mind. "Maybe we ought to go inside."

She arched a brow. "I don't think so. No one will overhear us in your backyard, but anyone who cares to can see an engaged couple having a pleasant meal. You're very good at hiding in plain sight. This is in keeping with your style."

He winced. Her words carried accusation, and rightly so. From the start, he'd discovered Rosemary was an intelligent woman. He needed to find out just how much she suspected or knew, then proceed with damage control—if that was possible. Slowly, he sat opposite her.

She looked directly at him. "You're smuggling." Her words hung between them as she drew in a deep breath. "I saw your desk. You're using the dolls."

When he didn't give any reply, she handed him a sandwich. "Eat that. It'll help keep up pretenses. That's all a part of the game, isn't it?"

The serenity he cherished about her was gone. Rosemary hadn't fled upon seeing the doll's tampered seams. Clearly she planned to give him the opportunity to explain himself. Even now as she asked for information, he would dole out as little as possible. Keeping secrets from her went against his grain. But he didn't have a choice. This underground operation was all that stood between those children and disaster.

"I never meant for you to be hurt."

"I have a lot of questions. I'm upset. I deserve to know what you've involved me in. It's not just me. You've drawn in my daughter and my nephew, too. You came to me asking for dolls for children. What are you really doing?"

"I've left you in the dark on purpose, Rosemary."

"No more. I expect answers."

"I'm not supposed to discuss this. I'm breaking confidentiality to say anything at all." He stared at her, willing her to open her heart and know the truth even though he'd have to limit his words. "The dolls are going to children."

"But what are you doing with the dolls? What are you putting in them, and why?"

He couldn't lie. In fact, he couldn't ask for more dolls if he didn't confess the truth. Most of all, he simply didn't want to conceal things from the woman he loved. "I'm inserting a little bit of gold or a small jewel. They go to a contact who uses that to fund forged documents and bribe or buy children's freedom."

"The Jewish children in Nazi Germany," she deduced softly.

"Yes."

"No one would expect you're carrying out this plot because you have the ability to travel under your Swedish passport and have a legitimate business. Your art purchasing serves as a perfect cover."

He gave no reply. He didn't need to. Sitting there, he could see her mentally shuffling the facts and reasoning out the puzzle.

Her eyes narrowed. "Axel?"

"Rosemary, I need to protect you and others. I can't reveal anything that would endanger any part of the operation. It's why I never said anything in the first place."

"On no account would I ever tell anyone."

He reached over and took her hands in his. "I trust you for that. When we started out, you were a mere acquaintance. I couldn't risk letting you know. Even now, we have to keep this between just the two of us."

"Promise me you won't involve Axel without his full knowledge."

"You needn't fret on that score."

Rosemary shook her head and let out a mirthless laugh. "No, I suppose not. I ought to know better. If anything, my mother or Annelise is just as involved."

He gave no reply.

"How bad is it?"

Paul looked down at their intertwined hands. "Very little is being revealed about the Nazis' actions. Jews' passports are stamped with a *J* now. They can't own businesses or eat at cafés. Torahs are being burned. They're rounding up Jews from several cities in conquered countries and shipping them into the interior of Germany. They've slaughtered all of the men in at least two villages and many women, too."

Rosemary's fingers tightened around his. "Why aren't people doing anything about it?"

"Nazi cruelty is unspeakable, and their capacity for evil is boundless. Jews, gypsies, people who are mentally or physically 'inferior'. . .they're all being mistreated or shipped to unknown destinations."

"Shipped?"

"Rounded up and put in trucks or railroad cars. I'm not talking about a one-time occurrence, though that would be bad enough. Amsterdam, Poland, Romania—every country that's been conquered by the Reich."

He saw the dawning horror in her eyes and hated stripping away the innocence that insulated her from such ugly facts. It sickened him to make her aware of the depths of evil in their world. She'd asked for the truth, and he prayed she was strong enough to handle it. Now that she knew, she also had to understand the risks that came with her knowledge.

"Warfare between the soldiers—I don't like it, but I understand that much. But they show no mercy to civilians?"

"None. Hitler's reign owes as much of its success to fear as it does to power or might. Europeans are frightened. If someone tries to be a good Samaritan and help what the Nazis term 'an undesirable,' they themselves are punished. Some people are trying to hide Jews; most won't."

"If a neighbor tattled. . ." Her voice died out.

He nodded. "Everyone lives in terror. Denmark is doing better than other countries at trying to shield the Jews, but I can't be sure how much longer they'll succeed. Sweden is one of the last safeholds—and that's because the Germans need Sweden's iron to make steel for their war."

"How can you make a difference, Paul?"

"One person can make a difference, and if I had to do it alone, I would. Praise God, there are others. Several people have organized. There's an underground."

"Like the Underground Railroad that helped Southern slaves to freedom?"

The faint twinkle in her eyes that accompanied the question made hope flicker in his heart. "Yes, Rosemary. We're doing our best to spare lives."

The twinkle disappeared, and wariness replaced it. "It's dangerous for you."

He hitched a shoulder. "I can't say there's no danger. I can't live with myself if I do nothing, though. Innocent children deserve mercy and help. I can't close my eyes to the need,

Rosemary. As a man, as a Christian—I have to be involved."

"Don't you think I'm willing to—"

"Rosemary." He sighed her name. "It wasn't a matter of whether I thought you'd be willing to take part. Fact of the matter is, I came to see very quickly that you'd jump in with both feet. But I wanted to shield you. The German Bund is exceptionally active in the States. We have no reason to believe they're on to this—it's a tiny operation. On the other hand, we don't want to underestimate their network. I didn't like withholding facts from you, but it was for your safety. The dolls are just a simple cottage industry—nothing more."

"I know that look in your eyes. I'm every bit as stubborn as you are, Paul Kincaid. Everything hinges on appearances. I'm making innocent dolls; you're an art dealer. I can play that game just as well as you can."

He watched her pick up a cup. "We need to end the conversation. I can't reveal any more details. I've already said far too much."

"I'm not a security risk, Paul." She tilted the cup to her lips.

Paul knew the cup to be empty. She was carrying on a charade, and the least he could do was play along. He picked up his sandwich and took a big bite. Something told him the matter wasn't settled yet.

She looked at him over the rim of her cup. "My sister's husband betrayed her trust. He left her for another woman."

"There's no other woman in my life!" He blurted out the words.

Rosemary set down the empty cup and nodded. A small smile tugged at her lips. "If I suspected such a thing, I wouldn't have stayed to talk." He nodded, and she continued. "When I thought about Frederick, I realized it was in his character not to be true to my sister. He always thought of himself first and was never satisfied with life. You are different."

In his line of work, patience was essential. Paul couldn't think of a time when his patience was so hard won.

"The first time I saw you, you handed your hymnal to someone else and sang by memory. Such a little thing, really." She shrugged. "But little things are telling. Like the way you listen respectfully to Valerie and the way you hold Mrs. Ainsley's elbow to help her. When we pray together, I feel in my heart that we are one. I don't doubt that you love me as I love you."

Paul felt part of the burden lift. They'd make it through this.

"Your character is clear to me. I fell in love with a man who has integrity. Old memories shook me for a moment, but I asked God to help me seek the truth. The one thing I don't understand is why you didn't trust me. Love means trusting, Paul."

He looked at her and let out a deep breath. "Love does trust, Rosemary. A man's love for his woman also compels him to protect her. I'd hoped to shield you."

"I understand your motive now."

"I'm glad, sweetheart. I know this cut you deeply, and I can't tell you how sorry I am. Now that you know I'm part of clandestine matters, I admit I kept a huge secret about myself from you." The words stuck in his throat. "It's only honorable for me to give you a chance to end our engagement."

Chapter 9

P aul!" Tears sprang to her eyes. "Is that what you want?"
"*No.*" He shook his head. "I love you more than I can
say. I just told you: You can always be certain of that
love. The only question is, is your love strong enough to survive the fact that I'll still keep secrets from you? If you still
want to be my wife, I'll have to rely on your trust, because I'll
never be able to tell you certain things. There will be times
you'll get curious. What I want you to know, through it all, is
that you can always be sure of my unwavering love for you."

"I love you with all my heart, Paul, and I'm not a young girl.
As a woman, I understand that the need for discretion must
come ahead of my personal interest. You can't keep from helping others—and that makes me love you all the more. Now that
I know what's behind your actions, it's plain that you never hid
who you are. You just concealed part of what your compassion
compels you to do. I wouldn't ask you to stop, and I'm not about
to let go of the man I love. I want to help in every way I can. I'll
be the best wife to you that I can, with God's help."

"And I'll be the best husband I can be to you, with His
help."

"Then you need to eat and keep up your strength." Finally, she smiled and slipped an oatmeal cookie into his hands, and he knew things were going to work out well. "I have a hunch God's going to keep us busy."

❦

"Yes, yes. Careful, now." Paul directed the purser as Rosemary stood by his side at the dock.

"Wow." She looked at the latest crate. "You managed quite a sizable transaction."

He patted the crate. "It's bound for the National Art Museum. They'll be more than pleased."

She nestled into his side, and he held her close. "I missed you," he growled.

"Not as much as I missed you." She laughed. "Valerie told me she was glad you were coming home. She said she's sick of me moping around without you."

"Moping, eh?" They walked alongside the cart containing his luggage and a few other smaller crates. The ship-to-shore phone allowed him to arrange with the museum to have a truck waiting. "And here I thought you were going to tell me all she wanted was my secret mashed potato recipe."

"You are the only man of my acquaintance who even knows a recipe."

"Keep it that way." He squeezed her tight and dipped his head. "I'm dying for us to get alone so I can kiss you properly."

Rosemary felt her face grow warm. "Me, too."

"Six weeks 'til the wedding. Did you get your gown yet?"

"I'm not sure I need one. I thought maybe my Easter dress. . ."

"Since when did a bride need an excuse to have a new gown?"

"I'd rather use the money for a project."

"Over my dead body. I brought back some Belgian lace."

"Belgian lace!" She blinked at him in amazement. "How?" She smiled and recovered quickly. "How thoughtful of you!"

"Anything for my girl." He saw to the truck being loaded, then took the keys to her car and drove behind the truck to the museum. "I'm sorry we're tied up like this, but some shipments require immediate signatures."

"What did you get?"

"There's a collection of incredible little carved ivory and jade kimono toggles that are called *netsuke*; a small bronze sculpture of a ballerina by Degas; a very Rembrandtesque painting that I suspect might be by Willem Drost; the central portion of a gilded medieval altarpiece; a few etchings; and a handful of other paintings. The Correggio "Madonna and Child" is the *pièce de résistance*."

"Are you serious? Paul, how can people stand to part with such treasures?"

"It's heartbreaking. So many of them are trying to sell, though. They know the Nazis will take anything of interest. Selling is the better of the two choices." He stopped. "The situation is already ugly. I want you to know I'm trying not to cheat anyone. I do my best to pay a fair price."

"That went without saying."

They stopped at an intersection. Paul leaned over and kissed her. "I want to haul you off to the church today."

She laughed. "Valerie would throw a fit, and Mrs. Ainsley would have a conniption."

He didn't laugh at all. "I'm noticing you didn't object."

"Paul, we can't do that." She blushed. "I'm not about to have anyone think I had to hurry up to get married."

The honk of the horn behind them cut short his laughter. "If we don't get going here, the whole town is going to think that's the case!"

He pulled into the back of the museum. "Sweetheart, it's going to take me a couple of hours. I want you to go buy a wedding dress now. Come back to pick me up, and we'll swing by to collect Valerie and go out for a bite to eat."

"I'll stay—" She stopped. "Okay. I'll go. You can unpack and do whatever you have to."

"But get your dress now."

"Why are you so worried about my wedding dress?"

He traced his fingers down her cheek. "You deserve a beautiful dress." He ran his thumb across her lips and added, "I like silk. I want you to wear silk."

"Any particular color?"

"Not especially. But the government is about to put an embargo on silk. I don't want you to get stuck without a choice."

"I'm getting my first choice. I'm getting you."

He groaned. "Are you sure I can't just haul you off to the pastor's house? His wife and a neighbor could be witnesses."

"Go play with your paintings. I have a dress to buy."

Valerie declined the invitation to go to dinner with them. She and "Grandma" Ainsley were "busy." Paul escorted Rosemary out to the car and muttered, "The two of them are thick as thieves."

"I know. I have a funny feeling they're up to something."

"If it were Valerie and her friends, I'd be worried. Mrs. Ainsley's involvement is reassuring."

Rosemary gave him an incredulous look. "Don't be too sure of it. Mrs. Ainsley can be feisty."

"That sweet old woman?"

She leaned close and whispered in his ear, "A spy ought to be more observant. Mrs. Ainsley is wearing nail polish these days."

He hooted. "Well, that makes her a floozie, doesn't it?"

They had a lovely dinner at Giovanni's. Afterward, Paul wanted to take a walk. They meandered through the park, and to his relief, she didn't pump him for any in-depth information about his trip. She asked general questions and didn't pry if his answers were less than direct. He told her how her relatives were doing, but most of all, he spoke of how he had missed her and how he was glad to be back home.

"How long do you get to stay home now?"

"I told them we're getting married. I figured I'd refrain from any more business trips until we come back from our honeymoon. If I do that, I'll need to slip away right after we return."

"I understand why."

He nodded.

"I'm taking you suit shopping tomorrow. Your blue suit is shiny."

"You're sounding wifely already."

"I'm out of practice. It's been almost eight years since I was married."

"I'm not worried in the least. You're the most practical

woman I've ever met. Speaking of practicalities, are there any of my furnishings that you want to bring on over?"

She grinned. "Now that you mention it, I love your oak hall tree. Wouldn't it look great by the front door?"

"Yeah, it would."

"My late husband used the small parlor beside the guest room as an office. We cleared everything out years ago. Would you like to bring over your desk, bookshelves, and picture of Christ?"

"That would be great!"

He took off his suit coat and slipped it around her shoulders. "You're getting chilly."

"Silly, isn't it? It's summer!"

"As long as you're not getting sick."

Rosemary turned and gave him a peck on the cheek. "I am sick—lovesick!"

The two of them sauntered all around the park, then drove back to Rosemary's. When they walked up to the house, Valerie pulled open the door. "You've been gone a long time. Mom, I need to tell you something."

"Okay, honey. Paul, would you please excuse me?"

Valerie shot her a wary look. "Could we go upstairs?"

Rosemary followed her daughter up the steps. What would be so urgent that her daughter would drag her away from Paul on their first evening back together? Valerie practically pushed her down the hall and into the master bedroom. Once inside, Rosemary fumbled with the switch.

When the lights went on, she let out a cry.

Chapter 10

S urprise!" Mrs. Ainsley crowed from over in the corner.
"Well, do you like it?" Paul slipped up behind Rosemary
and wrapped his arms around her.

"It's—it's gorgeous!" She stared in disbelief at the antique
bedroom set.

"I couldn't resist it," he confessed.

Valerie ran her hand across the front of the huge mirror-
fronted oak armoire. "Have you ever seen anything so beautiful?"

Rosemary turned and slipped her arms around his waist.
"How did you do this?"

"Valerie and Mrs. Ainsley helped. I called, and they
agreed to be here to tell the deliverymen where to arrange
everything."

"We put the old set in that empty bedroom down the hall,"
Mrs. Ainsley said. "It's nice and solid, but this—well, this is
something else entirely."

"I knew they were up to something!" Rosemary poked
Paul in the back. "You knew they were, too, and you didn't
let on."

"Some secrets, sweetheart, are well worth keeping."

He'd hoped he wouldn't have to go back for a while. Bill had arranged for a courier to take another shipment of dolls. Everything was arranged. Then the phone rang.

"We need to get together for lunch," Bill said.

He never called unless it was imperative. Paul straightened. "When are you free?"

"I just had a cancellation. Why don't we meet in an hour?"

"I'll be there."

Just like that, he was gone. He'd only been home four days. Rosemary kept a positive attitude. She understood they'd live by a capricious schedule and he'd dash off on trips without much warning at times. She loved him; it was a concession she'd make. Compared to the dangers and sacrifices others made, it was nothing.

Two days after he'd pressed her to buy her wedding gown, the government announced a silk embargo. Things like that made her aware of the fact that he had his fingers on the pulse of what was happening in the world. With all of those things weighing on his mind, he'd still made sure she'd have a silk gown. That thought made her love him all the more. He understood the little things that made a difference.

She went to pick up the suit they'd ordered. "It'll fit him perfectly. I guarantee it," the tailor promised.

"I hope so. What about the ties?" She'd selected some ties the day they ordered the suit. One, in particular, would look perfect for the wedding. The blue in it matched the wool in the suit exactly, but the pale blue stripe in it was precisely the same shade as the silk gown she'd be wearing.

"You're lucky I set them aside for you. Once they announced the embargo, folks have suddenly snapped up ties. Cost of wool's starting to hike. I've ordered some extra bolts just in case."

Rosemary studied the tailored lines of the suit jacket. "Why don't I go ahead and order another suit for Paul now?"

"I have his measurements on file. It'd be ready in a week."

"Wonderful."

Rosemary went home and sat down at the sewing machine. As it was Saturday, Valerie was home. *The Adventures of Ellery Queen* played on the radio as they worked together.

The bobbin thread ran out. As the radio touted the excellence of Bromo Seltzer, Rosemary suddenly jolted. *Paul knew about the price of wool. He made sure Mrs. Ainsley had a coat. He said he wouldn't quibble about an extra penny or two per yard of fabric for the dolls. . . .*

"Valerie!"

Valerie stopped stuffing a doll and looked up.

"We need to go buy fabric!"

By the time they carried the third load of fabric to the upstairs bedroom that evening, Valerie gave her a disgruntled look. "How many little girls do you think there are in Denmark, anyway?"

Rosemary diverted her by laughing. "I know you hate to sew, but complaining isn't going to make a difference."

"One yard. One stinking little yard of twenty different materials. That's weird enough, but you did that at—I lost count. How many stores did we end up going to?"

"Enough." The empty chest of drawers came in handy. Rosemary quickly tucked yard after yard into the drawers and filled all five. She'd also bought three bolts of muslin.

The clerks at the store all chattered about quilts. Rosemary didn't lie, but she hadn't corrected their assumptions, either. Paul had insisted on buying tires for the car because supplies would be distributed differently. Well, she figured she'd learn from his example. On Monday, she'd go buy wool yarn for doll hair.

Days passed. The closet in the spare room overflowed with dolls. Rosemary tried to tuck the dolls into the closet without her daughter seeing the "finished" product because she'd been leaving the one seam open. Since Valerie hated to sew, it hadn't been too hard to have her concentrate on sewing on button eyes and stuffing the dolls. Once, as they hugged good night, Valerie whispered, "I know something's up."

"We're up. We should have been in bed about thirty minutes ago."

Valerie gave her an indulgent smile. "Pleasant dreams, Mom."

That night, Rosemary's dreams were anything but pleasant.

"Ah, Captain von Rundstedt! I have a special package for you." Paul plowed through the crate and pulled out a small box. "For your niece."

"How very kind of you." The captain gave him a calculating look.

"Actually, I am in your debt. It was your idea."

The captain opened the box. Inside was another doll. This one was flaxen-haired and dressed in a long dress. A small copy of *Sleeping Beauty* accompanied her. "Very clever."

"The cleverness was yours, Captain," Axel said. "It's too difficult to import books right now, so I cannot carry this line, but Herr Lindhagen said he'd be happy to bring in one of each type when he can."

"That box has a red cape for your Red Riding Hood," Paul mentioned casually.

"My niece will be pleased."

"Good."

The captain looked around the warehouse. "I see you are still able to keep a fair business going, Herr Christiansen."

"I've changed some of the items I carry. A good business-man is always flexible. I'm thinking of dealing with a South American firm. They can fruits, vegetables, and jam. It might be a lucrative venture."

"Be sure such shipments do not end up on the black market." The captain stared at him. "I would expect careful book-keeping. Such things will not be tolerated."

"Naturally." Axel dipped his head in assent. "It occurred to me that certain products such as that might appeal to desirable persons."

"Keep me informed if they become available. Heil Hitler." The captain started to leave.

Paul cleared his throat. "Captain? Just one thing. I was asked by two families in Sweden to see if I might locate their grandchildren. Is there any assistance in such matters?"

"Give me their parents' names. I can have an aide check on it."

"Death notices were received. That is why the grandparents asked my assistance in finding the children. They're from Flensburg."

Rundstedt shook his head. "I cannot help you. It is not in my jurisdiction. It is a lost cause. Tracking orphans in a time of war is impossible."

"A shame, to be sure," Paul murmured.

"Indeed. Heil Hitler."

After the captain left, Axel gave him an incredulous look. "Do I dare ask what that was about?"

"No." Paul slapped Axel on the shoulder and walked off. He couldn't share the details of this mission with anyone. This time, he had nothing more than Paul Lindhagen's passport, an attaché case, and three dolls.

෴

Rosemary closed the door to the magnificent wardrobe, hiding her silk wedding dress from view. She caught her reflection in the mirrored front and forced a smile. She couldn't let Valerie see her concern.

Over the past few months, Valerie had finally begun enjoying life again. She'd gotten through the freshness of grief and was starting to mention Frank every now and then in casual conversation. "I need some of her resilience and spunk," Rosemary whispered to her reflection.

Paul had never been gone this long. It was supposed to be a short trip. He ought to have been back by now. . .only it had been four and a half weeks, and she hadn't heard a word.

The dangers of his profession loomed in her mind. It was just six days before their wedding, but she couldn't be sure he'd be home in time. . .if he came home at all.

She shuddered at that thought.

As the days passed, she prayed for him. She asked the Lord to protect him and to bless the dolls so children would find safety. Her prayers became increasingly urgent.

Mrs. Ainsley came to spend the day. They made applesauce together. As she added cinnamon to the sauce, Rosemary said, "This will give the applesauce a little zing."

"Like Paul Kincaid puts zing in your heart?"

Rosemary laughed. "Yes. He does that."

"Paul is wonderful." Mrs. Ainsley licked applesauce from her finger and gave Rosemary an impish grin. "I want to marry him if you don't."

"He's mine. You're out of luck."

Mrs. Ainsley pretended to huff. "Well then, I'm going to go home." She rose.

"Be sure to take some applesauce." Rosemary tucked a trio of pint-sized jars in a bag.

After Mrs. Ainsley left, Rosemary slumped into a chair and let out a sigh. No matter how busy she stayed, she couldn't distract herself. Worry gnawed at her. *Where's Paul? Is he okay?*

Soon Valerie arrived home from work. "Mom, you need to get out. You can't brood like this."

"Haven't you ever learned Danes are good at brooding?"

"Yuck. I never liked Hamlet. Let's forget about that and go outside." Valerie pulled her into the backyard and chattered as they gardened. The late August sunlight cast a golden glow around them, but Rosemary couldn't shake the feeling that something was terribly wrong. When they finished gardening, Valerie took the basket of vegetables into the house. Rosemary stayed behind. She knelt in the soil and wept as she prayed.

Two of them were out. Safe. Both little boys had the big haunted eyes of children who had seen far too much in their short years. Nonetheless, Paul knew they'd soon be nurtured by their grandparents back in New York. He'd passed them off to a contact who met them at the appointed time. Paul waded back to shore. Squinting at the horizon, he knew he had to hurry to find cover before the next patrol came by.

It was said anything could be bought for a price. Tonight, he almost believed that. The wealthy grandparents of those boys had gladly donated a sizable fortune—one that would fund the escapes of countless more children. The trip had been what Bill termed a "calculated risk." To Paul's way of thinking, the only calculation involved was that any child was priceless.

He rolled down his pant legs, donned his shoes and coat, and struck out walking. In the distance, he spied an overturned fishing dory. It would conceal him well enough. He ducked beneath it just in time. The patrol came and went.

Another several miles on foot, and he reached a thinly wooded area. The body of a man lay twisted in an unnatural position on the ground beside a thicket. A small sound made Paul take a second look. He knelt down and could scarcely believe his eyes. From beneath the undergrowth, a little child stared back at him.

He pulled her free and hastily checked the man's body for some identification. There was none. Young as she was, this little girl had become one of the orphans Captain von Rundstedt said were untraceable. Paul scooped her into his arms, and she clung to him. They'd barely gone ten yards when footsteps and a stream of harsh German orders sounded not far away. Paul shoved the girl between the gnarled roots of a tree and curled around her. *Lord, please make seeing eyes blind tonight.*

Chapter 11

F ive weeks. He'd been gone now far, far too long. Rosemary spent her days gardening and sewing. Friends from church dropped by with offers to help with the wedding. Rosemary pasted on a smile and acted as if Paul's prolonged absence was understandable. But batch after batch of cookies grew stale.

Inside, she was crying to the Lord with every breath. Once already she'd lost a husband. Was God taking Paul from her, too? She couldn't help fearing the worst.

Five days to go until the wedding. Rosemary sat down at the sewing machine and buried her face in her hands.

Lord, You know what's happening. I'm so confused, so scared. Love is such a rare gift. You gave Your Son as a gift of love. He said a man had no greater love than to lay down his life for another. Paul is risking his life. . .but, Father, please don't take him from me. I love him so much. I long to be his wife. You put us together—please don't tear us apart. Bring my beloved back safely to me.

"Rosemary."

She wiped the tears from her face. She wanted Paul so

much that she could hear his voice.

"Sweetheart."

She spun around. "Paul!"

He looked thinner and tired, but his eyes sparkled with love for her. In his arms, he held a little dark-haired, doe-eyed girl. "I'm sorry it took me so long to come home to you. I brought you a wedding gift. Her name is Rebekkah."

"And she's a living doll," Rosemary said as she ran to them with her arms open to pull them close to her heart.

one month later

"Up, Daddy. More." Rebekkah tapped her own little cheek to show him where he'd missed a spot.

"There can't be more flour on my face. I'm wearing most of it on my shirt!"

"I wearing flowers, too!"

Rosemary burst out laughing. "Yes, honey, your pretty new apron has flowers on it."

"She's smart as a whip." Valerie dried the mixing bowl. "Learning English fast as can be."

"Yes, she is." Rosemary hugged their little daughter and kissed the white fleck on Paul's cheek.

"Hey, stop that before the cookies burn!"

"I can't believe we only filled two cookie sheets." Paul made a face as Valerie pulled the treats out of the oven.

"Neither can I!" Rosemary wiped Rebekkah's hands. "As much cookie dough as you and Bekkah swiped, I didn't think we'd manage even one sheet."

"Be nice, or I won't share my family's secret recipe for mashed potatoes."

"You'll share it." Valerie laughed. "We *are* your family."

Bekkah's dark curls bounced as she nodded.

Rosemary and Paul exchanged a glance. They did that all the time now—carried on conversations with just a look. It never ceased to thrill her how deep their love had grown in such a short time.

"Rebekkah's eager for these cookies," Valerie said. "Look at her—she got the milk."

"That's buttermilk, sweetie." Rosemary knelt down. "We need the other milk."

Bekkah shook her head and handed the bottle to Paul. "Daddy. 'Tatoes."

He chortled. "This little scamp doesn't miss a thing."

"You use buttermilk?" Valerie gaped at him.

"Among other things. We need baking soda, cayenne pepper, white pepper. . ."

"Who would have guessed?" They all sat down at the table after he gathered the ingredients. Paul picked up the masher.

"Wait!" Rebekkah pressed her little hands together. "Pray. Pray first."

"Yes. Bekkah, would you like to say the prayer?"

She nodded and closed her eyes. "Thank You, Jesus. God bless all the boys and girls. Amen."

Rosemary looked across the table at her husband. Love radiated between them as they said in unison, "Amen."

CATHY MARIE HAKE

Cathy Marie is a Southern California native who loves her work as a nurse and Lamaze teacher. She and her husband have a daughter, a son, and two dogs, so life is never dull or quiet. Cathy Marie considers herself a sentimental pack rat, collecting antiques and Hummel figurines. She otherwise keeps busy with reading, writing, and bargain hunting. Cathy Marie's first book was published by **Heartsong Presents** in 2000 and earned her a spot as one of the readers' favorite new authors. Since then, she's written several other novels, novellas, and gift books. You can visit her online at www.CathyMarieHake.com.

Filled with Joy

by Kelly Eileen Hake

Chapter 1

December 1941

Roy Benson stared at the all-too-familiar turquoise wall. Some dingbat had decided the color was soothing, but that person certainly never stayed in traction for a month with nothing else to look at. It felt like living in a package of Blackjack gum, but the antiseptic smell provided a constant reminder that this was a hospital.

Martha, the grandmotherly nurse, bustled in to pick up his lunch tray. "Hello, Mr. Benson. Did you have a good day?"

He grinned. Every day she asked the same question, and his answer always stayed the same. "Yes, Miz Martha."

"Oh, please." Martha shot him a wink. "Ashley told me you've been restless all morning. Looking forward to tomorrow, I suppose?"

"True." Roy leaned forward as she fluffed his pillows. "A cast and crutches mean I can move around again."

"We're happy for you." She picked up the tray, stacked it on top of several others, and headed for the door. "I know you're itching to get out of here."

More than you know. Lying in bed for weeks on end was slowly driving Roy up the wall. He was accustomed to hard work and missed the sense of purpose he found in serving his country. The moment he'd turned eighteen he'd enlisted in the U.S. Navy, just as his father had done twenty-two years before.

His education at a Swiss boarding school stood him in good stead. Since Roy boasted fluency in English, Swiss, German, and French, in addition to having a knack for mathematics, he'd been recruited to serve the naval cryptography division OP-20-G. Now, eight years later, he'd immersed himself in decoding the Japanese naval code JN-25, as Japanese-U.S. relations became increasingly strained.

Entrusted with top-secret documents to deliver to the capitol from Station Hypo in Hawaii, he'd planned to return to duty immediately. Unfortunately, the spoiled son of a senator had climbed behind the wheel of his daddy's Benz as drunk as a skunk and lost control of the vehicle. As he plowed through the street, somehow the youth drove up on the sidewalk and rammed into Roy. After weeks of traction for his broken leg, tomorrow would bring crutches. Crutches meant recovery, and recovery meant getting back to work.

With those comforting thoughts, he reached over and turned on the bedside radio Martha had brought him. WOR broadcast live, up-to-the-minute commentary on football games every Sunday. This afternoon, the New York Giants played the Brooklyn Dodgers.

"You fellas ready for the game?"

"Yeah!"

Static from the radio mixed with the men's cheers; then the channel tuned in. "Wagner, can you hear it?"

Wagner waved from the far corner of the ward. "Yes, sir."

Roy settled in and got caught up in listening to the play-by-play calls, hearing the crowd roar, and wishing he could be out enjoying the day.

"We interrupt this broadcast to bring you this important bulletin from the United Press." The sudden news bulletin jerked him back to the present. *"FLASH, Washington—the White House announces Japanese attack on Pearl Harbor. Stay tuned to WOR for further developments, which will be broadcast as received."*

Roy's outraged bellow blended with those of his ward mates before a deathly silence fell over the room. *Pearl Harbor. It's not Station Hypo, but it's so close. Is my division okay? If only I wasn't stuck here in this bed. I could have been there helping break the Japanese code. This might not have happened.*

The bulletin repeated. The announcer also gave nonspecific information that the battle still progressed. Roy's hands clenched around the cold metal bed rail. *Lord, why am I in this bed when my country is under attack?*

"Ow!"

Valerie Fulton shot a commiserating grin at her stepfather as he set down the needle and popped a poked finger into his mouth. Paul had a difficult time sewing glass buttons onto the much-needed rag dolls—a fact that made her like him even more. She glanced down at her own much-pricked hands and sighed. "You'd think after making so many of these, we'd be pros by now. Whoever said practice makes perfect never took up sewing."

Her comment earned her a smile from Paul and a cheery

laugh from her mother.

"Maybe for some of us it's just hopeless," Paul agreed.

"No." Rosemary expertly tied a minuscule knot. "This project is all about hope. Every poked finger is another child rescued."

Paul and Valerie shared a purposeful glance and concentrated on the work at hand with renewed vigor. These weren't just dolls; they were the means through which the Lord looked after His own.

The dolls, and their lifesaving purpose, were what had brought Rosemary and Paul together this past year. Paul had come up with the idea after seeing Rosemary carry a basket of the dolls to the church nursery. At first, they'd simply made the dolls as requested, but eventually, Paul asked for Rosemary's hand in marriage and revealed the true mission of the dolls.

As the Nazis overran Europe, Jews were being chased from their homes or incarcerated. In an effort to help, Valerie and her mother stitched the dolls, and Paul made sure valuables were buried deep in the stuffing. When the dolls arrived in Denmark, the money funded the production of crucial documents. There, Valerie's cousins Axel and Annelise smuggled the dolls with the documents to Jewish refugees. Then the children were funneled to Sweden, where they would be safe from the Nazis.

On his last trip to Europe before the wedding, Paul had brought home a surprise—a Jewish toddler named Rebekkah. They'd adopted her, and she filled their hearts and home with a special joy. Rosemary called the little girl her living doll, and she'd just tucked her in bed.

To Valerie, Rebekkah was the sister she'd always wanted and the opportunity to help raise a child in the Lord's grace.

Every time she sewed another doll, she pictured another precious Rebekkah waiting to be saved.

As the days passed and political relations became more tense, the entire operation gained a frightening urgency. American imports to Denmark were already few and far between; the Nazi regime could stop accepting shipments of the dolls at any time. Every doll made was another child saved.

Valerie finished plaiting a doll's red yarn hair and held it up for a brief moment before placing it with several others in a crate by her chair. She threaded her needle with rose-colored floss and grabbed more material to embroider another face.

Moments later, as she pressed her handkerchief to the red stain spreading across her thumb, Valerie saw her mother watching out of the corner of her eye. "Well, practice makes patient, at least!"

After a shared chuckle, Paul became solemn. "Speaking of patient, what would you two say to bringing an injured soldier into our home for the holidays?"

"You know your friends are welcome anytime, Paul, but through New Year's?" At his nod, Valerie's mom asked, "What about the dolls?"

Valerie bit her tongue. This wasn't just her decision to make. She and her mom weren't alone anymore. Paul brought up the topic, but Valerie knew he and her mom would respect her opinion. Through Paul, God had blessed their home with continued harmony, but they were now a trio instead of a duet when decisions needed to be made.

"We'll have to guard our speech more closely, but we can still make the dolls and tell him we're sending them to Denmark to help Valerie's cousins."

"That's true. . .but what if he does happen to find out?" Valerie asked. Some things just weren't worth the risk.

"If it comes to that—and I'm not saying it will—he's a naval officer. I've known his father for over two decades, and whenever I was sent to Switzerland or the outlying area, I stopped by his boarding school to check on him. Right now he's laid up with a broken leg. Some drunken fool got behind the wheel and hit him. He's a bright young man and loyal as they come. We can trust Roy Benson."

Valerie could tell Paul had spoken his piece. She couldn't ask for a better reference. Clearly Mr. Benson must be an exceptional man. As her mother quirked a brow in silent question, Valerie bobbed her head.

"We'll do it." Rosemary patted Paul's arm. "I can't stand to think of anyone being alone in the hospital over Christmas."

"Besides. . ." Valerie grinned. "If all else fails, we can teach him to sew!"

Roy listened to the morning news. The announcer listed ships and carriers that had sunk to the depths of Pearl Harbor since yesterday's sneak attack. No matter what the government revealed, the information missing told Roy far more. The lack of statistics alone hinted at a devastation he could imagine all too vividly. He'd had a one-day stop in Pearl Harbor; he knew full well the size of the contingent there. The United States had moved the bulk of its naval force to Hawaii just last year as a show of power.

Though none would call the attack honorable or courageous, it had been brutally effective. *Still no word on the number of casualties, but that's to be expected.* The American naval fleet had been all but destroyed, and hundreds of families would bear the scars of what President Roosevelt named "the day which shall live on in infamy." These deaths would not be the last—America and Britain had jointly declared war on Japan.

As the news ended, promising listeners frequent bulletins and updates, the station began Benny Goodman's "There'll Be Some Changes Made."

Roy switched down the volume on the radio in disgust. His new cast itched, but not as much as he itched to rip it off and hop on the first plane back to Hawaii. All his antsy movement had caused a big wrinkle to form on his bottom sheet. He didn't want to bother the nurse, so he yanked at the sheet and let out a moan of relief. Bed. He hated it. This was the last day, too. After the cast dried, he'd be able to use crutches. . .and not a minute too soon.

He turned his head as footsteps clicked smartly down the hall. The tall honey blond in the doorway caught his eye immediately. It felt like years since he'd seen a woman wearing something other than a nurse's uniform. A leaf-green wool coat parted as she moved, revealing a beige sweater and brown skirt. The skirt flirted around the top of her calves, drawing his gaze toward trim ankles. She was a sight for sore eyes and well worth notice, but one of the men in the ward let loose a low, appreciative whistle.

"Show some respect," Roy growled and glared at the man before turning his attention back to the vision as she stepped into the room. She waited for an older woman and man to follow her. *Not timid. Bright enough to have backup before she gets in too deep.* She shot a questioning glance at the older man, who nodded in Roy's direction.

The man seemed strangely familiar. . .yes, more gray hairs, but that was definitely. . .

"Paul Kincaid." Roy broke out in a grin at the sight of his father's old friend. Paul used to bring him letters and news when he dropped by the boarding school.

"Roy." Paul strode over to his bed and clasped his hand in a warm greeting before frowning at the fresh plaster on his leg. "I just learned you were here yesterday, or I'd have dropped by sooner. Just get out of traction?"

"I got casted today."

c

Valerie followed Paul's lead toward the bed in the far corner, where a young man with an enormous cast sat listening to the radio. She listened quickly to make sure it wasn't a news update and caught the opening strains of Horace Heidt's "I Don't Want to Set the World on Fire."

Too late for that. This will be a world war, and none of us will escape unscathed. She pushed aside memories of Frank and smiled as Paul introduced her to Roy Benson. "This is my new bride, Rosemary, and her daughter, Miss Valerie Fulton."

His intense hazel gaze and full beard gave him an air of mystery, and the disreputably long, light brown lock of hair on his forehead lent a boyish charm that made her heart skip a beat. Despite the cast covering his left leg from foot to thigh, he struck her as a man of action, chafing at enforced inactivity. The smile that lit Roy's face couldn't completely mask his restlessness.

"I'm glad to meet you." Valerie dipped her head in acknowledgment.

"The pleasure's all mine. Paul, you're a lucky man." As the injured soldier gallantly kissed the back of her mother's hand, Valerie couldn't suppress a grin. Anyone who made her mother giggle was all right in her book.

"Would you like a stick of gum?" She fished a package of Blackjack gum from the pocket of her coat and held it out.

"Thanks."

Before she tucked the remainder of the pack into her purse, she noticed that the gum wrapper matched the teal walls almost perfectly.

"That's right." Amusement colored Mr. Benson's voice as he caught her glancing from the gum to the walls. "You'd better not drop that pack."

"I'd never find it, would I?" She chuckled and stashed it in her handbag. When Roy's smile reached his eyes, he seemed younger.

"Well," Paul began, "we didn't just come for a social visit. My new family and I would like to have you stay with us for the holidays. What do you say?"

Chapter 2

Mr. Benson hesitated, looking at their faces with a measured gaze. Valerie gave a slight nod to encourage him. She wasn't sure why, but she wanted him to feel comfortable coming to their home. He seemed so independent, she almost wanted to make sure he knew other people cared. Maybe it was because Paul had mentioned Roy had grown up in boarding schools. The thought of anyone being away from family for so long left her wanting to make up for the loneliness he must have experienced.

"Please say you'll come, Mr. Benson," Rosemary entreated.

He cast one last glance at the turquoise walls and took a deep breath. "I'd be honored."

"Good. We'll come by later this afternoon when your cast is set." Paul rubbed his hands together. "Dr. Reeves already gave his permission, since we promised to make sure you rested up."

Valerie didn't miss Mr. Benson's grimace at that last part. It seemed as though their new houseguest had had enough rest. Well, if he thought their home would be more fast-paced than the hospital, just wait until he spent a week sewing!

Roy rubbed his jaw and appreciated the brisk December breeze on the back of his neck. Paul had stopped at a barbershop on the way home and made sure Roy got a long-overdue haircut and shave. He didn't look like a bum now. What would pretty Miss Fulton think of his transformation?

Expecting wallpaper embellished with florid pink roses and lacy curtains blocking the window, Roy followed Paul through the house to the downstairs guest bedroom. Even if the room looked like a powder puff, it would be a welcome change. A room to himself was a luxury he'd hardly ever known. He'd shared quarters with other boys in boarding school, then during the first years of his service in the navy. Even the hospital ward packed several men along the long walls.

Now he'd have peace and quiet—time to think about what he would do with himself once he got out of this cast. The doctors told him he'd never fully recover. Cold weather would make his leg ache, and he'd always have a slight limp.

I won't be fit for active duty. Other men are marching off to protect their country, and I can't go with them. Ever. The sooner he could get back to breaking the JN-25, the better. *If I can't offer my life, my mind will have to do.*

He maneuvered his crutches through the doorway and surveyed his new home. Decorated in blue and white with sturdy walnut furniture, the room contained nothing that could be called purely feminine—except her.

Valerie Fulton looked up from the small vase of flowers she'd obviously just placed on the bedside table. She offered a welcoming smile and quickly stepped away from the bed.

The faint blush coloring her cheeks made her even lovelier

than he recalled from this morning. Honey-colored curls brushed her shoulders, and now he knew her eyes sparkled a deep emerald green.

Paul didn't notice the awkward moment. "That's nice of you, Valerie."

"Thank you," Roy added quickly.

"You're welcome, Mr. Benson." She came closer. "Why, you hardly seem the same person!"

"Is that good or bad?" He liked how easily she met his gaze. She stood at the perfect height. He didn't have to bend his head, and she didn't need to crane her neck to have a conversation.

"I don't think it would matter how you wore your hair, Mr. Benson, though this suits you well. It's more important that you seem so much happier. I suppose you're just glad to be moving around a bit?"

"Exactly." He grinned. Not every woman would have realized the true change—Miss Fulton looked to the core of a man and understood what she saw.

"Well, Mom asked me to tell you both that dinner will be ready in about twenty minutes."

"Something sure smelled good when we walked in. Nothing like good home cooking, eh, Roy?"

I wouldn't know. "I'm looking forward to it." Roy moved back as she moved toward the door.

"Well." Once she reached the hallway, she regained some of the energy he'd seen in her earlier. "We aren't having green gelatin!"

Roy watched as she whisked around the corner and heard her little heels clicking smartly on the kitchen linoleum as she joined her mother. Belatedly realizing he'd gazed after her like a fool, he snapped his attention back to Paul, only to find the older man giving him a knowing look.

"She's single. Not seeing anyone, either."

Roy scrutinized a painting of an old ship. Its sails swelled in the wind, and Roy could practically smell the salt in the air. *I may not be back on a ship for some time, but there are definite advantages to staying here for a while. Still, it does no good to foster expectations.*

"I didn't ask."

"You know that sometimes a man doesn't have to use the words to ask a question like that." Paul cheerfully ignored Roy's casual dismissal. "But she just lost her fiancé a year ago, so be careful."

"What happened?" Roy gave in to his curiosity. No man with a lick of sense would leave a woman like her.

"Frank signed up with the Canadian Air Force and was shot down over Germany. Valerie had a rough time accepting the loss." Paul's expression became serious, and he crossed his arms over his chest. "If you hurt her in any way, you'll answer to me."

"You sound just like we're back in Switzerland when the headmaster told you I'd hidden a puppy in my closet."

"Some things never change."

"And others do." Roy gestured to his cast. "I'm not in any condition to pursue your stepdaughter, so rest easy." *Besides, now that I'm lame, I can't be the brave young soldier she'd want.*

The older man raised his hands in mock surrender. "All right. But you've been warned. Now let's go get some food!"

"This is excellent," Mr. Benson complimented before loading his fork again.

"Thank you, Mr. Benson." Rosemary, ever the gracious hostess, refilled his iced tea.

"I helped!" Valerie smiled at her new sister's pronouncement. Rebekkah clapped her hand to her heart and explained, "I washed the 'tatoes!"

"Well, I'll bet that's why these are the best baked potatoes I've ever had in my life."

His compliment made Rebekkah positively beam. Their houseguest's personable charm and easy good looks made him a welcome addition to the table. Surely Paul appreciated some masculine company in the house as well.

"What's running through that mind of yours, Valerie Jane Fulton?"

"Nothing special, Mom. Why do you ask?"

"Even I know that satisfied little grin," Paul teased. "It means you're up to something."

"Honestly, I was just thinking how glad you must be to have another man around the house. You've been pretty outnumbered for a while." Valerie loved teasing her stepfather because he always played along without taking any offense.

"I manage to hold my own!" he protested.

"Of course you do, sweetheart." Rosemary's reassuring pat drove the point home, and Mr. Benson chuckled.

"I think Miss Fulton's got you there, Paul!"

"Traitor!" Paul shook his head. "I'd expected better from you, Roy. You're no help at all."

"Sorry." Mr. Benson's hazel eyes sparkled for a moment as he reached for the green beans.

That's the first time his smile has reached his eyes, Valerie realized. *I know these are hard times we live in, but if we forget the good, we do a disservice to those fighting to protect it! I want to see that smile more often.*

Her sister's yawn caught her attention and reminded her that the time was getting late for the little tyke. "Come on, Bekkah." Valerie scooted her seat out and lifted the three-year-old to the floor. "Let's go get the Advent calendar."

Rebekkah clasped Valerie's hand and toddled over to the living room, where she carefully picked up the colorful cardboard before scampering back.

"Here, Momma!" She raised on tiptoes to hand it over.

Rosemary scooped Rebekkah in her arms and laid the calendar, with seven little peekaboo doors open, on the table.

"See the pretty angel, Rebekkah? Up here," she said, tapping the corner, "is an eight. That's today."

"Why is it an angel, Momma?" Rebekkah traced the angel's wings.

"Do you remember what we already learned about Mary? This is when an angel came to talk to her husband, Joseph. Let's read what the angel says."

Rebekkah carefully pried open the tiny door, and Valerie read aloud: " 'And she shall bring forth a son, and thou shalt call his name Jesus: for he shall save his people from their sins.' "

"Jesus born on Christmas!"

"That's right, darling."

"Why did the angel come to tell him that, though?"

"Rebekkah, do you remember that Jesus is God's Son?" Rosemary waited until Rebekkah finished bobbing her head. "The angel is telling Joseph that it's all right to be Jesus' father here on earth."

"Oh!" Rebekkah's eyes shone brightly as she crawled down

from her mother's lap and tugged on Paul's pant leg. "Like God told you to be my papa."

Valerie blinked back tears as Paul scooped up the little girl and bounced her on his knee. "That's exactly right, sweetie." He smiled tenderly. "I think it's time to get you ready for bed. We'll hear more of the story tomorrow night."

"Yes, Papa." She willingly went into Valerie's arms but stretched out her chubby little arms for a few last hugs and kisses.

"Ni-night, Papa. Ni-night, Momma."

"Good night, sweetie. We'll see you in the morning."

"'Kay." Rebekkah circled her arms around Valerie's neck and leaned her head against her shoulder. Valerie planted a kiss on those soft brown curls and headed upstairs to the nursery, where she helped her little sister change into a warm flannel nightie before leading her to the bathroom.

"Open wide." Valerie squeezed a dab of Ipana toothpaste on a brush and gave it to Rebekkah, guiding her hand to make sure every tooth was brushed.

Tucked snugly in her new "big girl" bed, Rebekkah followed Valerie's lead and recited her bedtime prayer:

> *"Now I lay me down to sleep,*
> *I pray the Lord my soul to keep.*
> *Guide me safely through the night,*
> *And wake me with the morning light.*
> *Amen."*

Valerie hummed softly until Rebekkah's eyelashes brushed her cheeks. It was better to stay with her until she fell asleep—it cut back on the nightmares she'd suffered since her arrival.

Lord, You've blessed us so in Rebekkah. Every time I look at her, I see the reason You brought Paul into our lives and how important those dolls really are. If it isn't in Your plan, I may never have a child of my own, but this precious child fills such a void in all our lives. Thank You for letting Paul bring her to us. And while I'm at it, thank You for making my mother so happy with her new husband and second daughter! Amen.

She made her way downstairs and found her mother, Paul, and Mr. Benson drinking coffee in the living room, listening to the evening news on the radio.

The past two weeks had flown by far more quickly than even a single week at the hospital ever had. Tomorrow would be Christmas Eve.

He'd quickly gotten used to the routine around the house. Getting up and shaving took him far longer than it used to, but by the time he made it to the kitchen, Rosemary or Valerie had laid the table with something fresh and delicious.

Valerie would leave for the bank, where she worked hard promoting the new war bonds, and Paul would go to work as well. Between reading the newspapers from front to back and listening to the radio for news about the war, Roy had plenty to map out.

Determined to be back on his feet in the best possible condition, he'd begun taking daily "walks" around the house on his crutches. Unfortunately, the icy winter sidewalks kept him indoors. After lying in a hospital bed for so long, he needed to work up his strength again.

Aside from the freedom of movement—and good cooking—

the real bright spots were the people sharing their home with him. Rosemary fussed over him like a fond mother hen while Rebekkah would toddle up to him at various times clutching a children's Bible or her favorite game—Snakes and Ladders.

Paul had shared with him that he and Rosemary had decided to adopt the child but evaded going into any more depth. The little girl brought an innocent joy that lit the whole house, but at nighttime, Roy could hear Rosemary comforting her as unnamed nightmares haunted her sleep. Roy knew vague details of how the Third Reich systematically deprived Jews of their rights and even homes. The fact that they were just teaching little Rebekkah about Jesus made him wonder whether she could be one of those children. Besides, when Rebekkah cried at night, he heard her speak in German, and that bore out his suspicions as to why Paul had brought her here. Still, it wasn't his place to ask. They'd been more than generous and hospitable to him.

The days flew by, but his favorite hours were in the evenings, when Valerie and Paul would come home, bringing stories and smiles to share. After dinner, they'd open another Advent window before Rosemary or Valerie put Rebekkah to bed. Then they'd gather in the living room for coffee and news.

Rosemary and Valerie were forever sewing tiny rag dolls to ship to their family's business in Denmark, where they apparently needed every import they could get. Paul even pitched in, so Roy didn't mind picking up a needle.

After Roy spent a few minutes hemming a minuscule apron, Valerie realized what he was doing. She stared in astonishment before letting loose a muffled squeak. The small sound caught Paul's and Rosemary's attention, and they all watched him for a while before Paul guffawed.

"Well, if that doesn't beat all. Must be all those years looking after your uniforms, eh, Roy?"

"That's right. But I'll never be able to hold my own with Mrs. Kincaid. Some people just have natural talent at stitching."

"I know!" Valerie dabbed another spot of blood with her handkerchief and moaned, "And you're far better at this than I'll *ever* be!"

Chapter 3

I'm home!" Valerie unwound her blue scarf and hung it on the coat tree in the hallway.

"Sissy!" Rebekkah shot down the hall and squealed as Valerie hoisted her high in the air, then snuggled her.

Roy watched the sweet scene for a moment before clearing his throat. "Did you get more cinnamon? We sorely need it."

"Yes." Valerie gifted him with a wide smile.

"Tomorrow's Christmas!" exclaimed Rebekkah.

"Right you are. Come on, let's go help." Valerie cocked her head, including Roy in the invitation.

"Sounds good to me." Roy hobbled along behind them on his crutches as Rebekkah chatted like a magpie.

"Mr. Benson took me out, but I'm not s'posed to talk 'bout it." The child sent him an exaggerated wink.

"Is that right?" Valerie murmured as she slanted Roy a look over her shoulder.

"Maybe." He'd taken Rebekkah for a walk over to Mrs. Ainsley's place and given her a list of things to buy with the money he folded inside the note.

More than happy to oblige, the old lady trundled off

immediately. The only hitch in the plan came when he told her he'd included a bit extra for her to use however she'd like.

Mrs. Ainsley had puffed up like a pigeon, using every single bit of her four-foot-eleven height to glare at him with sharp blue eyes.

"Now, Mrs. Ainsley, you've been so good to me that I want to get you something for Christmas, but I've no idea what you'd like. Besides, this is such a big favor you're doing for me that I absolutely insist." With that spur-of-the-moment speech, he'd won her over. He'd just finished stashing the bags she'd brought him when he heard Valerie come in.

"I get the message." Her eyes twinkled up at him. "I won't ask any more questions."

"That'll be the day." Paul strode into the room with Rosemary right behind him.

"Oh, honey, I sure am glad you didn't have to work today!"

Roy couldn't agree more with Rosemary's loving words. Valerie's company made time fly faster than the snow.

"I could use help making gingerbread men for after the service tonight."

In no time at all, everyone became engrossed in the project at hand. Rosemary threw together the ingredients, then handed the batter to Roy to beat into dough. He passed it on to Paul, who rolled it out and waited for Rebekkah to help him press down the cookie cutter, while Valerie laid the little figures on cookie sheets and popped them in and out of the oven.

"I've never baked before." Roy sniffed appreciatively. "But I could grow to like it." He reached out to snag a warm cookie, only to pull up short when Valerie smacked his hand away.

"What?" He tried to look as innocent as possible.

"I saw that, Roy Benson. Seems to me like we don't have as many of these little guys as we should."

The warm fragrance of ginger and cinnamon filled the house as the final batch baked to a perfect golden brown.

"It wasn't me! That would've been only my fourth one." Roy poked one of the cookies. "They have legs, you know."

"Sure. I suppose they just walked off." Valerie plunked more cookies onto the table, where Roy mixed a large batch of frosting.

"If they didn't, I'd look at the other side of the table, if I were you." He pointed at Paul, who gave a noticeable swallow.

"Don't you be pointing at us!" Paul put his arm around Rebekkah's shoulders. "We haven't swiped very many at all, have we, sweetie?"

But Rebekkah, cheeks puffed out like a greedy chipmunk, just kept sticking red-hots on the tiny dabs of icing to serve as buttons.

After a hearty laugh, they packed up the remaining gingerbread men for the churchgoers. While they finished up, Rosemary laid out dinner in the dining room, since cookies covered every available inch in the kitchen.

After supper, they all piled into the red Pierce-Arrow, Roy taking the front seat since he couldn't bend his left leg, and rode down to Gethsemane Chapel for the Christmas Eve candlelight service.

"Merry Christmas!" Roy hobbled into the kitchen, where Valerie pulled cinnamon rolls out of the oven.

"Merry Christmas." She smiled to see him so full of energy. "Everyone else will be down soon. I expect they're just getting Rebekkah dressed."

"I'll get the coffee started," Roy offered.

"It's already done. But if you could grab some milk from the icebox for Rebekkah, I'd appreciate it."

He'd just put the milk on the table when the rest of the family filed in and took their seats.

"Dear Lord," Paul prayed, "we thank You this fine morning for all You've given us. Today we remember how You forsook Your powers to come as a man and save us. Please bless this food on our table and watch over our boys not at home as they protect this nation. Amen."

After they'd eaten their fill and the dishes were finished, they made a beeline for the living room, where bright packages waited.

Valerie turned on the radio, changing stations until she heard "God Rest Ye Merry Gentlemen."

She and Paul passed out all the gifts before anyone opened a single package. Rebekkah fidgeted but stayed polite as ever.

In no time at all, wrapping paper and ribbon lay scattered across the floor, and a barrage of "thank-yous" echoed.

"The diary is wonderful, Mom. You remembered that my two-year journal would be all filled up come January!" Valerie hugged her mother joyfully.

"You're welcome, honey. I love my little music box." Rosemary lifted the lid, and the spritely tune competed with the radio.

Valerie got up and shut off the radio, instead opening the Victrola to place her brand-new Jimmy Dorsey album on it.

"Green Eyes" filled the air as she thanked Roy.

"Every time I hear that song, I think of you—you're the first girl I've ever known with green eyes, Valerie." Roy's thoughtfulness tugged at her heart. He was such a special man—and it went beyond his thick hair and deep gaze. Despite his frustration over his leg, he stayed patient with Rebekkah, kind to her mother, and companionable to Paul.

Although Valerie had never heard him utter a single word of complaint about how much his leg must hurt, every time he heard about the war, the pain in his eyes deepened. The physical discomfort of his broken leg didn't hurt him half as deeply as the reminder that he wasn't out there protecting the country.

Lord, help me, but a part of me is glad his leg will never completely recover. It means he'll be safe from the war. I couldn't bear it if I lost another man I care for to the Nazis.

"And thank you for the Chinese checkers," Roy said as he set the box on the coffee table. "You'll have to give me a chance to try it out this afternoon."

"Gladly. It'll be fun." Valerie looked at the box. "You know, I think we could all play tonight—it says up to six players."

"Count me out." Paul held up two books. "I've got other plans. Thank you both—Roy for *Call It Courage*, and Valerie for *Daniel Boone*. I'm going to enjoy these."

"I'm up to a game." Rosemary pulled on her new fleece gloves and wiggled her fingers. "These are perfect, Roy. Thank you!"

"You can use my special Christmas table." Rebekkah dragged over a tiny chair and whumped her new teddy bear on top of it.

Valerie was glad Rebekkah liked Teddy. She hoped it would help to have another cuddly friend in bed when the nightmares came again.

"I'm gonna draw a picture for Uncle Roy with my crayons." Roy had given Rebekkah a set of Crayolas, and she busily scribbled on a sheet of scrap paper until it was time for lunch.

❦

"When are you going to tell me what's going on?"

At Roy's pointed question, Paul peered over the top of his newspaper. "You already know that Hitler took complete command over the German army and that Churchill arrived in Washington just before Christmas. . . . And as of the New Year, the U.S. and twenty-five other countries have signed a contract of war against the Axis powers and pledged no separate peace—"

"I'm not talking about what I can read in the newspaper or hear from the radio, Paul," Roy said, cutting into the older man's recitation. "Level with me."

"Listen," Paul said as he put aside the newspaper, "the news is about as accurate as we can get. You know that preliminary data is always sketchy. I will tell you that for the first time in our nation's history, we've established a federal office of censorship to filter information concerning the war, but that's more for the protection of our troops' positions than to keep anything from the public. It's not designed to infringe on our rights."

"Interesting, but that's still not what I mean." Roy held up a rag doll. "And you know it."

Paul shrugged. "We already told you—the dolls are sent to Valerie's cousins Axel and Annelise in Denmark, where they are trying to keep an export-import business afloat." He picked up his paper and raised it once more as he added, "They distribute them there. The dolls are quite popular, I hear."

"Don't try to pawn a surface cover story off on me. You should know better."

"What makes you think there's anything else going on?" Paul tried to sound casual, but Roy sensed the purpose behind the question. If he could convince Paul that his suspicions stood on solid ground, he'd be let into the fold.

"First, why can't they just transport the raw supplies and contract the work to be done in Denmark?" Roy led off with an easy question.

"Rosemary and Valerie are happy to help their cousins. This way, they don't have to pay for the dolls to be made." Paul explained. "It's better business."

"That's what I figured at first, but too many things don't add up." Roy dove in. "What about that letter Valerie received yesterday? She started to read it aloud but got slower the farther down she got. After the news that the Nazis were forcing Dutch physicians into serving them, she stopped altogether. What did she leave out?"

"How would I know?" Paul scoffed. "I don't read her mail."

Obviously Paul wasn't going to cave in easily. But the more he denied, the more important the matter truly was, and Roy didn't intend to be left in the dark. He brought out the big guns.

"Don't forget I was practically raised in Europe. Rebekkah is no little Danish girl. Even before I saw Valerie write her name yesterday as winning tic-tac-toe, I had my suspicions. She's Jewish. Those nightmares she has are part of the reason you brought her here. She was in danger." Paul met his gaze steadily and gave a slight nod. Good. He was making headway.

"So what do you think is going on?"

The question was more than a challenge—Paul had thrown down the gauntlet. If Roy's suspicions didn't come close to the truth, this conversation would be over.

Lord, You know how much I want to be a part of defeating the Axis. If this is Your plan for me, let my words be true.

"Rebekkah has one of those dolls. As far as I can figure out, they're used to smuggle something into Denmark—small things." Roy put the pieces together, building his case. "I would've guessed ammunition, but that'd be too heavy. For some reason, you're sending money over to Denmark. More than Valerie's cousins would need for just themselves. And the last time you visited, you brought home a Jewish child. You've worked out some system where you're using the dolls to save Jews from the Nazis."

"Well done, Roy. I'd hoped you would catch on. The navy can be proud of how well we trained you."

"What are the specifics?" Roy carefully kept his voice neutral and waited eagerly.

"We send valuables in the dolls. In Denmark, they take out the jewels or cash or what have you and use it to fund the creation of documents enabling Jews to leave the country. Rebekkah is one of the children who depended on us."

Roy sucked in a deep breath. "Do the women know?"

"Rosemary and Valerie do. Rebekkah doesn't understand it. She just knows that I came for her, and we're her family now."

More questions raced through Roy's mind, but he knew better than to push. "Then why are we sitting here reading the paper?" He stood up.

"You're right." Paul heaved a resigned sigh. "A man's gotta do what a man's gotta do."

"Sir, yes, sir." Roy saluted him, then grinned. "I'll go get the needles and thread."

Chapter 4

Y ou could just give up now," Roy suggested, looking entirely too happy with himself as he lounged in his chair.

I would be annoyed, but his eyes are sparkling again. If it makes him smile to win a game of Chinese checkers, that's a small price to pay. Not that Valerie would let him know, though.

"Never!" she shot back, giving her hair a saucy flip and reaching for the board as Paul walked into the room.

"Losing again, is she?"

"I don't think she'll ever admit that naval officers can't be beat when it comes to strategy."

Roy's comment proved to be the straw that broke the camel's back. Valerie pretended to ponder her next move; then, just when Roy shifted in his seat, signaling his restlessness, she sprung into action, hopping one of her green marbles over the "bridge" he'd just finished making for his own use.

"Nice one, honey." Rosemary walked up beside Paul.

"Well, what do you know? Maybe you're in trouble after all, Roy!" Paul teased, but their smug smiles faded when Valerie hopped her final marble into its slot, beating Roy by at least three moves.

"Well, Roy, I think you've met your match." Rosemary winked at Valerie before leaving the kitchen.

"I certainly have." Valerie's breath caught at the intensity of Roy's gaze. He gathered his pieces and gently placed them in her palm, the marbles still warm from the heat of his hand.

"It's time to go to the store, Val!"

"Coming, Mom!" Valerie held the marbles a moment longer before putting them away and rushing outside.

When they got to town, Rosemary took off the gloves Roy had given her and stepped into Nannington's General Store. "Hello, Abel."

"Good morning, Rosemary. What can I get you today?"

"A bit of everything, Mr. Nannington." Valerie laughed.

"I need a book of three-cent stamps, a loaf of bread, a gallon of milk," Rosemary rattled off, "two yards of green flannel, a dozen eggs, and twenty pounds of sugar—the ten-pound bags, please."

"See?" Valerie quirked an eyebrow at the shopkeeper.

"I reckon your daughter had the right of it, after all." Abel grinned as he rummaged through the shelves, plunking down the requested items. "But I'm fresh out of the ten-pound bags of sugar." He hopped down from his step stool. "Had a run on it since we declared war. People remember how it was with the Great War not so long ago. I have three five-pounders left. I can call you soon as I get more in, if you'd like. You're probably real low after all those cookies you made for the Christmas Eve candlelight service. Those sure were tasty."

"Thank you, Abel." Rosemary took out her wallet. "What does that come to?"

Valerie gasped when she heard the price.

"Sorry, ma'am. Prices have gone up a lot in the past month. Bread and eggs are a full cent more per order, and milk is on the rise, too," Abel explained. "It'll be worse before the war is over."

"I expected that." While Rosemary paid the bill, Valerie grabbed the box of provisions and carried it out to the car.

"I hate to break it to you, honey," Rosemary said, sliding into the driver's seat, "but a time may come when we can't get some of these things at all. War leaves no family untouched."

❧

The door creaked open. Roy hurriedly jabbed his needle deep into the doll he was working on and stuffed it behind his back just as Valerie walked into the room.

"What are you doing?" She gave him an odd look as he swung the Duncan yo-yo Rebekkah had given him for Christmas into a perfect cat's cradle.

"Nothing much," he evaded, reaching for the paper. "What were you gals up to?"

"We went to the store. Just finished putting things away." She strolled over and stood behind his chair. "If you're going to read, you'll need more light."

He caught a whiff of violets as she reached over to turn on the lamp. . .and instead snatched the doll he'd been hiding.

"I knew it!" she crowed triumphantly, only to have her grin replaced by a puzzled frown. "Do you really like sewing that much?"

"Not really." He prayed she'd drop it. No such luck as she spoke once more.

"So you figured out most of it, and Paul filled you in on the rest." She tossed the doll onto his lap.

"Yep." He cautiously lowered the paper. He waited for her to say something more, but she just started filling another doll with cotton batting. He put down the paper and resumed work on the one in his lap. They worked in companionable silence until he finally asked, "How'd you know Paul didn't just tell me?"

"This was our only concern about bringing you here. Paul promised he wouldn't tell you unless you figured it out, and his word is his bond. Besides, you're too smart for your own good." Her smile softened the words, making them a compliment. "Oh, and that's what happened with me, too. You have to put the pieces together yourself before anyone will tell you if you've done it right. Discretion is vital."

"Your secret is safe with me," he vowed.

"I know." She met his gaze in earnest, those green eyes giving her words meaning beyond the conversation. "I trust you."

The next evening, as the adults sat in the family room, stitching as rapidly as possible, the news came on the radio.

"As you all know, last Friday saw the creation of the U.S. Joint Chiefs of Staff. This week is shaping up to bear just as many historic occasions. Yesterday, Washington sanctioned the establishment of the National War Labor Board to oversee wartime economy. This sparks fears of rationing, as was the norm in the Great War, so women around the nation are flocking to their neighborhood stores to stock up on essentials such as sugar. . ."

The voice droned on, speculating about probable shortages of various items, until Valerie got up and changed the station.

"We went to the store yesterday, and everything now is just predictions anyway." She fiddled with the dial until cheery strains of bebop filled the room. "That's better."

"He's right, though," Rosemary noted. "Abel Nannington didn't even have twenty pounds of sugar on hand yesterday, and we bought him out." She handed Valerie a doll to fill with stuffing.

"It's all right, Rosemary." Paul worked at untangling his thread for the umpteenth time that evening. "If there'd been anything else important or new, they'd have covered it at the beginning. Every station is on the lookout for updates anyway, so no matter what we listen to, we'll hear whatever special bulletin comes along next."

"No sense rehashing what we already know." Roy set another completed doll in his nearly full box.

The next Sunday, Valerie stood in the choir as they led the congregation of Gethsemane Chapel in worship. The director had worked with the pastor to choose pieces befitting the sermon to come. As they sang the final piece before the pastor took the pulpit, Valerie closed her eyes at the power of the words:

> *A mighty fortress is our God,*
> *   a bulwark never failing;*
> *our helper He amid the flood*
> *   of mortal ills prevailing.*
> *For still our ancient foe*
> *   doth seek to work us woe;*
> *His craft and power are great. . .*

How true and right those words rang as a prayer set to music. Valerie became swept away by the music, and before she knew it, they were in the midst of the third verse:

> *And though this world, with devils filled,*
> *should threaten to undo us,*
> *we will not fear, for God hath willed*
> *His truth to triumph through us. . .*

Soon the song was over, and the pastor bowed his head in prayer. "Lord, please defend us against the war. Our cause is just. Bless those families pulled apart by it, and let our faith remain strong that Your will may endure. Amen."

The choir filed off the platform and took seats in the front pews. In light of the escalating war, the pastor chose to speak from Psalm 144.

He read the first two verses, speaking of faith and justice, recalling David's words when he faced war. "Blessed be the Lord my strength, which teacheth my hands to war, and my fingers to fight: My goodness, and my fortress; my high tower, and my deliverer; my shield, and he in whom I trust. . . ."

After drawing the parallel between David's situation when he wrote those words and the situation faced by the members of the congregation, the pastor exhorted his parishioners not to curse the consequences of the war but rather to pray to the Lord in thanks for His blessings of strength.

Roy listened intently to the pastor's words, drinking in the promise of strength as America fought in Christ's name to protect the innocents of the world. As the pastor led them in a final prayer, Roy took the time to offer his own request.

Lord, is there no way I can serve You and my country other than through those dolls? Have I truly spent eight years learning all I could to be of use in the navy only to be relegated to sewing during a war engulfing the entire world? Lord, help me understand Your plan—and to accept Your will, whatever it may be. Amen.

As Roy lifted his head after the pastor finished, he saw Valerie standing at the fore of the entire choir. The organist began strains of a familiar hymn before Valerie's clear alto rang throughout the chapel:

> *'Tis so sweet to trust in Jesus,*
> *and to take Him at His word;*
> *just to rest upon His promise,*
> *and to know, "Thus saith the Lord."*

For the refrain, the entire choir joined her, and the music swelled with life as they praised the Lord and asked for *"grace to trust Him more."*

Roy watched Valerie's eyes close as she sang the words to the second verse, her face lit with joy and hope. Her voice sounded pure and sweet above the others as the entire congregation rose to join her.

Lord, this woman means more to me than I ever would have thought possible, but what do I have to offer her? Help me trust in Your plan, for now more than ever I am nothing without Your grace.

Chapter 5

In the first week of February, Paul took Roy in to get his cast off, but the doctors told him he'd have to use the crutches for another two weeks, minimum, as he began physical therapy.

"Is there any way to speed this up, Doc?" Roy pumped the physician for information.

"You'll recover better if you take it slow. Too much too fast will do you more harm than good." Dr. Harwell fixed him with a penetrating stare. "First we'll work on stretching to get back your range of motion. Only then is it realistic to work on strengthening the muscle. You've been off this leg for over two months already; it isn't possible for you to just resume walking."

"I was afraid of that." Roy looked down at his legs and grimaced to see his left side so thin compared to the right.

"When you regain your muscle, they won't look so disproportionate." The doctor took a moment to jot down several notes on his clipboard before pronouncing, "I'll see you after two weeks of physical therapy. I want to be perfectly clear: You're still confined to crutches. On the bright side, it'll be a lot less unwieldy without that big cast. But no trying to walk on that leg yet. That's an order."

"Yes, sir." Roy grudgingly gave his word, seeing the wisdom in the doctor's order. He'd come too far to let a lack of patience land him back in traction.

❦

"Quit scowling, Roy." Valerie handed him a hot water bottle, which he gratefully placed on his shinbone. He put every ounce of determination he possessed into his daily exercises and received each measure of it back in stiffness afterward.

"Sorry, Val. I don't mean to be a grouch. I'll make it up to you with a game of Chinese checkers." His offer made her chuckle.

"All right. Who knows? You just might win this time." She opened the cupboard, grabbed the box, and set up the game on the side table next to his recliner. Since elevating the leg helped make him more comfortable, it had become his favorite chair.

"Yeah, yeah. Let's just play." He pretended to grump just a bit more to coax another smile from her beguiling lips.

"Listen." She perched on the chair she'd pulled up and rested a soft hand on his forearm. "In a week or so, Doc Harwell will decree you're ready to begin strength training. You'll be walking in no time."

He placed his hand over hers and gave it a slight squeeze. "Thanks, Valerie. I hope you're right."

"Well, I *know* I'm right." She tossed him a mischievous smile. "Now let's get this game going."

A short half hour later, Roy beamed over his hard-won victory.

"Hail the conquering her—o," Paul sang as Roy hopped over to the dinner table. "It's about time you won that game."

"Well, I hope you both learned a lesson." Rosemary ladled heaping portions of thick beef stew into bowls and passed them around.

"Oh, they'll think twice before they say anything about how women can't beat navy men when it comes to strategy." Valerie nonchalantly buttered Rebekkah's biscuit.

"True," Roy admitted. "I should've remembered that you work in a bank, so you're good with numbers and logic." He raised his iced tea. "To a worthy opponent."

"I'll drink to that." They all raised their glasses, then made a special to-do about clinking cups with Rebekkah, who giggled and sloshed her juice down the front of her dress.

Dinner remained a merry affair, and before she knew it, Valerie sat next to Roy in the living room again, listening to the evening news on the radio.

"Top news tonight, February 9. We'd like to remind everyone to set their clocks back an hour as daylight saving war time goes into effect. Although we'll all lose an hour's sleep tonight, we'll gain extra daylight every day. The increased productivity is expected to be a valuable contribution to the home-front war effort. When you listen to tomorrow's broadcast, you'll hardly believe it's actually eight o'clock!

"In other news, General Clinton Pierce, the first U.S. general to be wounded in action, has become an inspiration to our armed forces. Remember him and all our boys in your prayers tonight. . . ."

As the news broke into local headlines, Roy turned down the volume. "When they start changing the hours of the day, you know the war is getting serious."

"I think I'll like having an extra hour of light when I get

home from the bank," Valerie protested, determined to overlook the minor inconvenience of getting up an hour earlier and in the dark.

"If it doesn't work out, at least it's just for the war." Rosemary snipped her thread and tied another knot before passing the doll so Valerie could stuff it. This new system of having Roy take over her portion—and more, in all fairness—of the sewing and leaving her to stuff the dolls meant unpricked fingers and less tired eyes.

Roy Benson had proved a blessing in more ways than she'd ever imagined. Rebekkah had taken a shine to him; Paul obviously enjoyed having another man around the house; Rosemary got more help with the dolls; and Valerie got the satisfaction of seeing everyone be happy—not to mention the warm tingles she got every time he smiled at her with those deep hazel eyes. He wasn't going anywhere for at least another month, too. All in all, life was good.

⸎

"Come on, Valerie!" Roy called up the stairs.

"I'm coming!" She fairly flew down the stairs and gave him a quick frown before continuing along the hallway. "You do remember I'm the one who asked you about this?" she reminded him.

"I know." He stashed his crutches in the backseat. "And I'm glad you did."

Valerie shut the door and walked around the car to slide into the driver's seat. "I didn't mean to grump at you, Roy," she apologized as they made their way to the hospital. "It doesn't seem to matter how many times I give blood, I'm always happiest when it's all over."

"That's just because they give you juice afterward," Roy teased, knowing full well that Valerie gave blood out of nothing less than a deep determination to help others in any way possible. She'd inherited a fair portion of her mother's generous spirit.

"Ssshhh. If you tell them, they won't give me my favorite!"

"What's your favorite?" he wondered aloud. "Apple or orange?"

"I'm not telling." She pulled into a parking space and drummed her fingers on the steering wheel.

Despite her attempt to keep a lighthearted tone, he knew what she was thinking. "It's just one tiny needle. You'll be fine."

Half an hour later, they both sat at a table drinking juice and munching on cookies.

"You know, this reminds me a lot of Rebekkah's tea parties." Valerie lifted a tiny paper cup. "You're so good about attending those."

"I don't know what you're talking about." Roy feigned ignorance. "Soldiers don't go to tea parties."

"Oh, all right. I won't say anything more to spoil your image. I only wanted to thank you for how special you make her feel." She touched his hand across the table. "You have a knack for that."

"You are both special to me." He wasn't about to let the moment go. "Besides, don't think I haven't noticed how much better Rebekkah has slept since you gave her that teddy bear for Christmas."

"She's so sweet." Valerie smiled fondly. "She cuddles him on one side and her dolly on the other."

"See? You've made sure she knows she's always surrounded with love."

They simply looked at each other until a man sauntered over and plunked down onto another chair.

"Hello, Mr. Twisselman," Valerie greeted the stout fellow.

"Hello, Valerie." His moustache twitched as he spoke. "How are you?"

"Just fine. I don't like needles," she admitted to the older man, "but when I'm done, I always feel wonderful."

"Yep. Have to be careful, though." Mr. Twisselman hooked his thumbs in his suspenders and leaned back. "I come often. Good thing we butchers are hardy stock." He grabbed a paper cup.

"So true—" Valerie gasped. "Mr. Twisselman!" The butcher's face grew waxen as he slumped to the floor.

"Nurse!" Roy bellowed for help as Valerie dabbed Mr. Twisselman's forehead with a damp cloth.

"It'll be all right, miss." An orderly lifted the butcher off the floor.

"Happens all the time." A tall nurse brought out a blood pressure cuff. "He'll be fine."

"Would you like me to call his wife?" Valerie offered.

"No need. We'll keep him here a bit longer and send him on his way," the nurse assured them as she swept the now-empty paper cups into a trash can and mopped up Mr. Twisselman's juice.

As they walked out of the hospital doors, Roy smiled. *Well, Lord, I suppose being of "hardy stock" just might be overrated. If a fainting butcher can help in the war effort, why can't a lame soldier lend a hand? I'll ask the doctor at Monday's appointment just how much I can expect to be able to do.*

❦

"What did the doctor say?" Rosemary beat Valerie to the question before Roy so much as stepped into the room.

"Tomorrow I begin strength training." Roy's grin faded somewhat as he continued. "Of course, I'm still not supposed to try putting any weight on it."

"Bouncing is fun!" Rebekkah hopped in on one foot, a habit she'd taken to whenever the subject of Roy's leg came up. The three-year-old had to grab on to other things to manage it, but her special way of encouraging her "Uncle Roy" showed how much Roy had become a part of the family.

"Well, that's probably for the best." Rosemary's practical comment didn't seem to cheer him up any. "The streets are still icy, and we wouldn't want any accident to set you back."

"Look on the bright side," Valerie broke in. "It's a *step* in the right direction!"

Everybody groaned at her pun, but Roy smiled once again, making it all worthwhile.

❦

Roy looked out the window and, for the first time in months, saw a patch of blue sky. Mid-March brought the first hope of spring and the promise of change.

A lot had changed since he'd come here. The United States had declared war against the Axis powers, hundreds of soldiers had gone off to fight, and Roy had come to terms with the reality he would never be one of them. The dolls gave him a focus and purpose as his leg recovered, and he knew that although he couldn't engage in active combat, he could serve in other ways. No longer burdened by a large cast, Roy did so well in physical therapy that he'd graduated to using a cane this afternoon. He grasped it and rose from his chair, gritting his teeth and leaning heavily on the cane as he slowly made his way toward the kitchen. As his leg took the weight with only minor discomfort, he relaxed a bit and moved more easily.

Through all that, he'd become part of a real family. Roy would miss them when he left—Paul's guidance, Rosemary's mothering, Rebekkah's high-pitched giggle, and Valerie's. . .well, he'd miss everything about Valerie. Her honey curls, the mischievous sparkle in her green eyes when she teased him, the purity of her voice raised in song, how she cuddled Rebekkah, even the way she played Chinese checkers.

Before he went back, he would make a point of spending more time with her—alone, so he wouldn't have to see Paul and Rosemary exchanging smug glances. In a few days, he would be able to walk much farther. Maybe they could go for a stroll.

Lord, I complained so bitterly about my leg, but You've blessed me in so many ways through the injury. Physical strength is not the only way to be of worth. Thank You for showing me that truth.

Rebekkah tugged on his sleeve. "Snack time."

Roy grinned and took her into the kitchen, grabbing a couple of oatmeal cookies from the jar on the counter.

"Aha!" Valerie's exclamation made him turn.

"Mmmf—what?" he muttered around a mouthful of cookie. Rebekkah shoved her cookie behind her back and pressed up against the white kitchen cupboards, looking about as innocent as a girl with crumbs around her mouth ever could.

"I knew it!" Valerie's eyes flashed with suppressed laughter as she advanced into the room. "Caught you with your hand in the cookie jar."

Roy heaved a deep sigh and fessed up. "Guilty as charged, ma'am."

"I'll let you off with just a warning this time, soldier," Valerie intoned as she crooked a finger. "Hand over the contraband, and we'll call it even."

Roy winked at Rebekkah as his partner in crime crammed the second half of her cookie into her mouth. "I can't do that, ma'am. It's gone for good." He tried to keep a straight face as Valerie abandoned her role of authority figure to grab the green-trimmed ceramic canister and shove her arm in clear up to her elbow.

After groping along the bottom for a few seconds, Valerie gave up. "You ate the last one when you knew oatmeal cookies are my favorite?" She stared up at him in disbelief, sending a small pang of guilt through his chest. He hadn't meant to be so inconsiderate.

"Sorry, sissy." Rebekkah held up one tiny hand littered with crumbs. "All gone." Her lower lip began to quiver.

"Oh, sweetie!" Valerie scooped the toddler into her arms. "It's all right. We'll just have to break into the emergency supply!"

Roy watched in astonishment as Valerie nudged a cabinet open with her elbow and withdrew a round blue tin and set it on the counter. She popped off the lid and drew out three cookies before resealing it and nestling the tin behind some preserves.

"And you tried to make us feel guilty." Roy gazed fixedly at the cookies in her hand. "You've been holding out on us!"

She let loose a peal of silvery laughter before passing a cookie to him and handing another to Rebekkah. "When Paul moved in, we had to start making extra and putting a few aside," she explained.

"Good thinking!" Roy bit into the warm, buttery cookie and promised, "I won't tell!"

❦

"Here you go, Bekkah." Valerie handed her little sister a tiny shovel.

"I make holes." Rebekkah gleefully stuck her new toy in the dirt and made a shallow opening. "See?"

"Good job!" Valerie clapped. "Now do it again and make it deeper, like mine."

" 'Kay." Rebekkah rolled up her little sleeves, emulating Rosemary's habit for outdoor work, then dug in. The largest seeds, peas, sat in a bucket beside her. When Rosemary agreed the hole was deep enough, the little girl dropped in a seed and covered the hole with dirt.

"Done." Rebekkah clapped her hands and dirt powdered her little snub nose.

"One more thing. Now we have to make sure it's good and packed in there." Valerie walked over and pressed the dirt down.

"I can do it!" When Valerie stepped back, Rebekkah began stomping on the dirt.

"That's enough," Rosemary laughed. "If you keep it up, we'll never finish! Why don't you get going on the next one?"

More quickly than they would have thought possible, they filled the garden with hardy veggies like radishes, spinach, and peas. Later, when the weather warmed up even more, they'd make room for sweet corn, cucumbers, and beans.

Rebekkah hopped all around the garden for good measure as Rosemary helped Valerie rinse off their tools.

"Come on, Bekkah," Valerie called when they headed for the house.

"Comin', sissy!" She made a beeline for the house, practically zooming through the door before Valerie caught her.

"Oh, no you don't! Wipe your feet really good before you go in." Clumps of dirt dotted the mat before they all finished and trooped through the door.

"Why don't you go play with Teddy while Val and I heat up some lunch?" Rosemary watched her scamper up the stairs before fixing Valerie with a penetrating stare.

"What? I thought the garden went well." Valerie's stomach grumbled as it always did when her mother gave her that look.

"It did. I just thought it was time for a talk. Woman to woman." Rosemary sat down at the kitchen and patted the chair beside her. "While Paul and Roy are still at the doctor's."

Valerie's heart pounded in alarm. "I thought the doctor seemed impressed with Roy's progress. He's even starting to walk now! What's wrong?"

"Oh, it's nothing like that. Actually, I wanted to talk with you because he's healing so well." Rosemary reached over and clasped her hand. "He won't stay forever, you know."

"I know." Valerie didn't meet her mother's eyes.

"But he wants to."

"How do you know that? All his focus is on getting well so he can go back to the navy and risk his life." Valerie angrily swiped a tear off her cheek.

"Oh, honey, that's not true. Look at the way he's settled into this family—how wonderful he is with Rebekkah." She paused for a beat. "He'd make a good father."

"Don't say that." Valerie pulled her hand away.

"It's true."

"I didn't say you were wrong. He has other plans—he's never said one word to me about. . ." Her voice trailed off.

"About what? How deeply he cares for you? How much he appreciates this family? Honey, he's said plenty."

"Not to me. When did he tell you any of that?"

"Whenever he reads to Rebekkah or sews another doll, he shows his softness for children." Rosemary tipped her face up and smiled tenderly. "And every time he looks at you, it speaks volumes. You can't say you've never noticed it, Valerie."

"I know, Mom. I care for him, too."

"There was never any question in my mind about that. Show him."

Chapter 6

"I'll drive." Roy snagged the keys from the peg in the hallway.

"I don't think so." Valerie made a grab for them, but he moved too quickly.

"I like that zippy red Pierce-Arrow." He folded his arms across his chest, making his shoulders seem even broader than usual.

"You've only been walking for a week, and we're going to be walking all day." Valerie tapped her foot impatiently. She looked so adorable with that concerned expression that he conceded.

"Okay, but I'm driving home." He tossed the keys to her, and she snatched them in midair.

"So long as you feel up to it after a long day, that's fine with me." Her disgruntled look vanished as her eyes softened. "I just want you to be careful."

"I will be. Besides, I have a feeling today's going to be filled with fun. Bring on the fresh air!" He opened the door for her, and they walked out to the car.

"I must say it'll be nice not to have to carry a step stool

142

around with me. You're so tall, you can tack the tops of the posters."

Roy looked at the stack of war bond advertisements piled on the backseat. "Sure are a lot of them."

"Mmm-hmm." Valerie nodded. "It's a good thing, too. The last ones I put up didn't fare too well through the February storms. We'll take them all down and put the new ones up."

"Anything for the war effort."

"After all you've done, I believe it!" She pulled into a parking space. "This is a good block to start."

"Which ones do you want to hang first?" Roy flipped through the glossy ads. "The Statue of Liberty, Uncle Sam, battleships, or. . ." He stopped as he came across a poster of uniformed soldiers parachuting onto a battlefield with the words "BACK THE ATTACK—BUY WAR BONDS" emblazoned across the bottom.

"A bit of everything. It's best to have a variety on each block so the people don't see the same thing on every corner. We don't want to be boring!"

"As if you ever could be," Roy scoffed, grabbing an assortment so they could get down to work.

"All of these need to come down." Valerie gestured to sadly faded Christmas pictures reminding that war bonds were "the present with a future."

Together, they tore down the old and tacked up the new, keeping a companionable conversation going all the while as they looked at other posters.

"I like this one." Roy gestured to a red ad for stamps with caricatures of Nazis. It asked the public to help "lick the Axis."

"Pretty clever, aren't they? Catchy, even." Valerie shoved

the ratty old posters into a convenient garbage bin and strolled a bit farther with Roy at her side.

"Some of these are slogans we'll never forget." Roy stopped in front of a rendering of a battle cruiser with the reminder that "loose lips sink ships."

"I know. When you hear on the news how many ships have been attacked by U-boats and gone down, it reminds you how important it is to find the funds to replace them." Valerie tacked up another poster on a nearby fence.

"It's good to be out and doing something." Roy swiped the hammer and reached up to anchor the top. The crown of her head scarcely reached his shoulder.

"Especially when the weather's so nice." The crisp breeze put a healthy glow in her cheeks as the sunlight danced in her golden curls.

"It's beautiful." Roy drank in the sight of her as she turned to face him.

"We'd best get back to the car and move on to the next block. We're running out of posters."

❦

A few hours later, as she held up another one and Roy tacked the top, Valerie heard Roy's stomach rumble. "Hungry?"

"I could go for a bite to eat. I'm running on empty." He grinned. "Know anyplace around here with a good lunch special?"

"Hmm." Valerie thought for a minute. "Ella's makes the best chicken salad sandwich you've ever tasted. How does that sound?"

"Perfect. Let's go."

As they munched their sandwiches in companionable silence, Valerie caught sight of a newspaper. "Did you read the article about how the U.S. is moving native-born Americans of Japanese ancestry into detention centers?" She shook her head sadly. "In the midst of war so many people already lose their homes. It doesn't make sense to corral part of the population based on race."

Roy furrowed his brow. "How can we expect to have the Lord sanction our cause when we allow fear and prejudice to make us betray our own citizens?"

"I don't know." Valerie couldn't say anything to comfort him. The truth of the matter was that the discrimination against any person based on their heritage couldn't end well.

Every time she saw that determined glint in Roy's eyes, she knew she was that much closer to losing him. *Lord, he can do so much from right here. Please don't take him from me.*

After lunch they slid into the car. Valerie smiled at him. "Thank you for your help."

"I'm just glad I could do something to help." Roy grinned. "And the company's not bad, either."

"Why, I didn't peg you for such a sweet talker, Mr. Benson," Valerie drawled and batted her long lashes.

Roy laughed at her antics as she'd intended him to, then gazed at her intensely. "You know what I meant, Val."

Her breath caught when he stroked her cheek with the tip of his finger.

"You're an amazing woman."

"Roy, I—" An angry honk from an impatient driver shattered the tender moment, and Roy pulled out of the parking lot.

"I'm glad FDR asked the commissioner to continue baseball. All sorts of interesting things are happening with the game." Paul tapped the sports section the next morning.

"Sure was good of the Yankees to let five thousand uniformed soldiers in free to each of their home games," Roy agreed.

"Did you know that the Chicago White Sox just let two Negro players work out with them?"

"About time. It's not as though white men are the only ones who can play the game. Just look at the Negro American League! I hope they make the team."

"Time will tell. Remember the name Jackie Robinson—apparently he's pretty good." Paul folded the paper. "Not that we don't have other things to discuss, you and I."

"Like what?" Roy eased into a chair and kicked up his feet on the ottoman.

"Like Valerie. What happened between the two of you yesterday?"

Roy straightened and looked the older man in the eye. "Why would you think anything happened?"

"Because of the way you two were acting—skittish as newborn colts. Besides. . ." Paul frowned. "Valerie hardly spoke ten words last night."

Roy laughed. "So that's a dead giveaway, is it? We had a nice day together. She's a special woman."

Paul chuckled. "You know it!" He sobered a bit. "Remember what we talked about your first day here."

"I will." Roy took the pledge seriously. He had no intentions of toying around with Valerie's affections. She meant too much to him.

Two nights later, Valerie shoved the last bit of stuffing into another doll and handed it back to her mother. "We're out of filling."

"Already? But we just bought more!" Rosemary looked at the empty container in dismay.

"I think we have Roy to blame for that." Paul jerked a thumb at Roy, who busily affixed the finishing touches on a specialty Cinderella doll for Captain von Rundstedt's niece.

"Hey!" Roy took exception to being blamed.

"That's just because he's increased our productivity so much." Valerie patted his shoulder. "It's really a good thing, when you think about it."

"Not *that* good." Rosemary pulled out the list of stores where they'd purchased supplies. "I'm out of ideas on where to go. People are going to get suspicious if we keep buying cotton batting. With the war on, no one's sparing a dime for anything not absolutely necessary. We're starting to stick out like a red polka dot on a blue-striped shirt." She shook her head.

"I suppose we could travel farther," Valerie offered.

"We've already been anyplace we can reach in a day and be back before dark. It's not safe." Rosemary put a stop to that idea at once.

"I'll go with her," Roy jumped in.

"Absolutely not." Rosemary glared at them. "If you two disappear for a night, you'll both be ruined. The gossips will have a heyday, and how would you explain where you'd been?"

"We'll just have to figure something else out," Paul soothed. "What can we buy that we can use instead?" Silence fell as everyone pondered the question.

"You know," Roy mused, "mattresses are filled with stuffing to make them soft."

"That's a good idea!" Valerie perked up.

"It's too expensive," Rosemary sighed. "We can't buy a whole mattress just for the stuffing."

"Who said anything about buying?"

Blank looks met Roy's question. "We're not going to make off with mattresses, Roy." Paul glowered.

"No, of course not. We're not hoodlums. I meant going down to the junkyard and taking the stuffing out of old mattresses. Some of it will be in pretty bad shape, but the part in the very middle will work just fine."

"You can't beat free." Paul slapped his knee.

"Tomorrow's Saturday, so you and Valerie can go check it out. Just try and be as discreet as possible," Rosemary ordered.

"Sounds like we've got a plan." Roy winked at Valerie, and she couldn't help but think tomorrow would be a good day.

Chapter 7

Roy gaped as Valerie walked down the stairs early the next morning. "You're wearing slacks!" The getup made her slim legs look longer than usual. How could wearing a man's clothes make her seem even more feminine than when she wore a skirt?

"I couldn't very well go crawling around a scrap heap in a dress, now, could I?" She pulled on a pair of gloves.

"I suppose not," he grumbled. "What if someone sees you?"

"Now that women are working, slacks are far more standard. Besides, it's early and we're going to a junkyard, so I doubt I'll be running into many people anyway." With a gamine grin, she headed for the door, and Roy noticed she'd tied her curls into a shiny, bouncy ponytail. One thing was for sure—Valerie would never be predictable.

Half an hour later, they pulled into a deserted lot outside of town and opened the creaky gate to the junkyard. Piles of popped tires towered over smaller heaps of everything imaginable.

"This will be an adventure!" Valerie gawked around. "Let's get started."

"Let's walk the perimeter. Maybe there will be a pile of

them somewhere." He set about surveying the site in an orderly fashion. Valerie quirked a brow and headed toward the middle of the yard, then turned left.

"Over here!" In two minutes, she'd tracked down a stack of old mattresses.

"How did you know where they were?" Roy pulled out his pocketknife and slashed the first mattress.

"I don't know. I think the Lord just led me where we needed to go." Valerie pressed down on the edge of the mattress, and dirty rainwater oozed out. "Ugh. Maybe we should try the next one. This one bore the brunt of our storms."

Together, they hefted the monstrosity over to unearth a slightly smaller mattress already boasting a hole in the middle.

"That's more like it!" Valerie opened a laundry bag and held it out as he grabbed handfuls of the well-preserved stuffing and shoved it into the bag.

They'd already filled every bag they'd brought by the time they hit the last two mattresses. "Here, let's heft a few of the other ones on top so they'll still be all right when we need to come back." Roy and Valerie tossed the already gutted mattresses back on top, then carried their bounty back to the car.

"That worked well. You're very resourceful, Roy." Valerie smiled at him as they stood by the trunk.

"Oh, it was nothing." He shrugged it off.

"Roy." She placed a hand on his arm so he'd look at her. "I mean it. You need to hear what a great help you've been. Every doll you've made is another child saved. You know that. It's the reason you've been working on them practically nonstop and gone through all our stuffing. You could've just sat around complaining about your physical therapy, how you were taken away from your job, how much you wanted to leave, but instead you did something much better. Thanks to you, we've been able to help so many more of God's children." She took a deep breath. "Earlier you told me *I* was amazing, but you're nothing short of incredible."

With a low groan, he kissed her. She rested perfectly in his arms, her lips soft as she twined her arms around his neck. When the kiss ended, he held her close for a moment longer. "I love you, Valerie Fulton."

"I love you, too, Roy." She blushed sweetly. "Let's go home."

❦

"The Gallup poll has officially named this World War II." Roy gave Valerie an update as she hung up her scarf after work on Tuesday.

"That took longer than I'd expected. Anything else I should know?"

"Just that Paul's still at the docks overseeing another shipment of dolls, and your mother and Rebekkah took some fish to Grandma Ainsley for her cat."

"It's so sweet that you call her Grandma Ainsley now, too." Valerie gave him a peck on the cheek. "Any mail today?"

"It came late, actually. There's a letter from your cousins in Denmark." He handed it to her.

"Thanks." She slid her finger beneath the flap and cracked open the envelope before reading the message aloud:

Dear Rosemary, Valerie, Paul, and Roy,
   We are glad to hear that you are all doing well—we

*keep you in our prayers and hope by the time you get this,
Roy is completely off his crutches. Please write and tell us
how your latest addition to the family is doing! The merchandise is quite successful, and Captain von Rundstedt
requests a Cinderella package for his niece.*

*All our love,
Annelise and Axel*

*P.S. Our friend Mr. Wright wrote and said he is in poor
health. He's to see the doctor on April 30. Please keep him
in your prayers.*

"Who's Mr. Wright?" Roy studied the Danish stamp.

"We don't know a Mr. Wright, so it must mean something
important." Valerie frowned. "Paul will know."

"What will I know?" Paul boomed from behind them.

Valerie jumped. Her stepfather's silent tread had managed
to startle her on more than one occasion. "Axel and Annelise
want us to pray for a Mr. Wright. He's seeing a doctor tomorrow." Valerie handed the letter to him.

"I'll go see him day after tomorrow."

"I'm coming with you," Valerie and Roy insisted in unison.

"Roy will come, but you need to go to work." Paul took
Valerie's elbow and guided her away from the glass-paned door.

"If there's no other way. . .but I'll be jittery as a June bug
until I know what's going on."

Roy understood exactly what she meant. If the operation
was in serious jeopardy, not only would they be unable to
send any more dolls, but her cousins' very lives would be in
danger.

ॐ

"Good morning, Mr. Wright."

Roy noted that the mailbox designated the home as the Larson residence but kept that observation to himself as Paul introduced them.

"We're told you are in poor health."

"Come in, come in." Mr. "Wright" ushered them inside and locked the door.

"Annelise and Axel asked me to tell you that a secretarial associate with their import office has passed away, and they must find a replacement immediately. They specifically request someone who types well and knows German."

"Thank you very much, Mr. Wright." Paul shook the man's hand.

"I hope it helps."

"Your many contributions to our country will not be forgotten." Roy saluted the officer before they left and got back in the car. He waited until they were well on the road before speaking. "They can't provide the necessary documentation. That's what the message meant, right?"

"Yes," Paul affirmed grimly. "Finding a replacement will be tricky. It could undermine the secrecy of the entire operation, and with the Nazi presence so firmly established now in Denmark, they can't search on their own. Remember how last night we heard that Jews in the Netherlands are being forced to wear the star of David? Axel and Annelise's position is becoming more precarious." Paul stopped at a light and rubbed his temples. "We'll lose a lot of time while I find a permanent replacement."

"You already know someone who can fill in during the

meantime, Paul. I read, write, and speak fluent German and am more than familiar with official documents. I assume they have all the supplies I'll need?"

"Yes," Paul agreed slowly. "And you get around just fine now. . . ."

"But not enough to fight. I'll need to get back to the OP-20-G in about a month, but for now this is something I can do. Send me."

❧

"Well, what happened?" Valerie demanded as she bounded into the living room without so much as a friendly hello.

Rosemary called Rebekkah into the kitchen, and the little girl scampered off.

Lord, Roy prayed fervently, *please give me the words to help her understand why I have to leave, and grant me the grace to return to her.*

"Calm down, Val. Have a seat." Paul pointed to the couch.

"I've had a horrible feeling all day." She sank onto the sofa beside Roy. "Just tell me."

"The forger died, and they have no one to create the necessary documents." Paul brought her up to speed. He smiled. "Consider yourself debriefed."

"They can't find another one over there—things are getting worse every day." Valerie jumped to her feet. "If they try, they'll be discovered and executed."

"We know. That's why I'm going to track down a permanent replacement." Paul shot Roy a sideways look. "We're concerned about the time lost while we find one."

Valerie chewed her lip. "How long do you think it'll take?"

"A few weeks, at least. Discretion is key."

"Every moment is precious." Valerie paced behind the couch. "If only there was something we could do. . . ."

"There is. I've located a party willing to fill in until the permanent worker arrives."

"That's wonderful!"

"I'm glad you think so." Roy stepped in front of her and put both hands on her shoulders. Out of the corner of his eye, he saw Paul surreptitiously leave the room to give them privacy. "I leave as soon as they draw up my passport."

He watched the smile melt from her face.

"You?" Her whisper was barely audible.

"Yes, me." He held on as she tried to pull away, tears sparkling in her eyes.

He pulled her closer to wrap her into a hug. She sagged against him with a shuddering sigh, then pounded his chest with her fist.

"No. You're. Not. Going." She punctuated each word with another thump.

He captured her hands and kissed them. "It's the only way, darling."

"Don't you try to 'darling' me, Roy Benson." She glowered up at him. "You're not going to get me to say it's a good idea to send you halfway around the world to perform illegal rescue operations right in front of countless Nazis." Her face crumpled as the tears trickled down her cheeks. "We don't even know how the last guy died."

"Remember how the letter said everyone else was fine? They haven't been found out, Valerie."

He nestled her close as she thought for a moment, then

looked up pleadingly. "Don't go, Roy. I don't want to lose you."

"If I don't go, I've lost myself." The words sounded gruff to his own ears as he brushed his cheek against her soft hair.

"Why?"

"Do you remember what you said about me helping instead of sitting around complaining about my leg? I sewed all those dolls because it gave me a purpose. I even came to think that a lifelong limp was a small price to pay if my work saved even one child like Rebekkah."

"You've got a lot of nerve," she grumbled, "being so wonderful when you're telling me you're gallivanting off to risk your neck."

Encouraged, he continued. "I'll never be able to go off and fight with the other men, Valerie, but I'll always do what I can to serve God and country. It's who I am."

She gave a shuddering sigh and nodded. "I know."

He grabbed his handkerchief out of his pocket and wiped her face tenderly before pulling her into a deep kiss. "I'll come back to you."

"You'd better."

Chapter 8

Valerie stared at the blank page in her diary. *May 5, 1942,* she scribbled at the top.

I'm writing by lamplight with the windows shaded as nightly dim-outs along the East Coast continue. Last night my shade tore, so Mom and I hung up an old blanket to serve in the meantime. Today official sugar rationing was announced, and gas rationing is expected to begin any day now.

I can't get my mind off of yesterday's news that German troops have taken more than four hundred prominent Dutch citizens as hostages. Each day things become more dangerous in Scandinavia.

Has Roy really only been gone four days? I miss him so. He still won't be back for at least another three weeks. I can't call him, can't write him, can't stop thinking about him. I have no way of knowing he is well.

She shut her diary, turned off the lamp, and knelt by her bed to pray. *Lord, will You bring him back to me? Wherever he is, please keep him safe. Help me to concentrate on the good You've sent him to do, Lord, rather than be consumed by my worries. Hard as it was to work through the grief of losing Frank, I know losing Roy would be unbearable. Please, Lord, watch over him. Amen.*

※

Roy slung his duffel bag into the dinghy, then braced himself as the tiny craft was lowered into the water. The small splash sounded as loud as a tidal wave in the stillness of the dark night. They sculled toward the shoreline.

After five days at sea in the cramped cargo hold, he looked forward to being on dry land. He'd never managed to find his sea legs while compensating for his left knee. That, more than any other single thing, sunk home the fact he'd never serve on a naval vessel again. The dinghy hit a small, choppy wave, drenching his legs with icy salt water. The dull ache in his knee became a constant throb as he scanned the shoreline for SS officers.

They slid into a shallow bay beyond the docks, partially obscured by large rocks. With a dull scrape, the small wooden vessel met the beach. Roy shrugged his duffel bag onto his shoulder and picked his way across the sand.

By the time he reached the meeting point, his leg burned. Gritting his teeth against the pain and cold, he feigned nonchalance as he surveyed the dark streets.

A low voice from the shadows spoke in German. "Careful, stranger. Denmark no longer welcomes visitors. You must be Albrecht."

Roy shook his head and replied easily in the same language. "Jonas. Jonas Schwartz. Perhaps you know my uncle, Piet Schwartz."

His contact stepped into the light and matched the picture Paul had shown him back in the States.

"Axel Christiansen." He shook Roy's hand. "Let me show you where you can get a good night's sleep."

After a block or so, Axel casually slung Roy's duffel bag over his shoulder. As they maneuvered through dark, narrow streets, Axel changed directions frequently enough to assure Roy they weren't being followed. They continued to weave through the streets for a solid forty minutes before approaching a two-story home.

Silently thanking the good Lord that his leg hadn't buckled, Roy limped behind Axel into a blessedly warm kitchen.

"Jonas, this is my sister, Annelise and Grams, our grandmother." As Axel introduced them, Roy noted the fact that both siblings called him Jonas from the outset.

The clever tactic reduced the likelihood of either of them being overheard or slipping up within earshot of any enemies. It also underscored the grave truth that these people depended on secrecy for survival.

He gratefully took a seat and accepted Axel's help pulling off his soaked boots while Annelise set a bowl of stew in front of him.

"This is wonderful," he praised as he swallowed the first bite, the warmth of the stew quite welcome.

"We can take your things upstairs, where you can lodge with our other guests," Annelise spoke in hushed tones, "or, if you'd prefer, downstairs."

Roy swiftly assessed the options. Paul had briefed him about certain necessary details. The attic held two small hidden rooms where Jewish children and American servicemen waited to be smuggled out. The basement held another secret room where they could develop the requisite photographs.

With the work he intended to do, Roy would need to be in the basement, and going up and down stairs every day wouldn't work well with his leg. Furthermore, one of his footsteps sounded far more loudly than the other and would be difficult to mask if he stayed upstairs.

"Downstairs will serve well," he decided aloud.

As Axel grabbed his bag, Roy stopped him. "But first, a few things from your cousins." He tugged the drawstring to the duffel and pulled out the precious items.

Annelise smiled as he brought out powdered milk and a few chocolate bars, while Axel grinned to see the coffee and peanut butter. Many simple, everyday items had become scarce in Denmark.

"I've also brought typewriter ribbons, ink, and a few rolls of film." As they'd be placed in the basement, Roy left those in the bag.

"Good. I'll show you to your room." Axel stood up when Roy finished his soup. As he crossed the kitchen toward the basement door, a row of photographs in the hall brought Roy to a dead stop.

In a picture with her mother, Valerie smiled angelically, sending a pang through his heart. He'd asked for a portrait of Valerie to bring along, but Paul shot that idea down. Apparently Paul had shown Captain von Rundstedt a photograph of Rosemary and Valerie, and the SS officer commented on their Aryan features. If Roy underwent a search, such an item would immediately tie him to Paul and Axel, placing the entire operation in jeopardy.

"May I borrow this during my stay?" He pointed to the photograph.

"So that's the way things stand, eh?" Grams shook her head and bustled upstairs, returning with a photograph of only Valerie. "The captain could notice that one missing, so this should do." She pressed it into his hands and nudged him back toward the basement door.

Roy's socks squished on the steep steps and cold cement floor until they came to the back wall. Axel pulled aside an empty trunk and a few sacks of potatoes before sliding back what seemed to be a solid wall.

A narrow room lay beyond, hardly four feet wide. Axel folded down a wooden plank topped with a thin cushion before folding it back against the wall. Similarly, another fold-down piece of wood on the perpendicular wall served as a desk.

A lumpy pillow took up residence atop a pile of blankets in the corner. An old typewriter sat next to a chair buried beneath a stack of old magazines. Roy immediately made plans to place the magazines beneath the machine while he typed. They'd absorb some of the noise.

Against the opposite wall lay two tubs of fluid and a small clothesline and clothespins for developing film. A single bare lightbulb hung in the middle of the room with a pull chain.

"Perfect." Roy turned to Axel. "I think it would be best if I remain down here for the duration of my stay. It will be easier."

"Agreed. Annelise will bring you food and whatever else you will need, though you've brought your own supplies. I'll bring home more paper tomorrow, and I'll bring you the photograph film."

"One more thing." Roy caught Axel's elbow before he shut

the sliding wall and pressed a bundle into his hand. "Just in case."

Axel unwound the fabric to uncover a small pistol and box of bullets. He gave a somber nod, rewrapped the weapon, and tucked it deep inside his coat before leaving Roy. Roy propped up Valerie's photo on the desk and peeled off his sopping socks before sinking onto the bed. *Lord, please help us to be successful.*

❦

The weeks passed with agonizing slowness. Roy often slid open the secret door just to feel less shut in. Sure, the cellar didn't offer a fantastic view, but at least it eased the feeling of cramped confinement.

Each day bled into the next as he rolled off the wooden pallet and took up his station in front of the typewriter and forged official-looking documents again and again.

The only bright spots of his days were Annelise's fine cooking and Valerie's photograph. Her smile beamed upon him as a ray of hope, urging him to press on. The thought of holding her in his arms once more strengthened his resolve.

As he slid another sheet of paper into the typewriter, Roy heard Axel's booming warning from upstairs: "Grams, Annelise! Captain von Rundstedt is here!"

Roy sprang into action, pulling the wall shut and jerking the chain to plunge his small chamber into darkness. *Lord, shield us with Your presence and power.*

He stood stock-still, straining to hear the muffled voices coming from above him in the kitchen.

"Captain, to what do we owe this unexpected visit?" Annelise's voice remained steady, giving away nothing.

"It's been too long since you've visited your brother's work, Annelise. I haven't seen you in weeks."

Roy frowned into the darkness as thoughts whirled through his head. If the captain's interest in Annelise brought him to the house, there was precious little they could do about it. Annelise would have to visit the office more often in order to protect the children and airmen concealed in the attic, but at what cost? Encouraging the affections of an SS officer was risky, but rejecting him outright rated equally as dangerous.

"Besides," the captain continued, "I was going to give this Cinderella doll to my niece this week, but when I took her from my bag, I noticed she is coming undone."

That sealed it. Roy had sewn that doll specially just to keep the captain off their trail. There was no chance anything had begun to unravel—sewing might not be his favorite occupation, but no Benson could ever be accused of shoddy workmanship!

The captain obviously had sabotaged the doll as a pretext to visit Annelise.

Chapter 9

"Oh, I can fix that in just a minute. Let me grab my sewing kit." Roy listened to Annelise's footsteps fade as she moved toward the living room, then become louder as she returned.

"Something smells wonderful."

"Here you are. Just like new." Good. Annelise had finished repairing the doll. Now, if they could just get their unwelcome visitor out the door. . . .

Roy grimaced as he heard the captain's heavy boots thump toward the center of the kitchen, away from the door.

"It's been so long since I've seen anything this fresh. Home-cooked meals are hard to come by. I'll bet these are every bit as good as my mothers." Roy bit back a groan. The man was laying it on thicker than a jar of Rosemary's preserves.

"Looks as though you made enough to feed half a contingent."

"Have you seen how much Axel eats?" Grams's laugh hardly seemed forced at all.

"Yes, well, a hearty appetite keeps a man strong."

Roy's stomach rumbled at the captain's words. After all,

he'd requested tonight's dinner, a favorite dish from his child-hood in the boarding school. Obviously the captain wouldn't be leaving anytime soon.

"Well, I can't guarantee it's as good as your mother's, but you're welcome to stay for dinner, if you'd like." Annelise's begrudging tone was lost on her would-be beau.

"Wonderful!" A chair scraped across the floor.

Roy sank onto his makeshift bed and waited for the meal to end. In the dark, windowless cell, he couldn't judge the pass-ing of time nor look at his pocket watch. It seemed like hours before the captain finally took his leave and longer still before Axel judged it safe to come down to the cellar.

"Close call," Roy greeted him.

"You're telling me." Axel slumped onto the chair and held his head in his hands. "Annelise stopped coming down to the business because Captain von Rundstedt kept lurking around, and I don't want him near my sister. But since she left, he's become my shadow. Tonight he all but demanded to see her."

"We can't risk any more home visits, Axel."

"I know." He raked his fingers through his hair. "She'll have to start coming to the office again. I can only hope din-ner tonight dissuades him from wanting more home-cooked meals."

"Annelise and Grams are wonderful cooks. What do you mean?"

Grams came down the stairs with two peanut butter sandwiches.

"He means that I made the food saltier than the Dead Sea." She handed the sandwiches to Roy. "And he still ate every bite." She let out a sigh. "I do hate to waste good food, but we can't have him popping up all the time for meals."

"He didn't ask for seconds, though." Axel tried to point out a bright spot.

"That's good," Roy encouraged through a mouth full of peanut butter. "By the way, good warning."

"I had to do something." Axel gave a curt nod. "Didn't hear a peep from down here all night."

"Yeah, but I didn't get any work done, either." Roy gestured to the photographs hanging on the drying line. "I have so much to do. I'd like to set up a supply of documents that need only a photograph before I leave."

"We'll be sad to see you go." Axel started back up the stairs. "You're far more productive than the last fellow."

"Thanks." Roy smiled and glanced at the photograph on his desk. "But since my replacement is on his way, I need to be off soon."

Grams gave him a measuring look and followed Axel. "Home is where the heart is," she called over her shoulder.

And I left mine in Virginia.

❦

Valerie heard a tap on the door. "Come in."

Her mother poked her head through the doorway. "You're up late."

"So are you."

"I was just checking on Rebekkah, like I used to peek in on you when you were smaller." Rosemary stepped across the room to stroke Valerie's hair. "Sometimes I still do."

"I know." Valerie gave her mother a brief hug.

"You've been tired all month."

"I just can't seem to sleep when I don't know if Roy is safe." Valerie felt the too-familiar sting of tears prick her eyelids.

"Oh, honey." Her mother sat down next to her on the bed and nestled her close. "He's in all of our prayers."

"I pray and pray," Valerie confessed, "but still don't have any peace about it."

"Even if you pray diligently, so long as you don't give your cares to the Lord, you won't be at peace about it."

"I just can't." Valerie grabbed her handkerchief. "I thought I'd finished grieving over Frank—that I'd come to terms with the loss."

"I thought this was about Roy!" Rosemary tipped Valerie's chin with her hand.

"It is! Don't you see? Frank is gone, and nothing will bring him back—I accept that. It's not because I miss Frank! When I fell in love with Roy, I thought he'd always be safe in spite of the war. He couldn't fight because of his leg."

"So you thought his injury made him safe for you to love." Her mother knew exactly what she meant. "You didn't have to worry about losing him."

"And now he's in Europe risking his life!"

"Valerie, do you love Roy because he can't fight or because of the man he is?"

"I love him because he's strong in Christ and kind to others, and he made me feel as though everything would be all right. And now he's not here."

Rosemary just held Valerie tight and let her cry. When the sobs subsided into tiny hiccups, she spoke again. "Honey, if you wait to love someone until you're certain your heart is safe, you'll never love. Love is the greatest gift God granted us and the heaviest responsibility." She placed her hands on Valerie's shoulders and looked her in the eyes. "If you live in fear of loss, you never really live at all."

"But I am afraid. I'm afraid for Roy. I'm afraid of being without him."

"You need to give that fear to the Lord. If you don't, you're saying you don't trust Him with what is most important to you."

"How can I?" Valerie whispered brokenly. "How did you when Paul was away?"

"Who better to trust than the one who made you? The Father who sent His Son to die for you? Didn't He assure us of His plans to prosper each of us?"

She pulled out of her mother's arms and blew her nose. "I don't know what those plans are, but I've got some praying to do. I was wrong, Mom."

"We all are, honey. That's why we need Jesus." She kissed her daughter's forehead. "Good night, Valerie."

"Good night."

☙

Valerie stood on tiptoe at platform 3C as she heard the train whistle. "It's coming!"

The nine o'clock train chugged into the station. Rosemary stood next to Paul, who carried Rebekkah atop his shoulders. A stream of passengers swarmed out of the cars, blanketing the platform. Valerie peered around as best she could, but Rebekkah spotted Roy before any of them.

"There! Roy!" The toddler flailed her arms so wildly that Paul tightened his grip so she wouldn't fall off.

As Roy made his way through the throng, Valerie couldn't stand still. She'd waited five long weeks to see him again—even one more minute was too long. She took off to meet him halfway. When she reached him, he wrapped her in a warm hug. She rested her cheek on his shoulder. "I'm so glad you're home!"

"Me, too."

She kissed his cheek, then stepped back. "Let me just look at you for a minute!"

"I get the better end of that bargain." His eyes drank in the sight of her, making her feel beautiful and blessed beyond imagination.

Lord, thank You for bringing him back to me safe and sound. I'm sorry I didn't put my faith in You sooner!

"My turn!" Rebekkah stretched toward Roy, wiggling her fingers.

He gave an easy laugh and swept her high into the air, grinning at her merry giggle. "Good to see you, too, Bekkah!"

"All right, all right, enough with the mushy stuff." Paul swiped Rebekkah and passed her to Rosemary before clapping Roy on the back. "Good to see you, Roy."

"Good to see you, too." He turned to Valerie. "Paul and I have some business to attend to, so we won't get home until this evening."

"Oh." She couldn't hide her disappointment. He'd been gone for five weeks, and "business" was more important than spending time with her?

"But I want you to be ready. I'm taking you out to dinner so I can have you all to myself." His smile made her heart pound. "Then we're off to the seven o'clock showing of that new Disney movie."

"Perfect!" She gave him one last hug before Paul led him away.

❦

"Roy, this is William Donovan."

Roy shook the stranger's hand before pulling up an office chair. "Nice to meet you, Mr. Donovan."

"You, too, Mr. Benson." Mr. Donovan leaned back and tented his fingers. "You must be wondering why we brought you in here."

Roy nodded but said nothing as Paul's friend pulled out a rather thick file and plopped it on the desk before leafing through it.

"Fluent in four languages, served the navy for eight years now. Ascended the ranks quickly to become an officer of cryptography in the OP-20-G. Very impressive, Mr. Benson." Mr. Donovan shut the folder and peered at him.

"Why so dedicated to America when you were raised in Europe? This is no time for divided loyalties."

"My father has served the United States Navy my entire life." Roy refused to let the probing question raise his temper. "Benson loyalty is steadfast, and I'm proud to follow in his footsteps. It's my heritage, my duty, and my honor to protect my country."

Mr. Donovan leaned back and gave Paul a curt nod. "Excellent. Mr. Kincaid speaks quite highly of you and your father. Let's get down to the reason for this meeting.

"As you know, we live in dangerous times when intelligence and preparation for homeland security are vital. Up until now, there has been no cohesive intelligence unit functioning at the behest of the government since the MI8 was disbanded in 1929.

"The separate cryptography divisions of the army and navy are no longer sufficient, as the Signal Intelligence Service and the OP-20-G have not established a free flow of communication. President Roosevelt has authorized me to establish an American intelligence service, which I've dubbed the Office of Strategic Services. Our mission is to collect and analyze strategic information for the Joint Chiefs of Staff and to conduct certain special operations not handled by other agencies. For instance, Latin-American intelligence will be handled exclusively by the FBI." Mr. Donovan paused for a moment, but Roy remained silent.

Lord, can this be another way You've answered my prayer to do Your work in this war?

"If you're interested, we could use a man of your background and talents."

"It sounds very worthwhile, but I have obligations to the OP-20-G, Mr. Donovan. Mr. Kincaid already had to make extensive arrangements regarding my leave of absence."

Donovan broke into an approving smile. "That Benson loyalty, eh? I already attended to the matter. Admiral Rochefort tells me that Station Hypo is now consistently breaking the Japanese naval code and has graciously consented to my request."

"In that case, sir, I'm your man." Roy rose to shake his hand again.

"Good." Donovan chuckled. "By the way, my friends call me Wild Bill." And with that, the three men went off to enjoy a fine lunch before Wild Bill left to attend to other concerns.

"So." Roy cleared his throat as Paul pulled out of the parking lot. "Where do they sell rings around here?"

Valerie dabbed a bit of perfume on her neck as she heard Paul's car pull into the drive. She grabbed her jacket, gave her hair one final pat, and made her way to the top of the stairs.

"He'll be out in a minute." Rosemary met her at the bottom, wiping her hands on a dish towel. "You look lovely, honey. Have a good evening."

A few minutes later, Roy came out of his room, dressed in full uniform. He seemed so tall and handsome that he made Valerie's breath catch as he gazed at her appreciatively.

"You look stunning." He gallantly offered her his arm as he took her outside. On their way to Giovanni's, she learned of his time in Europe.

"I stayed in the basement the whole time. It was cold, cramped, quiet. . ." He reached over and gently clasped her hand. "And lonely. I missed you."

"I missed you, too. I prayed for your safety every day." Her grip tightened.

"Thank you." He grinned as he led her into the restaurant.

As they enjoyed warm, fragrant bread and lasagna, Valerie could tell something else was on his mind. When dinner was over, she broached the subject. "You're probably tired after your trip. We can skip *Bambi* and go home if you'd like. I'll sleep better knowing I'll see you tomorrow."

"Oh, no," he refused quickly, then gazed at her intensely. "But there is something I need to tell you."

"What is it?"

"I know how you felt about me going," he began, "but I'm called to my work. Can you support me in it?"

Valerie didn't need to think it over. "Yes, Roy, I can. I know it's a part of who you are, and I accept that. I trust you, but more than that, I trust the Lord with our love. I won't try to stop you from doing His work again."

He knelt down before her and pulled a small box out of his coat pocket. "Then, since you've captured my heart, will you do me the honor of becoming my wife?"

"Yes, Roy." She trembled as he slipped the small diamond onto her finger and swept her into his arms to seal the promise with a kiss.

"You've made me a happy man, my love."

"No happier than you've made me." She stroked her fingers through his wavy hair and smiled. "With God in our hearts and you by my side, our home will always be filled with joy."

KELLY EILEEN HAKE

Kelly is a recent high school graduate who is fast aspiring to her lofty dreams of writing and teaching by attending college. She is currently majoring in English and spends her free time writing, baking, and playing with her dogs, Skylar and Tuxedo.

A Thread of Trust

by Sally Laity

Chapter 1

Copenhagen, Denmark, Spring 1943

The growing darkness outside added gloom to the deserted interior of Christiansen Enterprises, casting murky shadows against the plain office walls. The eeriness heightened Annelise Christiansen's nagging sense of fear for her brother. She began pulling outdated letters from the customer files—anything to keep busy.

She checked the wall clock again. Where was Axel?

Something creaked.

Closing the file drawer, Annelise glanced through the interior window to the warehouse floor. The employees had left for the day, and only patches of light cast by dangling bare bulbs kept the blackness at bay. Stacked rows of crates and boxes of goods heading to or received from Germany and Sweden created shadowed canyons in the cavernous space.

Someone could easily hide out there. A chill prickled the fine hairs on her arms, and Annelise tugged her lightweight cardigan closer as she dismissed the notion. Being alone in this big place made her uneasy.

When she followed her brother from America to Copenhagen to take over their dying grandfather's import-export business, she never dreamed they'd be caught up in a whirl of intrigue. Imagine smuggling forged documents and money to facilitate the escape of downed British and American pilots—and more dangerous, harboring hunted fugitives! With the Nazis rounding up Jews in Germany and Poland and shipping them off to death camps, more unfortunates were flooding into Denmark needing to be hidden and given transport to neutral Sweden.

So far, Danish Jews had been spared, but for how much longer, no one knew. Everyone suspected that the Germans occupying the country were merely pretending to be friendly trading partners as they moved armed troops in "to protect the Danes," while gradually taking control of the government.

Underground resistance came into existence early on, and of course Axel had to be in the middle of it. Only the Lord knew what he'd left the warehouse three hours ago to do, since he assured Annelise her safety lay in not knowing.

Strange that he had no qualms about taking her to Nazi gatherings, convinced that a guileless female could gain useful information. She and Axel were scheduled to attend the foreign minister's dinner party in less than an hour, and they needed to go home and change. *If* he ever got here.

And *if* he hadn't been arrested.

Shaking off the thought, Annelise forced herself to focus on deciding which of her four gowns she'd don this evening. The very thought of another Nazi party with all the free-flowing schnapps and beer made her cringe. Smuggling for the Allies was hazardous enough without having to rub shoulders with those arrogant officers of the Third Reich.

Annelise exhaled, directing her thoughts to the words of a psalm she'd read in her morning devotions: "Fret not thyself because of evildoers, neither be thou envious against the workers of iniquity. For they shall soon be cut down like the grass, and wither as the green herb."

The passage still soothed her anxious mind. God's presence through these troubled times was almost tangible. He had power over all. He was stronger than the German forces, even when the opposite seemed true.

The bell above the shop's main door trilled, bringing a wave of relief. Only Axel had a key to that entrance. *Thank You, Father, for looking after him, for keeping him safe.* Breathing the silent prayer, Annelise rushed to the showroom to greet her brother.

Halfway through the furniture and artwork displays, she stopped short. The light streaming from the office illuminated not Axel, but a tall unkempt stranger in dirty seaman's clothing. Her gaze quickly assessed his unshaven face and muscular frame as she detected the stench of rotten fish and recoiled from the odor. "How did you get in here? That door was locked."

Erik Nielsen hiked his brows and stared at the most enchanting woman ever to cross his path. Endless days aboard a British fishing trawler, hours waiting in a muddy coastal marsh for his contact, suddenly lost importance. Before him stood a vision silhouetted in a glow of backlight gilding the golden hair around her face like sunshine outlining a cloud. Only the smell of cod and herring proved this was no dream, and for some unfathomable reason, he sensed his life would never be the same.

"I said, where did you get that key?" She stepped toward him, her movements graceful. Puzzlement crested her delightfully feminine features as they came into focus, revealing eyes clear and blue as the heavens.

"Huh?" Entranced by the alluring sight, he couldn't pull his thoughts together. He'd never entertained the notion of dating, much less marriage, wanting no distractions from the life God had called him to. Now a yearning toward hearth and home, of caring for someone besides himself, swirled through him. Did the Lord have someone for him after all? Was she the one?

"The key. In your hand."

Erik glanced down. "Oh. Right." She must consider him a numbskull. He cleared his throat. "Your brother sent me to get you."

"Axel?" She frowned. "Where is my brother? Why didn't he come in?"

"He's outside, miss. Someone driving past stopped to talk. He should be along any second. He said you were late, that I should hurry you up."

"*I'm* late?" Her rosy lips tightened with a huff. "Well, wait here. I'll be back."

Gaining control of his faculties, Erik tipped his head politely and feasted his eyes on her willowy grace as she hurried away. Her light steps made whispery sounds, like the rustle of her skirt.

She returned shortly with her coat and handbag. "Might I ask your name? I don't believe we've met."

"Oh. Forgive me. Erik Nielsen, at your service." After wiping his fingers on his grimy trousers, he extended his hand.

Her nostrils flared slightly before she clasped it.

The bell announced another arrival, and easygoing Axel strode in, doffing the hat atop his fair head.

Behind him came. . .a Nazi.

Eric quickly surveyed the import shop for the nearest exit. Surely Axel hadn't ratted on him. He mentally calculated the distance to the door in case he had to make a dash for it.

"Captain von Rundstedt has honored us with a visit on his way to this evening's party," Axel announced nonchalantly, his voice and expression typically calm and collected. "He wondered why I was still in street clothes. I explained that the boat bringing my sister's fiancé was late coming in, and I had strict orders to bring him straight to her." A jaunty grin crested his callow face. "And so I have. You've kept poor Annelise waiting nearly a year, haven't you, old man?" His blue eyes twinkled with mischief.

Somewhat relieved, Erik played along, praying that the officer hadn't sensed his fear. He glanced back at the woman whose hand he still possessed. *Annelise. No one could have chosen a more perfect name for such a beauty.* "Right. Almost a year. But so far my Annelise has been keeping me at arm's length." He tugged her closer, cringing as she stiffened. "You've yet to give me my welcome kiss, love."

Impeccable in his gray uniform and spit-shined jackboots, dark-haired Rundstedt observed the exchange, his expressionless demeanor exuding the typical measure of Aryan superiority displayed by the military force occupying this small country. "How curious, Miss Christiansen. You never mentioned your engagement. Curious indeed." The crisp words, in German-accented Danish, were controlled and authoritative as his close-set, hooded eyes assessed Erik. Cold and gray they were. Like death. "So many times you conversed with me, danced with me."

Erik felt her ease slightly away. "Would that be polite, Captain? Discussing my fiancé while dancing with another gentleman? Expressing my fear for his life while he's at sea? I think not." She smiled warmly up at her intended.

Some tense seconds passed as the long-nosed Nazi continued his scrutiny. "Where, exactly, have you been fishing to be gone so long, seaman?"

Erik wondered if the man was jealous, suspicious—or both. "Mostly between Faroe Island and Norway. But this is my last trip. Our boat was boarded at gunpoint on three occasions. Once by the English and twice by you Germans." Hoping his answer implied that his papers were in order, he drew Annelise closer and gazed down at her, drinking in her beauty again. "I know I promised to stay at sea until we had enough money for that house you set your heart on, sweetheart, but—"

Annelise touched her fingertips to his lips. "I wouldn't hear of it, love. Not with the war raging at sea these days. You've taken too many chances as it is. No amount of money is worth your life. We'll find somewhere else to live."

"If you're sure. Your brother has offered me a job here as long as I need it."

Her expression brightened. "Here with us? Wonderful." Rising to tiptoe, she kissed Erik's stubbled cheek. "Welcome home, darling. I've so much to tell you, I hardly know where to begin."

Though it was all for show, the tenderness of her soft lips

touched Erik deep inside. He wondered if he could trust his voice to speak.

Captain von Rundstedt inserted himself into Erik's brief interlude. "Does this mean you will not attend Foreign Minister Scavenius's party?"

Axel gestured toward the door and ushered him toward it. "I doubt my sister would enjoy partying this evening on her fiancé's first night home. I'll be along myself, though, once I change into appropriate attire. I understand there'll be an assortment of lovely, unattached young women there, as always."

The captain halted at the entrance and raised his chin a notch as he turned to glance at Annelise. "None as lovely as your sister, to be sure."

Erik felt Annelise grow rigid.

"Until we meet again, Miss Christiansen." With a click of his heels, the officer raised his arm. "Heil Hitler."

Positively seething, Annelise moved out of Erik Nielsen's grasp and glared in wordless fury at her too-handsome brother. What kind of mess had he gotten them into *this* time? Really. Having to take part in the pretense that this. . .this *smelly sailor* was her betrothed!

She glanced up at the man, gratified he had the grace to look as uncomfortable at this turn of events as she. Refusing to favor either of the males in the shop with another word, she huffed out to their car. At least their enterprise was valuable enough to the Nazis that they were still permitted a personal vehicle, she conceded with a twinge of guilt, since few Danes still enjoyed that privilege.

On the homeward drive, Annelise debated whether her emotions were ruled by anger or embarrassment. She'd already endured one disastrous engagement—a humiliation she never intended to repeat. The pain caused by that debacle helped her decide to leave her familiar world behind and follow Axel to Denmark.

Axel. Hmph. Once more he'd proven that no man—not even a brother—could be trusted. Compressing her lips into a determined line, she let her gaze settle on the broad shoulders of the seaman up front. Neither the stubble on his square jaw nor those fishy clothes could detract from such heart-stealing features. He had the most compelling eyes—light brown, with tiny gold flecks. And when he'd gazed down at her with them, her knees—

"By the way, sis. . ." Axel interrupted her wandering thoughts. "Erik was sent here by our American contacts to forge documents for the Allied pilots shot down over enemy territory. Originally I'd planned to set him up in the attic so he could keep out of sight. But now that the Nazis are aware of his presence, that won't be possible."

"Surprise, surprise," she groused. "So I assume this. . .forger will be working right out in the open with us. As my fiancé."

"Well," he teased, "you always claimed you didn't like being pawed by the members of Hitler's elite. Now there's someone who'll spare you that indignity."

She grimaced, though she knew they couldn't see her face. And lucky for them, she couldn't begin to put her indignation into words.

"At least spare her until Herr Captain figures out how to get me out of the picture for good," Erik added. "From the look on his face when you introduced me, I'd say the man is on the make and wants your beautiful sister all to himself."

Beautiful? Annelise allowed herself no more than a second to dwell on the compliment. "The captain has tried to get me alone lately. He's been quite persistent." *And Erik Nielsen thinks I'm beautiful, too. . . .*

"But I'm proud of the way you've handled things," Axel commented. "You did inform me he's the most loose-lipped of all those strutting Nazi peacocks." He switched his attention to his new friend. "By the way, Erik, what qualifies a person to become a forger for the U.S. government, if you don't mind my asking?"

Nielsen shrugged a shoulder. "My former occupation wasn't nearly so notorious as this one sounds. Before the war, I had a normal, run-of-the-mill job, teaching art at a college in New England. Turns out I'm particularly adept at calligraphy."

The news roused Annelise's curiosity. "How is it you speak Danish so fluently and without any hint of an accent?"

He chuckled. "It's my first language, actually. My family emigrated from Sjaellands Point, on Ise Fjord."

"Really. Where did you live in America?" Axel asked.

"The northern coast of Maine. I'm the first in my family not to make a living off the sea. I worked my way through university fishing during the summer months, though, so I know my way around a boat."

"So the smell of herring is not foreign to you," Annelise couldn't help adding.

A chuckle rumbled from deep in his chest. "You would bring that up."

"My sister and I were raised in America, too," Axel

explained, seemingly unaware of the thread of tension between his passengers. "I returned in '37. Annelise came over in '39, just before the Nazis invaded Poland. I tried to convince her to go back home where it was safe, but she'd have nothing to do with that."

"My life is no more valuable than yours, brother dear. I just try to take better care of it." After a pause, she spoke to their soon-to-be guest. "No doubt Axel has informed you we do more than help downed Allied pilots. Hundreds of Jews have escaped out of Germany. Often, though, parents manage only to get their children to safety. We have a young boy and girl hidden in our basement right now. All they lack are some authentic-looking exit visas. Perhaps you've come in answer to our prayers."

"I'll do what I can. Which reminds me. . ." He slipped into English. "Before I completed my training in Virginia, your Aunt Rosemary's new husband gave me some rag dolls to bring to you. They're in my duffel bag. He told me to guard them with my life."

"I must caution you never to speak English, my friend," Axel urged. "Not even when we're alone. You're not an American, remember. You're Erik Nielsen from Sjaellands Point. I don't even want to know your real name."

"That *is* my real name," he returned, reverting to Danish. "My relatives here have already been informed about this. They're all sympathetic to our cause. I am now the son of my uncle, and I've got the documents to prove it. . .even if they are my own handiwork."

Annelise smiled, despite herself. "You're also my fiancé. But. . .may I ask what a young woman of class, like myself, would be doing engaged to a lowly fisherman?" Suddenly aware he might construe her statement as flirting, Annelise felt her cheeks redden. *Don't forget how badly you were burned,* she lectured herself.

Nielsen didn't appear to notice her discomfort. "You know what the Bible says. Love is blind and all that."

"I've never come across that particular statement in any Bible I've read," she returned. "Sounds more like a myth to me."

He chuckled softly. "Maybe it just said *hopeful.*"

Annelise filled her lungs. *This one is too much of a charmer. Almost as charming as Tony was—before he dumped me for the next pretty face. So like Father. I'd better take care. There's far more danger here than merely being caught by the Nazis.*

Chapter 2

The city streets lay dark and still, and as the chatter inside the car petered out, Erik felt weariness envelop him. He remained alert by making mental notes of the route Axel took home, the landmarks illuminated faintly by the downward-slanted headlamps. At last they pulled into a narrow street and stopped before a substantial two-story house which, in the dim glow, appeared similar to that of its neighbors. He only hoped that somewhere inside it had a bed made up and ready for him to collapse onto. He hadn't eaten since early that morning, but exhaustion prevailed over all desire for food.

"This is it," his new friend announced, dousing the lights and turning off the engine. "We live with our grandmother. I'll open the boot so you can grab your bag, and Sis will introduce you while I dash upstairs and throw on some glad rags. I should've been at that party ages ago."

Erik opened his door and climbed out, unable to discern any unique features in the dwelling since blackout shades shrouded every window along the street. He stepped to the rear of the vehicle and retrieved his duffel bag, then followed Annelise up the front steps. "You're sure I won't be imposing?"

"Not at all," she said, turning the knob, her tone indicating she'd resigned herself to his presence. "Come on in. Grams is used to our showing up at odd hours with strangers."

"At least she won't have to hide you," Axel said, bringing up the rear.

Hooking her coat onto the hall tree, Annelise shot him a stern look. "I do wish you'd stop plunging us headlong into your schemes. We can't afford to draw such constant attention."

"Point taken, sister dear." He rolled his eyes and started down the entry hall for the staircase.

Annelise straightened her shoulders. "This way." She moved toward the squared archway leading into the front room.

From a step behind, Erik assessed the well-appointed parlor with its fine upholstered furnishings and dark, gleaming woodwork. An assortment of framed watercolor seascapes adorned the walls. The plump sofa looked especially inviting to his travel-weary bones.

Then he noticed an older woman in black, seated in a padded rocking chair, peering up from a child's sock she'd been darning. She had a pleasant enough face, and silvery hair drawn into a French roll gave a frail quality to her that reminded Erik of his favorite aunt. Her small blue eyes gazed over rimless reading glasses perched on her nose.

Annelise bent to kiss her parchmentlike cheek. "We have a guest, Grams. This is Erik Nielsen. The American military sent him to provide the exit visas we need so desperately. Erik, I'd like you to meet my grandmother, Margarethe Holberg."

The woman set her work aside and began to rise.

"Please, don't get up, Madam Holberg." He touched her surprisingly firm shoulder. "I'm afraid I reek of the sea. But I'm most honored to make your acquaintance."

"Thank you, young man." Her speculative gaze took swift measure of him.

"We don't even have to hide him," Annelise added. "He can use the guest room. There's one other thing I need to tell you, though." She colored delicately. "We're supposed to pretend Erik is my fiancé come to live with us."

The woman's shrewd eyes gravitated between her granddaughter and him, and her pursed lips flattened. "This, of course, would be Axel's doing."

Annelise nodded.

Her bosom rose and fell as she studied Erik. Then her nose crinkled. "Well, take the man upstairs and draw him a hot bath. He needn't take his luggage along. It probably smells as bad as he does. We'll wash everything up in the morning, make it all fresh."

"Thank you kindly, madam." Erik gave an appreciative tip of his head. His original impression of her had been way off the mark. For all her fragile appearance, she was deceptively strong. Even persuasive. "But I shouldn't let my bag out of my sight. It contains my forging supplies and some rather. . .important. . . rag dolls."

Nothing fazed the old gal. "Don't worry. You're perfectly safe here, and so are your belongings. But this is my house, and I won't tolerate the whole place stinking like the docks."

He acquiesced. "As you wish." His glance at Annelise caught the amusement on her face.

"And to pay for your lodging, you will make exit visas for our other guests." Mrs. Holberg's expression made it a statement of fact.

"Certainly. Once I finish those needed for a downed bomber crew, I'll do the others. I believe your granddaughter mentioned there were two children here."

"That is correct. How long do you expect it will take you to get to their papers?"

Her unwavering stare nettled him. "A week maybe. Two at the most. Then I'll get right on them."

"You'll do them first," she countered, arching her eyebrows. "Planes are being shot out of the sky every day, and adults can fend for themselves. At least temporarily. But we cannot keep youngsters hidden indefinitely. They've already been shuffled around too much, been exposed to atrocities no human, let alone a child, should witness. Their trust has been shattered. They live in constant fear of never seeing their parents alive again, and the poor dears think somehow they're to blame. You'll do their papers first, so at least a fraction of their childhood might be salvaged. Otherwise, you can find someplace else to stay." She reached for her sewing supplies and resumed her chore.

Stunned by the woman's declaration, Erik recognized dismissal when he saw it, and her threat was more than a little discomfiting. He looked to Annelise.

"Come on, Grams. We can't put Erik out on the street after the Allies sent him to us. I'm sure he'll do his very best for us *and* the cause."

"Nevertheless," she insisted, "I'll do what I must. Army people think this war business is more important than anything else—this shooting at each other and anyone else who happens to get in the way. Well, these children are getting *out* of the way. This I say, and this I mean." Setting down her work once again, she crossed her arms.

"Put like that, I can understand your feelings," Erik admitted. "I'll start on those visas first thing tomorrow morning. I'll need to have their new names. Pictures, too, if you have any. You can fill me in on their ages and so forth."

Annelise shook her head. "The underground hasn't found anyone to take them to Sweden yet, so we don't have names for them. Sorry."

Perhaps it was the unwelcome news or the close confines. Maybe even a few too many hours without sleep. Erik's head began to swim. He raked his hand through his hair and gave himself a mental shake, grasping at the first idea that came to mind. "What if one of the pilots pretends to be their father? A couple kids would make good cover. . . ."

"What?" The old woman poked her needle into the sock and dropped the darning egg. "I never heard of anything so daft! You'll not risk those dear little children to rough soldiers who can't even speak their language. Just get to work on those visas. I'll find someone myself." Muttering under her breath, she continued her work.

"I'm sure Axel will come up with somebody," Annelise suggested. "There's no reason for you to endanger yourself, Grams."

"Hmph. After this latest brainstorm of Axel's? I'd best take care of the wee ones. I've many trusted friends at the church. We'll find someone willing to accompany them to safety."

"Did I hear my name being bandied about?" Axel peeked through the archway in his crisp white shirt, bow tie, and dark slacks. His blond hair was freshly slicked back, and a dinner jacket lay over the crook of his arm. He quirked a smile at Erik. "Everything all set for you, old man?"

"Yes. Couldn't be better." Though spoken facetiously, Erik knew he'd stated the truth.

Annelise hurried to her brother's side. "Be careful. Promise? And for once, please don't do or say anything that will dig this hole any deeper."

"Whatever you say, little sis." A peck on her cheek, and he dashed off.

Mrs. Holberg frowned and sighed. "We'd better spend a good part of this night in prayer for that boy." Then her cool gaze fastened on Erik. "I assume you are a praying man."

"Yes, madam, I am." *But even if I wasn't, I'd tell you I was. I wouldn't want to be on your bad side.*

"Good. I can't abide heathens under my roof."

Erik had to grin. For a lady he'd first considered small and defenseless, she sure had spunk. And he liked spunk. In fact, he liked *her*. He liked her a lot.

Annelise observed the banter between her grandmother and their new guest—who anyone could see was dead on his feet—and admiration for the sailor-forger rose several notches. He was holding his own in the face of a woman many considered to be domineering and formidable. Perhaps it wouldn't be so bad having him around for a while to keep Grams occupied.

Still, the man *was* a perfect stranger, and beguiling smiles were something Annelise would never be fooled by again. Even if the military bigwigs considered him trustworthy, he had yet to prove himself to her and her relatives. She'd best stay on her guard. "I'll take you upstairs now," she offered, maintaining a businesslike tone.

He nodded and bid her grandmother good evening, then followed Annelise to the staircase, where portraits bearing a strong resemblance to the family members he'd already met lined the walls.

Once they reached the top landing, she gestured to her right. "That will be your room as long as you're here. Directly across the hall is the bathroom. You'll find everything you need in the cupboard. I'll bring some of my brother's clothes for you to use till yours have been laundered. Leave your soiled things outside the door, and I'll take them down to the cellar to wash."

"Thank you. . .Annelise. I. . .hope you don't mind my familiarity."

She grimaced. "Why should I? It would appear we're an item, thanks to my big-mouth brother."

"Ah, yes." He flashed a completely disarming grin.

It made Annelise conscious of her less than friendly manner. Realizing she'd been nearly as gruff as her grandmother to the poor man, she softened her tone. "Look, I know we've made things difficult for you, and I do apologize. We're all working toward the same objective, and it would benefit the lot of us to be friends."

He nodded. "I could live with that."

"Good. Well, I know you're tired. Hungry, too, I'd imagine. I'll bring a tray to your room so you can have a bite to eat when you've finished. Is there anything else you might need tonight?"

"You've about covered everything for now. Tomorrow, though, we should get together and work on our. . .relationship. Since we're *engaged*, we need to know a little about each other, decide when and where we met and all."

194

She looked down. "Let's wait for Axel to get home. No telling what story he fabricated for the Nazis this evening."

"Good idea. Oh, one other thing. I had planned to visit my relatives in Sjaellands Point as soon as I can get away, to familiarize myself with the area. That part of my story needs to be kept straight, too."

"Sounds wise."

His lips spread into a knowing smile. "Of course, as my fiancée, you should probably come along and meet the folks...."

A maddening sense that things were spinning out of control jolted Annelise. For a fleeting moment, all she could think of was throttling her brother.

☙

A ray of sunshine drifting through the edge of the drawn window shade warmed Annelise's face. She opened an eye and checked her bedside clock, then bolted upright. Normally she awoke before daylight. Yesterday's stress must have taken its toll. Wasting no time, she made quick work of her morning ablutions and dressed in a white blouse and navy skirt, then hastened for the stairs. Her devotions would have to wait.

Male voices drifted up from below. "The guys had to separate," Axel said. "Only five made it to a safe house."

"That's not good news," Erik answered. "Maybe a few others will—" He clammed up when Annelise entered the dining room.

"Good morning," she said brightly, masking the irritation she felt over always being kept in the dark about everything.

"Well, well," Axel teased. "If it isn't Miss Punctuality. Your clock stop or something?"

She glowered at him. "You could have rapped on my door when you got up." Even as she spoke, her gaze took in their freshly shaved guest. Axel's checked shirt and wool slacks suited Erik, though a touch small and tight-fitting. And his easy smile did strange things to her insides.

"I figured you could use the sleep, sis. Besides, this way I get to repeat what I told Erik about my conversation with the distinguished captain last night."

"Which was?" She drew out a spindle-back chair from the table and took a seat.

Her grandmother came in from the kitchen just then, bearing plates of sausage and eggs and dark rye toast for the men. She directed her attention to Annelise while setting the food before them. "I see you finally decided to make your appearance this day."

Annelise bristled as Axel and his new friend swapped amused grins.

"I'll start some more toast and eggs while you go down and fetch the children for breakfast," Grams said, returning to the kitchen.

Something about the smiles the two men had sported stuck in Annelise's mind as she headed for the cellar door beneath the staircase. Her father's smiles—just as roguish, but deceitful as well—had caused the family untold heartache. Tossing off the unwelcome reminder, she opened the door and flicked on the light to illuminate the wooden steps.

The cellar's space had dwindled when Axel enclosed secret rooms on either end, disguising the change with floor-to-ceiling storage shelves. Windowless walls made the close confines even drearier as Annelise picked her way through the cluttered maze of washtubs, food stores, and castoffs from the main floor. She carefully opened the secret door concealed with shelves of canned goods.

Two narrow cots occupied one end of the long, shallow room. A small table with chairs sat at the other end, and in between, a bookcase held schoolbooks and picture books. An assortment of worn toys lay about the rag runner covering the floor.

As always, when hearing the door opening, the children ceased their activity and huddled together in mute silence, their chocolate-brown eyes round with fear. Six-year-old Rachel peered up at Annelise, a froth of soft dark curls surrounding her heart-shaped face. She'd taken a protective position in front of her brother, Moshe, already a charmer at three. Both wore faded clothes, with their shiny curls neatly brushed.

Annelise's heart contracted at the sight of their too-thin frames. "It is all right," she crooned in the high German dialect. "I've come to get you for breakfast. Grandmother has scrambled some nice eggs for you."

The boy's brown eyes glinted, and he looked about to say something, but his sister put a finger to her lips. She relaxed her hold on him and stood, then bent to pick up his missing shoe and help him put it on. "There," she whispered. "We are ready now."

No smile accompanied the statement, but then, only on the rarest of occasions had Annelise seen either of the little ones smile. They seemed to know instinctively never to make noise, never to speak unless spoken to, never to touch things that did not belong to them. She longed to gather them into her arms and love them to pieces. . .but Grams, in her wisdom, felt it would only cause the children more grief to become attached to yet more people who'd be shipping them elsewhere. So she restrained her motherly instincts and settled for being pleasant and warm, trying to instill trust in their hearts, showing them that kind people still existed in the world.

"The cold days are almost over," she remarked as they exited the secret room. "I've been making over a new dress for you, Rachel. A pretty one with flowers, for when you're free to play in the park again."

The child's sable eyes misted, and the hint of a tiny smile appeared. But Moshe's rosy lips plumped with a pout.

"And I haven't forgotten you, sweetie." She ruffled his dark curls. "You'll have a new shirt and vest to wear."

Suddenly the door at the top of the stairs opened.

Annelise automatically reached for the children.

"It's that Nazi!" Erik said, closing the door after himself. "He and a truckload of armed soldiers just pulled up out front. Get the kids outta sight!"

Chapter 3

S haken by Erik's announcement, Annelise maintained her composure but pressed a finger to her lips. She scooped up Moshe and made her way quietly down the steps to the secret room, its shelf-laden door left open for such emergencies. Rachel trailed silently behind, clutching Annelise's skirt. "Don't make a sound, my darlings," she whispered, ushering them back inside their haven. "Though we walk through the valley of the shadow of death, we fear no evil, for God is with us."

Rachel, ever the protector, put her arms around her brother, and the pair huddled together on one of the cots. The sight of their huge, dread-filled eyes cinched Annelise's heart as she carefully closed the door on the little ones. What a pathetic existence they lived, silent, invisible. Would they ever get to be carefree children? She breathed a prayer that God would be with them. Surely He would send His angels to surround and protect such sweet darlings.

Some jars rattled from the movement of the shelves. Grabbing a bottle of her grandmother's plum syrup as an excuse for being in the cellar, she joined Erik, who waited on the top landing, his ear to the cracked door.

The sound of knocking carried from outside. "At least they aren't pounding with their fists or rifle butts as they're so fond of doing," she muttered.

"Not yet, anyway. That's their second summons. Your brother's taking his time answering."

"*God morgen*, Captain von Rundstedt," came Axel's greeting at last. "You're up and about early after last evening's festivities. What a pleasant surprise."

"*Ja*. We are on our way to Kirkgarde Engine Works to aid your authorities in breaking up a strike. Three stoppages this month alone. Traitorous agitators think they can thwart us by stirring up the workers, turning them against the cause. We will put a stop to it."

Annelise breathed more easily. The soldiers hadn't come to conduct a raid on the house; they were waiting for their captain. But before she completely let down her guard, her gaze fell on Erik's duffel bag still slumped where he'd left it last night—the bag containing forging tools, money, and stuffed dolls from America! Effecting serenity she didn't feel, she took his hand and stepped with him out into the hall to draw Rundstedt's attention.

Resplendent in his immaculate uniform and polished jackboots, the Nazi officer had his military hat tucked under his elbow. "Ah." A subtle hiking of his brows lengthened his thin face. "I see the lovebirds are also early risers."

Erik draped an arm around Annelise's shoulders, its warmth steadying her. "Why, Captain," she said airily, "we were about to sit down to breakfast. Won't you join us?"

"*Nej*. I am on duty. I stopped by to invite you all to tea on Saturday. Just a small, intimate gathering. Nothing grand."

Always stiffly proper, he never revealed emotion in his hard features, and little about the man inspired confidence. Annelise sensed his true motives were far from friendly. Certainly he suspected something amiss here. Nevertheless, refusal was no option. She smiled up at Erik. "That would be lovely, wouldn't it, sweetheart?"

"Wait a minute, sis," Axel interrupted. "We've already made plans for the weekend. Erik placed a call early this morning to the pay telephone in Sjaellands Point. A neighbor was dispatched to inform Erik's family he's back and that you'll be driving out there on Saturday to visit."

"Yes," Erik confirmed, "and Willem Larsen, who took the call, is worse than a town crier when he hears a juicy bit of news. You'll be meeting more than my family, my love. You may end up greeting the entire neighborhood."

Annelise seriously doubted that possibility would be much more enjoyable than having high tea with a German officer who was infatuated with her. "Oh, dear. I must make a good impression on your parents, your relatives, *and* the whole town?" But lest she sound too anxious, she turned to Rundstedt. "Then you must come to our home the following Saturday for tea, Captain. Surely things will have settled down by then."

"I beg to differ." Her grandmother entered the hall from the kitchen, the black attire she'd insisted on wearing since her husband's death adding to her austere demeanor.

Knowing that the outright contempt Grams had for the overbearing Nazis gave the woman a tendency toward bluntness, Annelise felt another twinge of panic.

"Not with an upcoming wedding to plan," Grams elaborated.

Eric hugged Annelise closer. "And the sooner the better." He tipped his head politely at the officer. "We hope you'll grace us with your presence on our happy occasion."

"Ah, yes. A wedding." His steely eyes fastened on Annelise. "Have you chosen the date? I should like the honor of throwing your seaman a bachelor party, if your brother has not already commandeered that duty."

"That's very generous of you," Axel replied. "But I fear the nuptials will have to wait awhile. My sister still has crucial shipments to process this month to a number of cities in Germany. It is imperative they be arranged before she leaves for her honeymoon."

"Honeymoon." Erik nuzzled against Annelise and kissed her cheek. "I like the sound of that."

Embarrassed and caught off guard by circumstances over which she had no control, Annelise eased out of his embrace. She needed time to think. Time for life to get back to the way it was before this stranger descended upon the household. In the meantime, however, she had to keep up the senseless charade. "Regardless of our wedding plans, we will make time to entertain our friends a week from Saturday."

Rundstedt took her hand and bowed over it, staring intently at her. "In appreciation, I will cancel my plans for Saturday and drive you all to Sjaellands Point in my touring car. It is far more comfortable than yours, Axel, and there'll be no necessity of using your petrol rations." He returned his full attention to Annelise. "What time shall I come by for you?"

The Nazi had yet to relinquish her hand. As Erik moved up behind her, Annelise responded with an even tone. "We'll expect you at eight o'clock. And *tak*. Thank you so much. This is most kind."

His thin lips spread into a mirthless smile. "So far from the

Fatherland one has so few loyal supporters. It is the least I can do for true friends." He finally let go of her. With a click of his heels, he straightened, then raised an arm. "Heil Hitler."

A heavy silence reigned after Axel closed the door. He led them into the dining room, where they waited several tense moments for the captain's car and the open lorry lined with helmeted troops to rumble away down the cobblestone street.

Erik let out of whoosh of breath and slumped into the nearest chair. "Well. We really will have to contact my relatives now. Let them know they're going to have unexpected visitors to entertain—me, my fiancée, and a nosy Nazi."

"Do you mean to tell me," Annelise demanded, folding her arms across her chest, "you haven't even placed that call yet?" She cut a glare to her troublemaking brother. "You made the whole thing up?"

He flashed a sheepish grin. "Don't give me all the credit. Nielsen, here, added a few creative touches."

She couldn't decide which man infuriated her more.

"Breakfast is getting cold," Grams announced, breaking the strained moment. "Sit down. Eat. Axel, go get the children while I bring out their plates again. And take that putrid bag with you." She turned to Annelise. "As for you, young lady, you and that fiancé of yours need to get busy on wedding plans."

Annelise didn't dare glance at Erik. She was upset enough as it was. "But—"

Grams allowed no opportunity to protest. "That will keep you occupied so you won't have time to think about entertaining any church-burning disciples of Satan in my home. I declare. Your grandfather would roll over in his grave." With a huff, she returned to the kitchen.

"Is it ready yet?" Axel mouthed through the window separating the warehouse from the office.

Annelise shook her head and held her hand aloft, fingers splayed. "Five more minutes."

He frowned, then turned back to the loaded truck waiting near the vehicle entrance.

Amazed she'd actually found space for the carload of cabbage on a barge to Amsterdam, in the Netherlands, Annelise hurriedly finished typing the shipping manifesto. More than likely those large crates held more than produce, since Axel displayed undue concern. He'd already come twice to hurry her along.

Erik, instead of working out in the warehouse, had spent the last few hours behind the filing room's closed door, creating documents for some downed fliers who faced the possibility of being intercepted by the Gestapo in Holland. The Nazis didn't bother with any pretense of friendship with the Dutch. They'd overrun the tiny lowland country in four days in 1940 and now occupied it with an iron fist. The active Dutch underground did all it could to arrange transport for the airmen to England, but the risks were incredibly high. Annelise prayed silently for the brave souls in Holland and Denmark, as well as the Allies.

Besides the perils involved with this venture, Annelise had to contend with having an attractive man living at home. He not only had taken all his meals with the family over the past three days, but he also constantly pumped her for personal information. That was the hardest of all: being expected to lay her heart out on the table as if it were an open textbook to be read aloud, every painful detail discussed.

She understood the reasoning behind the questions.

Tomorrow they'd travel to his hometown in the company of a distrustful German officer. Something about Erik's tone and manner implied he was truly interested in her. But considering her past experiences of being betrayed first by her father and then by her former fiancé—two men she'd loved—she was hesitant to give these new allusions about Erik much credence. It didn't help having him assigned duties in the warehouse, either. All he had to do from any area of the open space was look through the office window to observe her every movement. She'd caught him doing just that on a number of occasions.

The door to the filing room opened, making Annelise jump like a nervous cat.

"Finally." Erik smiled disarmingly, devastatingly handsome now that his own clothes had been laundered and pressed and he no longer had to wear Axel's things. His grin turned smug when he patted the bulge of papers in his inside jacket pocket. "Shipping papers all set?"

"All but the bottom line." Giving the carriage return lever a last shove, she pounded the keys hard enough to print the total number, weight, and price of the cabbage crates on all four carbon copies. Then she rolled the forms up another line and leaned closer to proofread them.

Erik moved to stand behind her. "I know this whole marriage thing has you on edge," he said gently, his fingertips resting lightly on the chair back. "Especially with our having to drive to Sjaellands Point with the captain tomorrow. But since you're just now being introduced to my family, there's not much you'll be expected to know. As long as we keep our own story straight, about meeting at church—a place where a Nazi would never be caught dead—and how I was attracted by your beauty and shyness, how I kept making a point of sitting by you until you couldn't ignore me any longer, we should fare just fine."

Annelise didn't trust herself to look up at him. Not when his voice held that quiet sincerity that made the words sound true, even to her.

"And how I finally convinced you to take Sunday afternoon walks with me," he went on.

"Yes," she said, repeating the story they'd rehearsed so often, "and how on that last walk before you sailed, you asked me to marry you."

"And how you kept me on tenterhooks for the longest minute of my life before giving me that beautiful yes."

Her gaze drifted up to meet his eyes, and she lost herself in the sincerity of their light brown depths.

Axel pounded on the window.

The fragile dream popped like a soap bubble. Annelise swung back to her typewriter and ripped out the invoice forms. Fingers trembling, she tore off the last copy for her files and handed the rest to Erik. "The two of you be careful."

"Count on it," he said, hurrying out the door.

That was close, Annelise conceded. *I was almost starting to believe that pretty story he concocted.* She tightened her lips and sniffed, draping the typewriter cover over the machine. *But he was so near. And his words sounded so—so real. But that's just it. They're entirely made up, a script he wrote in his mind. He's merely a good actor, no more sincere than Tony. I must not succumb to such fantasies again!*

The worn passenger seat squeaked as Erik jumped into the

truck. He thought it odd that Axel, the boss of the factory, would undertake a menial chore like delivering produce. He'd seemed unusually keyed up all morning. "Is there something I should know in case there's trouble?" Erik asked as they pulled away from the warehouse.

Axel shook his head. "Not really. I just needed to stay busy, keep my mind off things." He paused. "I received some bad news. Nazis captured a flight crew—one that passed through Copenhagen last month. Some of our Norwegian contacts were trying to sneak the guys across to England and were intercepted by a wolf pack of U-boats. The Nazis removed the airmen, then sank the fishing boat with its crew still aboard."

"Oh, man. That's insane." Disturbed at the horrible news, Erik nudged the brim of his cap back and scratched his head. He switched his attention to the ancient city buildings lining both sides of the old cobblestone street.

"The submarine captain has since turned our boys over to the Gestapo in Belgium."

"I hear the Gestapo is quite accomplished at, shall we say, *persuasive* interrogation. Will this put you and your sister in danger? I can't imagine someone as delicate as Annelise at the mercy of those brutes."

Axel glanced over with a half-smile as he guided the truck toward the wharfs. "Don't worry about Sis. Only one person— her contact in case something should happen to me—knows of her involvement. The Resistance has extremely strict rules. Information is given out only on an absolute 'need to know' basis. I have no idea myself how many people are connected to the underground. I do believe our ranks are swelling every day."

"So you're sure Annelise is safe? She acts so. . .guarded

around me. So jittery. Maybe you put too much on her, having her pretend to be my fiancée."

He didn't answer right away. "Actually, I think it'll do her some good. Since she arrived in Denmark, she's been on a crusade to make her life count for something more substantial than being 'some man's doormat.' She used to be a naive little innocent. Now she's lost all trust in men. I guess I've only made things worse, dragging her into the middle of Nazi society."

Erik rubbed his chin in thought. "I can't imagine anyone deliberately hurting someone so lovely as Annelise, causing her to be so apprehensive."

"You can't?" Axel grinned. "Sounds like you have something in common with the captain—an infatuation with my little sister."

Erik averted his gaze, noting that the dock area was crowded with vessels, many of which were German. Pleasure boats no longer had permission to sail, but fishing trawlers, ferries, tugs, and other working boats stirred on the water. Here and there on the walls of buildings he spotted scrawled *V*s, victory signs that mysteriously reappeared again and again no matter how often the Germans painted over them. He glanced back at Axel. "Even if I did find myself attracted to her, being thrust at her out of the blue as I was hasn't endeared me to the poor girl."

"Nevertheless, I'm beginning to think throwing the two of you together was the smartest thing I've done in a long time. Annie needs her safe little mind-set shaken. It was a shock when she finally woke up and realized our dad had a number of women on the side. Then to have her fiancé do the same thing to her. . ." He shrugged. "But hey, no one gets a free ride through this life. Just ask those little urchins in our cellar or the flyboys being interrogated by the Gestapo as we speak." He inhaled a sharp breath. "I can't let myself dwell on them. All we can do is pray our guys going out today will have more luck taking the inland waterways."

As his friend reverted to silence, Erik mulled over the new revelations about Annelise. One concept his father had hammered into Erik's head since boyhood was that he really get to know a young lady before considering developing a serious relationship. He could still hear his dad's voice, see him counting off the items on his fingers as he spoke: *"Is she a believer? Is she as beautiful on the inside as she is on the outside? Seek God's approval before venturing forth and choosing a wife. Bear in mind, this will be the mother of your children."*

But one thing he could not escape. Everything within him yearned to stay close to Annelise, to shield her from ever being hurt again. *Father God, if You don't want me to choose this woman, please take these feelings from me. . .even if she's like a warm, fragrant breeze after a cold, hard winter.*

"Better quit daydreaming," Axel chided, halting the truck. "Let's get these crates unloaded for the crane. The ship'll be out of here with the tide."

As Erik reached for the door handle, he spotted Nazis in pairs patrolling the docks, some with vicious dogs on leashes while they checked and poked into the various loads of cargo. *And here we are, trying to smuggle some men out with a shipload of cabbage!* Time to get his mind on what was important. And forget this romance nonsense.

Chapter 4

Though a little early for spring to eradicate winter's drabness, gentle new greens tinted the rolling countryside as Rundstedt's shiny black touring car purred past tidy farms and red tile-roofed villages between Copenhagen and Sjaellands Point. Annelise tried to relax and enjoy the scenery, despite feeling trapped between her alleged fiancé and the German officer whose attentions she'd practically encouraged over the past several months.

"What did you say kept you away so long?" the captain asked in his heavily accented Danish. He leaned around her to focus his shrewd gray eyes on Erik. "An entire year fishing? The North Sea is rife with hazards in the winter months, is it not?"

Erik gave a casual nod. "That's what delayed us. Whenever the sea became too rough, we'd make for the nearest friendly port and sell our fish there, but for much less than we'd have gotten at home. Then we'd go out to replace our catch, only to be forced back to the nearest little fishing hamlet. The crew was determined to stay out 'til we could return with a big profit. Myself, I'd have given up sooner. I was desperate to get back to my Annelise."

"Meanwhile, I was at home," she breathed on an airy sigh, "imagining you'd thought better of your proposal or found someone else."

"Never." He smiled at her and squeezed her hand, a gentle reminder that he'd been a perfect gentleman from the first, always respectful and considerate. She returned his smile, noticing the way his dark hair caught the light among the thick strands, complementing his healthy complexion.

Annelise saw the captain's fist tighten, and knew he hadn't missed Erik's possessive gesture. Her gaze drifted ahead to the truckful of armed soldiers escorting Rundstedt's vehicle. Another followed behind them, their presence adding to the discomfiting reality that she, her brother, and their American friend were completely at the mercy of the Nazis.

She wondered how Erik viewed their current predicament. The assignment that brought him to Denmark had been risky enough without this. But to his credit, he seemed entirely at ease, answering the captain's almost nonstop questions while they covered the nearly seventy miles to Erik's hometown. Surely she'd have picked up on any nervousness he felt, sensed it in his grip. He'd held her hand in that protective way since they'd left Copenhagen. Farce upon farce. How much more would they have to endure?

Seated up front with the driver, Axel, the conjurer of this entire mess, turned around. "Looks like we're coming up on Sjaellands's Point. We've made pretty good time." Nothing about his demeanor indicated nervousness, Annelise noted. Her brother seemed made for this intrigue business.

She glanced down the gentle slope to the picturesque fishing port tucked around a sheltering cove in Ise Ford Bay.

Beyond it the Kattegat Strait led out to the North Sea. With Nazi restrictions added to the danger of being at sea during wartime, idle fishing trawlers and ferries crowded the docks. No doubt countless idle seamen would be lazing about on this pleasant sunny morning.

Annelise's chest tightened as she pondered her present situation. She was coming into this town in an enemy convoy, supposedly betrothed to Erik Nielsen, a local lad whom no one here had ever laid eyes on. She needed her head examined!

The vehicles slowed to a crawl behind some milk cows plodding down the road. The herder, a gangly young man in a worn cap, turned and saw the trio of official vehicles. He gave a sharp whistle in the direction of his dog, then started purposefully for Rundstedt's car.

Annelise held her breath. Had this ruse been discovered? Had he purposely blocked the road to inform on them?

"So this is the little bride-to-be." The lanky redhead's freckled nose nearly touched the car window as he spoke through the glass, giving the interior a once-over.

Erik's heart hammered against his rib cage. Betrayal? He manufactured a smile.

The stranger grinned roguishly as he looked Annelise over. "No wonder you've kept this doll to yourself. She's too good for the likes of you, old man."

Erik released a pent-up breath and winked at Annelise as he rolled down the window.

"Seems my friend has lost his tongue," the fellow said. "But I'm quite capable of introducing myself." He reached inside to shake Annelise's hand. "Jakob Kirkgarde. You must be the mysterious Miss Christiansen we've heard so much about."

"Call me Annelise. It's a pleasure to meet one of my fiancé's friends. Erik hasn't been nearly so forthcoming about you."

A cocky one-sided grin accompanied Kirkgarde's raised brow. "Now I know why."

"Driver, move on," Captain von Rundstedt abruptly ordered.

Kirkgarde stepped back. "Guess my dog's cleared the cows off the road. I'll drop by later to meet the rest of your party." He tipped his cap, and his gaze grazed the others in the car, revealing nothing.

As the vehicle drove past the herder and his cows, Erik saw Rundstedt extract his hand from a holstered pistol. He squelched a smirk. Apparently the Nazi had some fears of his own due to the growing tensions between the Danes and the occupying forces. But then, the Germans had good cause to sweat. There was scarcely a Dane in the entire country who didn't abhor their haughty presence. Just last night an explosion lit up the sky when yet another shipyard was sabotaged. This little caravan easily could have been ambushed.

Nearing the port of Sjaellands's Point, Erik prayed that everyone in town was in on his charade. The last thing he needed was for someone to try something stupid. . .or divulge his true place of origin.

The lead German truck turned onto the side street Erik had indicated, and Rundstedt's driver followed suit. A smiling couple standing on the corner waved as they passed.

"More friends?" The captain sounded already bored with the day's agenda.

"That's right. It's a small town."

Axel turned and grinned. "Methinks we're all gonna be excess baggage for you and Sis today. Perhaps after we've eaten, the captain would like to accompany me to the docks while I look for some vacant warehouses to rent."

Knowing his friend was attempting to ease the tension, Erik resisted the urge to thump him on the back.

Rundstedt seemed oblivious to the undercurrent. "We find it prudent to make our presence known wherever we go, check through a few crates, make sure all is as it should be."

The Nazi caravan drew up to a well-kept, two-story house where a group of people waited outside, smiling and waving as their returning "son" arrived.

Eager to greet them, Erik hopped out. He'd never actually seen these relatives face-to-face but had heard stories about them his whole life.

An older man bearing a strong resemblance to his real father stepped forward. Even with the receding hairline and somewhat hunched shoulders, Erik recognized his dad's younger brother from family photographs. There was no mistaking those kind hazel eyes or that Nielsen smile as the man engulfed him in a bear hug. "Welcome home, son. We've missed you."

"Don't forget about me," a feminine voice cajoled from behind. Turning, Erik saw his aunt, another familiar face from the family album. A bit shorter than he'd expected, she wore a dark skirt and white blouse, and her graying blond hair was pinned neatly in place. Already he was adjusting to thinking of the couple as his parents.

"Mom." He wrapped his arms around her plump little form and kissed her soft cheek. "I missed you, too. *And* your cooking. I sure hope you've made some of your famous *frikadeller* and *rabarbergrød*. I've been craving them for ages." His mouth watered at the thought of the Danish meatballs and rhubarb pudding, specialties of his family.

"Well, they are your favorites." She didn't bat an eye. "Your father and I are just glad you've come home in one piece. Such foolishness, venturing out to sea to fish during wartime. Tsk, tsk."

Some individuals on the sidelines surged toward him then, all talking at once. Three of them were his cousin and alleged sister, Bergitte; her husband, Svend; and their baby. The others he recognized as another aunt and her husband, the local baker.

"Bergitte, Svend." He hugged the petite blond beauty and shook hands with her burly, Viking-like husband. "Don't tell me this strapping towhead is little Thor, big enough to walk already!" Then he turned to the other couple. "Aunt Lisbet. Uncle Karl. Wonderful to see you both again." Trying to respond to everyone's comments amid all the hugs and greetings, Erik suddenly remembered Annelise. He turned to see her already emerging from the car, utterly feminine in a flowy silk dress of rich violet and a gray cashmere coat with matching hat. Awed as always by her exquisite beauty, he offered his hand. "And this, everyone, is Annelise Christiansen, the beautiful woman I wrote you about, who has agreed to become my wife."

"Oh, come here, my dear, come here," Erik's "mother" crooned as the group surrounded Annelise and started introducing themselves.

"Looks like Annie has found herself among friends," Axel remarked, coming around the vehicle from the opposite side with their Nazi escort.

At the appearance of the hated uniform, the collective exuberance dimmed a fraction.

Erik cleared his throat. "Mom, Dad, everyone, I'd like you to meet Annelise's brother, Axel, and Captain Franz von Rundstedt, who graciously offered us the use of his personal car today. Axel, Captain von Rundstedt, may I present my parents, Magnus and Gjerta Nielsen. Next to Annelise are my sister, Bergitte, and her husband, Svend Dinesen, along with my Aunt Lisbet and Uncle Karl Kristoffersen."

Erik's "father" placed an arm around his wife's waist and drew her toward the newcomers. "My Gjerta and I are honored to meet you," he said cordially, extending his hand. "Welcome to our fair town."

"Yes. Welcome to our home," his wife added with a polite smile. "We're so pleased to have the pleasure of your company for the noon meal."

Watching the exchange and noting the tiny lines of strain near their eyes and mouths, Erik sensed the huge effort it cost the older pair to feign friendliness toward the German intruder. He made a mental note to express his profound gratitude later.

The group headed for the house, Annelise and Erik's pretend sister chatting about baby Thor's latest accomplishments. Erik hesitated, waiting for Axel and Rundstedt. The Nazi had gone to speak to the driver of the lead truck. Erik could not make out the conversation, but when the heavy vehicles started up and made a U-turn, he figured the troops were being dispatched to the docks to conduct searches on the various cargoes, warehouses, and ships. Meeting Axel's cagey expression, Erik prayed they'd all survive this day.

"I'm afraid the parlor isn't large enough to accommodate all of us," Mrs. Nielsen said as they crowded into the home's appealing and homey confines. "Let's gather around the dining table instead. It's time to eat, and everything is ready."

Annelise felt Erik move up beside her and take her arm, leading her through the comfortably furnished front room and into the next as if he were familiar with the layout. She glanced around the charming dining room, where a lace tablecloth accented a long oval table already set with blue underglazed Royal Copenhagen china and his aunt's best silverware. Trays of fancy Danish pastries awaited on the buffet along the wall.

"Do I smell roast beef?" Erik's dark brows arched high on his forehead.

"That's right," his father affirmed. "Our neighbor butchered one of his cows a few days ago, and I talked him out of a sizable roast. He owed me a number of favors."

Erik chuckled. "That would be Lars, the persistent borrower of tools, no doubt."

"And before the meat dries out," his mother added, "we must serve the *klar suppe*."

"Ah, yes." Erik's cheery tone indicated how much he anticipated the clear soup with carrot bits and thimble-sized dumplings and meatballs. Annelise, too, enjoyed many of the traditional Danish dishes she'd first tasted at her grandmother's home.

"I'll help you, Mother," Bergitte said, "once I put Thor down for his nap."

Annelise watched her hurry toward the stairs as speedily as Erik's mother had left the room. Obviously the family was anxious to rid themselves of the great *honor* of wasting precious food on a Nazi officer. "I'd be glad to help, if I may," she offered.

At his place at the head of the table, Mr. Nielsen put his hand on her shoulder. "That's not necessary, my dear. Perhaps next time Erik brings you home, we'll impose on your good nature. Today you are our very special guest, and I'd like a chance to get to know my new daughter better." He paused. "My son tells me your brother has a shipping business, and you handle all his correspondence. Will you and Erik stay in Copenhagen after the wedding, or will we enjoy the pleasure of having you here near us? This is a lovely little town, coastal climate, salty breezes. . ."

It was a question neither of them had anticipated. Annelise could feel Rundstedt's perceptive stare from across the table. She chanced a glance at Erik, devastatingly handsome today in a gray tweed sport jacket and charcoal trousers, his gold-striped tie accenting the gold flecks in his brown eyes.

"With the war on," he answered, "we feel we'd be of most use in the city. Axel is too busy to get by without us."

"Oh, yes," Karl the baker chimed in, the overhead light shining off his balding pate. "Import-export. Any chance you might import some sugar our way?" He glanced at his plump wife sitting beside him. "We've exhausted our month's ration already with all the baking for your visit. Even our flour is running low. We may have to lock the bakery doors."

Axel brushed crumbs from his silk tie and gave a thoughtful nod. "Flour I can get you easily. Sugar? I'll do what I can. After all, we're family. . .or will be soon enough." His too-easy grin and twinkling blue eyes nettled Annelise. What new scheme was taking form in that handsome blond head?

Mrs. Nielsen and Bergitte returned with trays of steaming

soup bowls and took their places.

Ignoring the presence of the austere German officer, Mr. Nielsen offered a brief prayer of thanks; then his wife met Annelise's gaze. "Erik never told us the date you've chosen for the wedding. Will you marry here or in Copenhagen?"

"We'd be happy to arrange for the local church," Erik's sister added. "It's lovely, in a quaint sort of way. I've always preferred the traditional-style building, don't you?"

It took extra effort for Annelise to swallow the small meatball in her mouth. Surely these people knew she and Erik weren't planning to go through with an actual wedding. Or had her *fiancé* conveniently forgotten to mention that little technicality? She smiled sweetly. "My grandmother's already making the arrangements. It keeps her happy to feel. . .useful."

"But you're all invited," Erik assured them. "The Christiansens have a large house. There's plenty of room for the family to come and stay for the festivities." He set his spoon down and sat back.

His mother, noticing that everyone had finished the first course, sent a pointed look at Bergitte, and the two cleared away the bowls in preparation for serving the main dish. The platter of beef they brought to the table moments later was richly decorated with gravy, bits of bacon, parsley, and pickled beet and garnished with green pepper and lemon slices. Potatoes browned in butter and sugar occupied one end of the large platter, and tossed red and green cabbage added a dash of color, enhancing the dish as a whole.

"It's truly beautiful," Annelise murmured, as appreciative as everyone else seemed over this respite from endless meals centering around fish.

Mr. Nielsen carved the roast and passed plates to everyone, then retook his seat. "I don't believe I caught the wedding date you mentioned." He directed his comment to Erik.

Annelise noted Captain von Rundstedt's heightened interest as he paused in eating.

"Our other son, Mikkel, is stationed over on Jutland," Erik's father went on. "He'll need to apply for a leave of duty to attend the ceremony."

"You sound like our grandmother," Axel cut in. "I've been trying to arrange time off for Sis and Erik, but with so many wartime orders hanging over our heads, it's almost impossible. Maybe by the end of May I'll be able to spare them for a short time. That's the best I can do."

Erik's Aunt Lisbet beamed as she rested her forearms on the table. "That would be perfect! The flowers will be in full bloom. And we'll bake you the most beautiful cake"—she switched her attention to Axel—"*if* your brother manages to get us some sugar, that is."

"Then it's settled," Mrs. Nielsen declared. "The last Saturday in May it is. Of course you'll wear my grandmother's wedding gown. All the women in our family have worn it. The lace is most exquisite. I'll send it back with you so you can have it altered to fit."

Of course! The reason for all the talk about the wedding dawned on Annelise. There must be something that needed to be smuggled along with the gown. How comical, she decided, sneaking contraband beneath the nose of an officer of the Third Reich. "I'd be honored to be part of that family tradition."

A span of silence followed while everyone ate with enthusiasm.

At length, Axel turned to Mr. Nielsen. "The wedding brings up a much more pleasant subject—the honeymoon."

Svend Dinesen poked his wife in the ribs with his beefy arm and winked. "That's the whole purpose, right, honey-girl?"

Annelise watched Bergitte's cheeks flush and felt her own blush climbing to her temples.

Erik grinned and took her hand with a not-so-subtle squeeze, adding to her distress.

"Sis has been working pretty hard." Axel's mischievous smile matched her soon-to-be brother-in-law's. "I'd like to gift the newlyweds with a honeymoon they'll never forget. Annelise has always wanted to sail up the coast of Sweden, and late spring would be ideal for that kind of thing." He looked to Svend. "I understand your father has a yacht for charter, right?"

Flaxen-haired Dinesen flicked a stilted glance at the Nazi before answering. "It's in dry dock, same as all the other leisure boats. There's not much call for pleasure cruises with the war on." His full lips tightened at the edges.

"How about it, Captain?" Axel challenged. "Any chance of you persuading some of our naval friends to allow safe passage for a honeymoon ship? At least until she's well north of Bornholmsgat Strait?"

Annelise's insides sank. Her brother's big mouth was digging them into another hole. Honeymoon cruise. Right. No doubt he planned to help refugees escape to freedom on that yacht. Taking a sip of water from her crystal goblet, she directed a wistful look at the Nazi officer. "Oh, would something like that truly be possible? Could you actually arrange it?"

He swallowed, then blotted his mouth on the linen napkin. "I do have a few friends in the naval office." Never one to miss an opportunity to be the big man, he shifted in his chair and hiked his chin. "Perhaps I could manage something—particularly if we invite them to the wedding. If they know there will be more young ladies as lovely as the ones in this room, they might be agreeable."

Axel's good-natured laugh broke forth. "No problem, Captain. Surely you've noticed the women of Denmark are every bit as lovely as our spring tulips."

Rundstedt's cool glance slid from Annelise to Erik, and his polite smile vanished.

For what purpose had the Nazi insisted on coming along today? Annelise wondered. This family gathering couldn't be pleasant for him. It was hardly a secret that he'd love to rid himself of Erik in a way that might elevate him in her opinion. But as long as the man wore that hated uniform, nothing he could do or say would make him appealing—to her or any other patriotic Danish woman.

"Coffee and pastry, anyone?" The lady of the house nodded to Bergitte, and the two rose to clear away plates and the remaining food. In moments, the younger woman returned and set the assortment of fancy treats on the table, while the hostess poured fresh coffee. Then the two retook their seats.

Erik's uncle Karl stood to his feet and lifted his goblet in a toast. "May the good Lord bless our nephew and his lovely betrothed. May they raise a houseful of healthy children in a world of peace and harmony."

Erik draped his arm affectionately around Annelise and hugged her.

Mr. Nielsen also got up. "And may God bless this feast He provided for us on this most joyous of occasions."

Annelise heard the captain heave a weary sigh at what he undoubtedly considered an ignorant old man's ravings. But she knew that he was the real fool for thinking the Nazis could snub their noses at the Creator of the universe and get away with it forever. Retribution would one day be upon them.

Meanwhile, Axel was pulling her ever deeper into his whirl of intrigue—and Erik with her. Somehow, though, the American's presence beside her instilled her with confidence. She truly enjoyed the feel of his arm about her. And as she grew to know him, she realized she was discovering more to appreciate and like about him. Despite everything, she felt safe and loved in the midst of his warm, generous family.

Even with a Nazi staring straight at her.

Chapter 5

Emerging from the other secret room in the Christiansens' basement, Erik stretched a kink out of his back and neck. To avoid chance discovery by the Nazis, his desk and forging supplies had been brought over from the warehouse, and now he shared the hideaway with newcomer Charles Bridgeport, a lone escapee of a downed American plane. Erik's eyes burned from hours of the meticulous work, and his fingers ached when he slid the shelf-lined door partially closed behind him.

A commotion echoed from the other end of the shadowy cellar as Axel's voice impersonated a high-powered engine. "Varoom! Varoom!"

Erik worked his way to the kids' doorway and stopped at the entrance. He smiled at the sight of two grown men on the floor trying to keep pace with an energetic boy racing cars around a makeshift racetrack of boards and books.

They all glanced up, then returned their concentration to the race.

He shook his head and chuckled. "I'm going to the kitchen for a snack. Anybody else hungry?"

"We could use some of those cookies Annie baked this morning," Axel said, stopping his miniature car, "and milk. Racing's a thirsty business, buddy." After checking to see if the others agreed, they resumed the competition. "Varoom! Varoom! Varooom!"

Erik smirked and started for the basement stairs. When he'd left America for this assignment, he envisioned himself hiding out in some cold, dismal cave, suffering the life of a mole. Instead, he lived openly in this snug house with warm, caring people. People he'd quickly grown fond of. . .one in particular.

Thoughts of Annelise played through his mind in a collage of pictures, from his first glimpse of her exquisite beauty to her stunning appearance while visiting his relatives at Sjaellands Point. And her many moods—being flustered when she'd slept in on his first morning here; being annoyed when put in risky situations, yet willing to see them through; being patient and determined. And she cared for people: her aging grandmother, her foolhardy brother, children who'd been ripped away from their families, even total strangers imposing on their hospitality. *Like me.*

What a pity the wedding they talked so much about was a sham. The more time Erik spent with Annelise and the better he got to know her, the more he realized she met every single qualification his father had rattled off. And he cared about her. Really cared. Problem was, she needed a man she could trust to be with her no matter what. With a war raging around them, Erik couldn't promise to be that man.

Yes, he was going upstairs to get a snack, all right. In truth, he was yearning for some time alone with his fiancée. Reaching the main-floor hallway, he heard feminine murmurings from the dining room, where the ladies were making a new dress for little Rachel. Annelise's enchanting voice drew him down the gloomy hall toward the golden lamp glow spilling from the room.

In the archway, he feasted his eyes on his betrothed as she concentrated on pinning puffy sleeves to a small floral and lace bodice. Grams Holberg sat at the treadle machine nearby, sewing what resembled a wide sash for a dress pretty enough to be worn by a flower girl in a wedding.

His and Annelise's wedding.

No one among the family's church friends knew anyone who could take the children to Sweden, so Erik and Axel concocted the daring plan to have Rachel and Moshe march down the aisle as flower girl and ring bearer, right under the noses of the Nazis. The little pair would then accompany the wedding party to the reception on the yacht and conveniently disappear below deck before time to sail. The newlyweds would personally transport them to safety. Annelise had scoffed at the insane idea at first, but now even she was caught up in the wedding plans. Maybe in time her new enthusiasm might extend to him, too.

Erik's gaze meandered to the curly haired darling perched on her knees in a chair by Annelise, fussing with a doll's dress made to match Rachel's special one. The rag doll was from the batch he had brought from America stuffed with money for refugees, and Rachel had latched on to one whose yarn hair was as dark as her own. Absorbed in dressing the dolly, the slight child looked so small. So vulnerable. He prayed that God would see them all through this dangerous escapade.

His attention gravitated to Annelise again, and his heart swelled with tenderness. Maybe after they'd accomplished their mission and were sailing the Gulf of Bothnia, they'd be free from the wartime tension for a while. He imagined them just being together, getting to know each other. One day she might come to trust him. To love him. . .as he was growing to love her. There was no use denying his feelings.

But who was he kidding? They'd be watched day and night by the Germans.

"See how pretty Abigail looks?" Rachel's eyes shone as she held out her stuffed doll for Annelise to see, dressed up in her fancy attire. "May I please hold my Abby under the canopy while you and Mr. Erik get married?"

Annelise smiled, admiring the treasured doll. "We won't be having a canopy, sweetie. Our wedding will be different from the ones you've seen. You'll just walk down a long aisle to the front of the church and wait quietly. Mr. Erik will already be standing there, waiting for me." A wistful smile—or *wishful*, Erik dared to hope—softened her expressive features. When she raised her lashes, her beautiful azure eyes locked on his.

For a second, he thought he detected undeniable joy. . . until her cheeks pinkened and her expression settled into one of mere politeness.

"I. . .uh. . .came up to get something to eat for me and the race-car drivers downstairs," he stammered.

Mrs. Holberg gave a wry grimace. "That's just where Axel belongs. In the cellar playing with cars instead of out in the world concocting endless messes for the rest of us to clean up."

"Did Uncle Axel spill some milk?" Rachel asked in that cute but perilous Hamburg accent. Her brown eyes rounded with dread.

"No, my dear. Nothing like that." The older woman slanted

a glance at her granddaughter. "Annelise, why don't you go to the kitchen and help Erik fix a nice tray for the boys? Maybe one for us, too." She surprised Erik with a sly wink as Annelise placed her work carefully on the table.

Erik's respect for the old gal went up another notch. For all her disapproval over some of her adventurous grandson's schemes, it seemed she was in Erik's corner when it came to him and Annelise. Yep, he liked that dear lady.

☙

Acutely aware of Erik's presence in the kitchen with her, Annelise filled the water kettle and set it on the hottest part of the stove, then moved to the icebox for cheese and other snack items. "Would you mind fetching a tray and a few napkins?" she asked to keep him busy. "And there are crackers in that cupboard behind you. Cookies, too, for the children."

Erik took out a tin of cookies she'd baked earlier and brought them to her. He didn't even ask where things were! He'd gotten to know his way around the kitchen and the rest of the house amazingly quickly and seemed at home now. How had Grams put it yesterday, those old eyes of hers sparkling? *Such a good fit, he is.* Already the opinionated lady treated him like part of the family, just one more grandson. A person would think that her granddaughter and Erik really were engaged—and that the mock wedding mere days away now was legal!

Smiling at the ludicrous thought, she conceded that the American was more than pleasing. He was charming, witty, and intelligent, and he displayed a rare gentleness whenever he was around the children. Still, it seemed that Grams and Axel were caught up in a fairy tale.

How many couples really lived happily ever after? Sure, her own grandparents had enjoyed a long and wonderful life together, but that was back when marriage was considered a sacred trust, when a man presented himself to his true love's family, vowing to honor and protect her till death parted them. She couldn't imagine Erik approaching her father with such a pledge. Frederick Christiansen lacked a single honorable bone in his body.

She shook off the bitter thought. *I'll never forgive him. Never.*

"Is this everything, Annelise?" Erik interrupted her musings. . .and her idleness at the worktable.

"Hmm?" Her gaze collided with his, only inches away. "Oh." She tried to regain her poise as she surveyed the tray. She couldn't remember slicing the cheese or laying out the pickled herring, let alone arranging the apple slices, cookies, and crackers so artfully. What was wrong with her? "Yes, that's fine, except we need cups."

Erik studied her for another excruciating second before turning toward the china cabinet.

Her heart racing, Annelise asked a needless question. "The little ones will want cookies and milk. Do you think the airman will prefer those or the cheese and fruit?"

"Oh. You don't care what Axel or I want, is that it?" He looked askance at her.

"I already know that."

A mocking expression met her as he brought over the cups. "You do, do you?"

She answered too quickly. "Whenever there's something sweet, you're Johnny on the spot."

His teasing grin broadened.

"And as for Axel, he's a true Dane at heart and adores herring. But considering the wedding fiasco he's gotten us into, he doesn't deserve better than bread and water."

Erik's smile faded.

Had she hurt his feelings? She swallowed. "But you—you've been a wonderful sport about all of this. You really have."

His gaze didn't waver as he seemed to consider her words—or was it the meaning behind them? Abruptly his demeanor brightened. "Hey, for your brother to come up with a plan for me to smuggle several people out of the country by sailing up the coast in the company of Denmark's fairest flower. . ." He shrugged and gave a lopsided grin. "I'm not about to complain."

Denmark's fairest flower? He was so very entrancing. . . which only increased her jitters. For a heartbeat, a small part of her wondered what it would be like to really be married to Erik Nielsen. And part of her wished she could find out. Filling plates methodically, she changed the subject. "But Rachel and Moshe. I'm so afraid for them."

Erik exhaled a spiritless breath, as he did whenever she dodged personal subjects. "No matter when the children go, it'll be dangerous. Wouldn't you rather it was the two of us taking them out, instead of handing them over to someone who doesn't love them as we do? How much would a stranger risk to keep them safe?"

"You're right." Annelise paused and turned to face him. He'd grown as attached to the youngsters as the rest of the household had. "Whenever I look into their big brown eyes, I want to wrap my arms around them and promise them the world, make them believe everything will be all right."

With an understanding nod, he moved closer. She almost expected him to take her in his arms. . .and kind of hoped he would. Instead, he reached out to brush a tendril of her hair away from her eyes with the backs of his fingers, his touch sending a tingle down to her toes. "You've made things much easier for them while they've been here. Especially little Rachel, who understands more of what's going on. That pretty dress for her, and one for her doll. . .you'll make a wonderful mother someday." He took her hand, caressing her palm with his thumb as he gazed from it to her eyes.

Her heart skipped a beat. Unless her imagination was getting the better of her, Erik was looking at her the way a man looked at a woman he cared about in a truly special way. Her pulse throbbed in her ears.

"My dad always told me," he went on, standing much too close, "a man should search for a woman who'll be a loving mother to his children. Not just a pretty face but someone with a beautiful heart. Someone he could love for a lifetime."

Annelise could scarcely breathe.

"I—"

A deafening explosion rocked the house.

Instinctively, Annelise swayed against Erik, and he crushed her to himself.

Rachel screamed and flew in from the next room, trembling with terror.

Erik bent and lifted her up between them. "You're safe," he crooned, hugging them both close. "I'll never let anything happen to you."

Somehow Annelise sensed he was comforting her along with the child.

And somehow she believed him. She closed her eyes, reveling in their closeness.

Footsteps pounded up from below as Grams rushed in from the dining room. "From the front window, it would appear the crystal factory has blown up."

"They must have used enough explosives to level the entire block," Erik grated.

"Probably did," Axel affirmed, bursting in from the hall. "The SS stored arms there." He opened the back door and stepped out onto the porch. "Would you look at that!"

"What?" Annelise, with Erik's arm still around her and Rachel, joined him.

The night sky was ablaze. Copenhagen, beautiful, ancient Copenhagen, was being destroyed bit by bit—by its own people. And it couldn't be helped. Every Dane knew if the underground neglected to go after the Nazis, British bombers would do it for them. RAF planes roared over the country almost every day on their way to bomb strategic German sites. At least this way, the Danish people could pick and choose their targets.

"We must pray, all of us, for God's protection on all the innocent victims," Grams murmured and began to pray aloud.

Annelise pondered the fragility of life, how quickly it could be snuffed out. Within the warmth and strength of Erik's arm while they stood watching flames lick the sky, Annelise wished fervently he truly could keep her and the little ones safe. . .that he could be that fairy-tale man, the one she could trust until death.

Annelise blew her bangs out of her eyes and peered closer at the itemized columns she'd entered in the ledger, making sure the figures matched the shipping manifests from the latest delivery truck. Axel would want the accounts up-to-date when he returned from wherever his latest "business" had taken him. She hated it when he was delayed.

The shrill of the street doorbell carried above the warehouse racket. Hoping it was her brother—or Erik, who also had been gone overlong—she glanced out the office window. How she resented Axel for risking other people's lives.

At the thought of Erik, her mind drifted to the previous night in the kitchen, to the things the dashing American had said to her. And the things he hadn't. Unless she was mistaken, he'd come pretty close to. . .to asking her to marry him for real?

Her breath caught. She had to stop this foolish daydreaming. Even if her imagination hadn't been far wrong, his actions could be attributed to high wartime emotions. Likely he was caught up in the rush of danger and excitement, the same as Axel.

Sigrid Thomsen, the birdlike woman who ran the front shop, rapped on the office door and came in, all fluttery and nervous. "Captain von Rundstedt is here to see you." She glanced toward the main entrance.

Before Annelise could respond, the Nazi brushed past the woman and strode right in. "*God morgen*, Miss Christiansen," he said in his stiff, condescending way, while Mrs. Thomsen took swift leave.

What business brings him here? Annelise wondered. Perhaps Axel or Erik had been discovered, and he'd come to inform her. . .to interrogate her. She drew on her practiced calm, returning the greeting. "Good morning, Captain. How nice of you to come by."

He gave a curt nod. "I did not see your brother's sedan outside." He peered out the inner window, scanning the warehouse.

Annelise followed his gaze, relieved that the shipping clerks had paused in their work to watch him. He'd be obliged to maintain proper decorum. "Axel's down at the harbor master's office arranging sailing permits."

He continued his scrutiny. "Let us hope it is for those mechanisms that were to have been shipped last week." He returned his attention to her.

She knew he referred to the remote homing devices for some new type of bomb that the BBC reported was being tested in Germany. Axel had been stalling the shipment while the underground made "minor adjustments" to them. "I do believe they went out, but I haven't received the paperwork yet," she answered nonchalantly. "Perhaps he'll bring it with him when he returns."

The captain gave a speculative nod. "I do not see the prospective groom around, either. Perhaps he, too, is bringing the papers." His tone dripped with sarcasm, but then, he always acted and sounded suspicious of everything and everyone.

"No," Annelise answered evenly. "He's gone to the train station to pick up a carload of fresh produce ferried over from Jutland."

"So I have you all to myself."

His insinuating leer in no way put her at ease. This threat was more personal. She attempted a small smile. "So it would seem."

Rundstedt pulled up a chair and plunked it uncomfortably

close to hers, mostly below the view of the curious warehouse workers. "Now that your fisherman has been around on a daily basis, I thought you might be growing bored with him. It would not be uncommon for a young woman such as yourself to be having second thoughts about now."

When she did not respond, he spoke again. "Surely you are aware that it has been difficult for me seeing one as refined and socially elevated as you wed to such a. . .common fellow." He leaned closer. "Consider for a moment the life you would enjoy with a man of my breeding and taste. The clothes, the jewels, the finest villa. As you know, I am highly regarded in the party. And I intend to see that remains so. Once the Fatherland is victorious and controls global commerce, you could have anything in the world. Anything your heart desires. . .as my wife. Travel. . ."

Stunned by his unwelcome declaration, Annelise knew she had to be extremely careful not to offend him. She hoped her forced smile appeared sincere. "Why, Captain, I hardly know what to say. That would be a tempting offer for any woman. I haven't the slightest doubt you'd be a thoughtful and loving husband. But what my heart has desired, for a very long time, is Mr. Nielsen. Despite his humble family, my love for him has not diminished at all. Nor, I truly believe, has his for me. He is the deepest desire of my heart. All else pales by comparison to the love we share."

Rundstedt's face hardened like his rigid posture. "I see." A corner of his mouth lifted sardonically. "But surely you understand my reason for doubting this *great love*, at least on his part. I have seen no marriage announcement in the newspapers nor an application for a marriage license posted."

Annelise feigned surprise. She snatched the opportunity to

stand and step back from him, her hands to her face. "You're right! We forgot all about the license. Thank you for bringing it to my attention. We must go to city hall this very day, the minute Erik returns. We've been so busy trying to keep all the warehouse orders current while making wedding plans, writing out invitations, we've—" She forced herself to take the captain's hand. "We've even put off having you for tea as we intended. But once we return from our honeymoon, you'll be our very first guest. We'll have you to our new home, you and all of the other kind people who'll help make our wedding such a memorable event. Especially those at your naval headquarters."

The door opened just then, and Axel entered, the huge smile he always flashed on the Nazis fixed in place. "Well, well. We have a most esteemed visitor, I see."

Annelise extracted her fingers from the officer's grip.

"You'll be pleased to know, Captain, that shipment you've been concerned about is headed for Lubeck as we speak," Axel announced proudly. He patted the briefcase he carried. "I have the shipping manifests right here. I'll send your copy over with the others this afternoon."

"Good." His typical brusque nod accompanied the word. "I will inform the authorities when I return to my office." His demeanor softened a fraction as he turned to Annelise and recaptured her hand, applying pressure. "I enjoyed our little talk. Do reconsider what I said."

"Thank you again for that timely reminder," she managed, tugging free with some difficulty.

He stepped back and nodded to Axel, then clicked his heels in a smart salute. "Heil Hitler."

Axel moved to the door and cocked an ear as the Nazi's

footfalls receded. Then he swung to the warehouse window, deadly serious.

Following her brother's gaze, Annelise spied two of the workers nodding purposefully at the captain and gesturing toward her and Axel. The Nazi did the same. Obviously he had issued some kind of order to them. But what was it? To watch her when he was gone? Did they have concealed weapons they'd use against her or her brother? The very thought turned her blood cold.

"What did the Kraut mean?" Axel asked. "What did he want you to reconsider?"

"Marrying Erik. He thinks I'm much better Nazi-wife material," she replied dryly.

"That's nothing new."

"Maybe not. But here's something that is. He noticed we haven't bought a marriage license yet."

"Never misses a beat, does he? But that's easily remedied. Where's Erik?"

"What do you mean, *where's Erik*? You're the one who keeps sending him out on the streets."

Axel grimaced and turned away. "I take it he's not back yet."

"Oh, no you don't. You're not getting off that easily, big brother. From what Erik told me, he didn't expect to be gone more than an hour or so."

"Things don't always go as planned," Axel hedged.

"What things?" How she detested this constant secrecy! How *could* he think so lightly of endangering a friend? Her fear for Erik intensified. "What have you got him doing this—"

He clamped a hand onto her shoulder. "Look, sis, Erik is a soldier. It's his job to do whatever he can to help win this war."

"No!" she raged back. Then, remembering they could be seen by the warehouse workers, possibly even heard, she switched to an intense whisper. "His job is to forge papers. If he's caught running errands for the underground, he won't just be shipped off to a POW camp. He'll be shot."

Axel's chuckle lacked humor. "Won't we all." His head jerked up, and he stepped nearer to the window. "Thank the Lord. That's him now." Wheeling around, he headed for the office door.

Vastly relieved, Annelise chased after him through the shop and out the warehouse door as he went to meet the truck.

Her fiancé, as maddeningly relaxed and handsome as ever, hopped down from the cab. Spotting her, he grinned.

Axel was not half as calm. "What kept you? Did you make the delivery?"

His gaze lingering on Annelise, Erik nodded. "Yep. They're all safe."

Releasing an exasperated breath, Axel gripped his friend's shoulder, drawing his attention. "Then what took you so long?"

Erik shrugged, unconcerned. "I had to take care of something." He turned back to Annelise and withdrew a tiny velvet box from his trouser pocket. "This is for you."

Realizing it was from a jewelry store, Annelise accepted the little box and opened it with trembling fingers. Inside she found a simple yet exquisite wedding band. "Ohh. . ."

"I wish I had the money to buy something more elegant," he added softly. "One that would do justice to your beautiful hands."

His tone and expression were so tender and sincere, she had the strongest urge to melt into his arms as she had last night. She tore her gaze from his and back to the ring. "It's just perfect in its simplicity. Exactly what I would've chosen."

"Really? You're not just saying that?" He released a huge whoosh of air as if her approval was of utmost importance, then plucked the golden band from its container. "When I told the jeweler you had delicate fingers, this is the size he gave me. I hope it fits." Taking her hand, he slipped the ring on her third finger.

The wedding band fit fine. . .but another band, an invisible one she could only feel, squeezed the air from her lungs. There they stood, the two of them, as if no one else in the world existed. Her hand rested in his much larger one, both of them fully aware of the ring's significance, this symbol of something so very elusive. . .never-ending love.

A tiny thought swirled through her head as delicate and iridescent as summer's first rainbow.

A girl could do worse than marry a man like Erik Nielsen.

Chapter 6

This day, their wedding day, had come so fast. Standing with his "father" at the front of the sanctuary while the ushers seated arriving guests, Erik felt his nervousness increase with each peal of the church bells. Normally the beautiful Danish chapel he attended with the Christiansens on Sundays instilled him with peace. Constructed of cut stone with a steep slate roofline, the structure's tall arched windows of jewel-like stained glass bathed the interior in a warm glow, even on dreary days. In today's sunlight they sparkled like diamonds, casting miniature rainbows everywhere. A bounty of ferns and flowers added lush fragrance that mingled with the perfumes of women dressed in their finest. So many people had come to see him and Annelise get married.

He tugged at the too-snug tie of the black suit Axel insisted on having made for him. Erik knew he looked dashing in his first tailored outfit, but that hardly soothed his nerves. Anyone would think this ceremony was the real thing!

The side door swished quietly open, and Axel came to join him, equally elegant in his own tailored attire. He was accompanied by Bergitte's husband, Svend, whose size made him appear oafish next to suave Axel. Bergitte's brother Mikkel was unable to obtain leave from military duties to be best man because of heightened tensions between the Danish army and the Germans.

Svend caught Erik's eye and patted his breast pocket with an affirmative nod, indicating the presence of the wedding license. Unknown to him, it would remain unsigned to prevent validation.

A bittersweet sadness came over Erik, but he dared not let it show. He diverted his attention to the mostly unknown faces occupying the pews, their conversations hushed against the subdued music from the pipe organ.

He easily picked out his relatives. About a hundred other trusted folk from Sjaellands Point also had come, expressly so the American, Charles Bridgeport, and several British flyers could blend in while "hiding" in plain sight. Erik spotted Charles coming to take his seat, flanked by two locals chatting brightly in Danish, little of which Charles understood. Erik tried to see if he could detect anyone who appeared British, but no one stood out.

What did stand out were the sharply dressed Nazis positioned in the back row on either side. Despite their futile attempt to maintain their superior attitude, they had to know most people detested their very presence.

Dear Lord, Erik prayed, *those particular "guests" possess terrible power. Please take control of this day and all its events. May everything go smoothly as planned, and may the Nazis leave the wedding celebration every bit as unaware as when they got here.*

Erik's "father" slipped an empathetic arm around him. "Bridegrooms are supposed to be nervous," the older man whispered, "but you look like you're about to face a firing squad." He gave Erik's shoulder a bearlike squeeze. "Put those other concerns out of your head. My friends and I will see you and your beautiful bride through all the pitfalls of this day. Just do what your grandpa told me on my wedding day." He chuckled under his breath. " 'Forget about the pomp and ceremony. Keep your mind on the prize. The honeymoon.' "

Erik knew no such prize awaited him. Yet hating that he'd deceived his relatives on that point, he mustered a grin. No one except Annelise's family and the minister knew this was a mock wedding. With so many lives at stake, Axel insisted that the fewer people who were in on the ruse, the better.

One niggle of guilt did assault Erik. His bride-to-be would be coming down the aisle in a gown worn by every bride in his family for generations, making light of a sacred tradition. In truth, she had no choice. It had been forced upon on her. . .as had this entire wedding. . .and him. He grimaced.

Three fashionably dressed young women arrived and took the pew directly in front of the Nazis. One of them turned and smiled coyly at the officers—to provide feminine diversion, Erik surmised.

He couldn't help noticing an abundance of very attractive girls sprinkled throughout the sanctuary. More of Axel's doing, he figured.

His uncle/father jabbed him in the ribs, obviously drawing a similar conclusion. "That new brother-in-law of yours must be a very persuasive fellow, to persuade so many available young ladies to attend."

Erik slid a glance at Axel and grinned. "You have no idea."

The organist abruptly increased the volume, heralding the

start of the ceremony. Erik's heart leapt into his throat. The minister, garbed in his traditional formal robe, came to join him and his groomsmen, while Erik's "father" took his seat beside his wife in the front pew.

The talking ceased, and everyone focused forward.

Bergitte stepped to the doorway at the back, then started down the aisle, her steps measured to the meter of the music. His cousin's gown of rose taffeta edged with velvet and lace complemented her fair coloring and golden hair, a lovely contrast to the slim brunette who followed in a matching dress, a friend of Annelise's from church. From their dreamy expressions, neither had an inkling this wedding was anything but real.

It could have been real, Erik conceded, if Annelise would have provided the smallest bit of encouragement. He'd almost come right out and proposed to her that night in the kitchen, only she hadn't taken the hint, just gazed up at him with those incredibly sad eyes.

As Bergitte took her place at the front, Moshe started down the aisle, an adorable little tyke decked out in a new Sunday suit, his curls slicked back and shiny as he proudly carried a small satin pillow bearing a ring tied with a satin bow.

Erik watched for any indication of suspicion on the part of the Nazis to the Jewish boy's distinctive eyes and coloring, but they had yet to quit gawking at the pretty girls in front of them.

Then fragile little Rachel entered in her floral dress with its velvet sash, her sable hair a mass of ringlets and ribbons. She scattered pink and white rose petals from a white basket looped over one arm. The child took her job very seriously!

Erik almost choked when he spied the rag doll in the basket. Halfway down the aisle, she caught sight of him and gave a shy wave, her sweet smile cinching his heart.

He winked and waved back, vowing silently to protect those two children with his life. Them and Annelise. He would die before he'd let one of them suffer at the hands of those ruthless Nazis.

The music segued into the formal bridal chorus.

Pulse racing, Erik turned his attention to the rear.

On the arm of her grandmother's brother, Annelise, the vision of his heart, paused on the threshold of the sanctuary for a breathless moment before stepping forward. Her golden beauty shimmered through the misty veil, her glory lighting up the room as she came toward him, a bouquet of pink and white roses and trailing ribbons in her other hand. The Victorian heirloom gown of handmade lace accented her fragile, priceless elegance.

Erik could barely breathe. How had he gotten caught up in a charade of this magnitude? To think he'd entertained the notion that someone like him was worthy of the perfection now coming to him on satin-slippered feet! Feeling a deeper sense of loss than he'd ever known, he let out a ragged breath.

The first sight greeting Annelise as the congregation rose in honor of her walk down the bridal runner were the Nazi uniforms flanking either side. The second was the captain's ever-suspicious stare. She took a firmer hold of her great-uncle's arm, and he gave her hand an affectionate pat and a smile. Not in on the plan, he doubtless considered her a typically nervous bride.

Avoiding so much as a glance at Rundstedt, she focused straight ahead, and her gaze collided with Erik's. He stood tall and resplendent against the flowers and ferns, adoring her with his eyes. She almost forgot her own name. How unutterably sad that this whole ceremony was nothing but a charade. She'd have given anything for it to be real, to have that incredible American love her as much as he appeared to, enough to be faithful always. She almost sighed audibly.

When she reached the front, her great-uncle raised the edge of her veil to kiss her cheek, then let it fall back into place as he put her hand in Erik's and stepped away to await his line about giving her to be married.

The bridegroom took both of Annelise's hands in his and smiled at her, then turned slightly toward the minister, his gaze never leaving hers. The tenderness in his expression, the soft warmth of his touch brought a sheen of tears. She blinked to clear her vision. Intent in her struggle for composure, she scarcely heard the minister droning on in the background.

Erik repeated his vows with his eyes as much as his lips, his apparent sincerity almost tangible.

Then it was her turn. Annelise succumbed to the moment, imagining the wedding was real. But with emotion clogging her throat, she could barely murmur her own responses.

Before she knew it, the groom was putting his ring on her finger—the simple band he had chosen for her with great consideration. He gently rubbed his thumb over it, sending such a sensation of love through her that her knees felt weak.

A few final words by the minister, and Erik lifted her veil and drew her to him in a kiss so astoundingly gentle yet passionate that it was like being kissed for the very first time. Now her knees actually did wobble. Only Erik's strong arms prevented her from sinking to the floor.

He hugged her, chuckling quietly in her ear.

The receiving line seemed excruciatingly long as Erik and his beautiful bride greeted the individuals inching past, most of whom they had never met. Still, the congratulations and good wishes seemed sincere—even those from the German officers. In their case, the joviality probably resulted from being invited to a gathering where so many unattached lovelies graced the hall.

Only one person gave him pause for concern. Rundstedt hung back on the sidelines, observing everything in silence. Did he suspect something? Or was he just being his usual overbearing self?

When the Nazi finally stepped to the end of the line, Erik felt Annelise grip his arm. Though she appeared outwardly calm, he knew she was thankful that church members had whisked the children out of harm's way, at least for now.

"I read your wedding notice in the newspaper a few days ago," the captain remarked, reaching them. He shook Erik's hand in grudging courtesy. "So I must concede the ceremony makes it official. I won't say the best man won. Perhaps merely the lucky one."

"Speaking of official," Svend piped in from down the reception line, extracting a folded document from his breast pocket. "We need to catch the good reverend and get this marriage license signed."

Erik heard Annelise's slight gasp. "You're right." He draped his arm around her shoulder, pretending to look around for the minister.

"I see him." Svend gestured to draw the man's attention. "Excuse me, sir. We require a moment of your time." He waved the paper in the air.

Observing the Nazi as he approached, the pastor maintained a pleasant expression. He smiled at the newlyweds. "Of course. Come into my office."

"And since you're standing right here," Svend tipped his head at Rundstedt, "would you mind being the second witness?"

Annelise didn't dare venture a look at Erik as the foursome traipsed after the minister into his office. She fixed her attention on the man's black robe instead. He knew what was at stake here. He'd even been reluctant to be a party to a fake wedding. But now *this*.

He took his place behind the desk and held out his hand.

Svend, completely unaware of the ramifications of the affair, grinned broadly and handed over the official document.

The reverend took his good-natured time smoothing it out just so before turning it around for Erik and Annelise, as if even yet hoping for a last minute reprieve for them. When none came, he picked up his fountain pen and offered it, his demeanor bland in the pregnant silence.

Erik took the pen and with surprising confidence bent and signed his name. He then turned to Annelise, that bravado losing a little of its power as he locked gazes with her and held out the instrument to her.

She knew she couldn't show any hesitation, either. She took the pen.

As she did, Erik closed his hand over hers. He brought her

fingers to his lips and kissed them, his gaze never wavering.

The romantic gesture stopped her heartbeat for a second. But had he done it for her benefit, or the captain's?

When he released her hand, her fingers trembled. She steadied herself with her other hand and wrote her name below Erik's.

"Good going!" Svend boomed, snatching the pen from her. "That's the last time you'll ever sign your maiden name. From now on, you're a Nielsen." He scribbled his own signature, then handed the instrument to Rundstedt, who added his name and dropped the pen on the desk.

The tiny sound echoed inside Annelise's head like the closing of a great door. It was done.

It was official.

She was now Erik Nielsen's wife.

For real.

"Time's wastin' away." Svend Denison slapped one arm around her and the other around Erik and steered them toward the door. "Time to go to the yacht club for the party."

Chapter 7

No one spoke in the big black touring car transporting Captain von Rundstedt, the newlyweds, and Svend to the marina. Nearing their destination, Erik noticed wedding guests already milling about. How ironic that he, the son of a lowly fisherman, would have his wedding reception at a yacht club and honeymoon aboard a luxurious pleasure craft. But then, nothing about this wedding day had been normal, not the least of which was that he had actually married Annelise. That, of course, would have to be dealt with later. . .after the honeymoon.

Honeymoon. What an absurd thought.

Beside him, Annelise stirred, and he filled his lungs with the tantalizing scent of her perfume.

The car pulled into the parking area and stopped in close proximity to an immense yacht aglow with faint lights. Having expected a small, sleek, but cramped sailing boat, Erik could only stare at the beautiful ship. No wonder Svend's family chartered out this incredible vessel. The upkeep alone must be exorbitant.

Then Erik spied the German sentries, and grim reality returned full force. Since the Nazis no longer allowed the

Danes to police their own docks, soldiers were positioned every dozen yards along the boardwalk. German naval officers were numbered among the guests, so the guards would likely remain in the background, but they appeared edgy while the throng of revelers gravitated between the yacht and the open French doors of the clubhouse.

The driver turned off the engine, then got out to assist Annelise. Erik followed close behind. As he straightened, he spied a German patrol boat anchored beyond the marina slips. It was enormously gratifying to realize that with an official escort, no other Nazi ships would bother them in the heavily patrolled southern waters of the Baltic. Obviously Rundstedt had more influence than his rank would normally grant. According to a recent BBC report, the Germans shouldn't be wasting military equipment on nonessential pursuits when they were having such a rough time trying to conquer Russia.

Axel, smiling expansively as he emerged from the club, intercepted the arriving foursome. "I've got everything running smoothly," he told Erik and Annelise. "You two go in and enjoy yourselves while you can. You'll be sailing with the tide, and that's barely an hour off. What took you so long, anyway?"

"The photographer insisted we pose for a formal portrait before we left the church," Annelise answered. "What a perfectionist. He must have taken a dozen different shots before he was satisfied."

"And they wouldn't be legally married if it wasn't for me," Svend chimed in. "We almost forgot to get their signatures on the marriage license. But it's all official now. Captain von Rundstedt and I acted as witnesses."

Axel cut a glance to his sister, then grinned in his easy way at Svend and the officer. "Lucky you two were there."

A wave of guilt over having signed the document swamped Erik momentarily. Sloughing it off, he put his arm around Annelise and steered her toward the music wafting from inside the building. "I do believe my beautiful bride owes me a dance."

☙

"Thank you ever so much for the lovely wedding cake," Annelise gushed, giving Erik's aunt and uncle a parting hug. "I've never seen such a pretty one in my life."

"Think nothing of it, dear. Karl and I rarely have an opportunity to do something special for our Erik. It gave us such pleasure." She beamed with pride, her heightening color glowing against her best navy dress.

"And it has been our pleasure," Erik said, "having you here today. Thank you for coming."

What if they knew this dream wedding was just part of the war effort? Annelise wondered, fighting tears.

Axel strolled toward them, arm in arm with a fashionable young brunette Annelise had never seen before. "It'd be great if you two would board the yacht. Svend and his crew are waiting."

Annelise knew the meaning behind his casual statement. The clandestine switch of crew members had been successful and the children were tucked safely away below deck. As usual, her brother managed everything without her help. With that horde of people in constant motion, the guards couldn't possibly keep everyone straight. Still, so many lives were at stake. "We should say our good-byes. It would be rude just to walk out."

"Don't worry, little sis. I'll take care of it." Axel gestured to Erik with his chin.

Erik slipped an arm around her waist. "Let's be off, sweet-heart. I can't wait to check out that boat." Without waiting for her to respond, he ushered her out a side door leading to the boat slips.

The German soldier at the gate didn't bother checking their identification. "Congratulations!" he said in a thick Bavarian accent as they breezed past him.

"Thank you," Annelise called over her shoulder and clutched the long skirt of her gown in her hands. Her heels clicked on the hasty ascent up the wooden gangplank. Some wedding guests she didn't recognize were coming down just then, and she exchanged pleasantries with them. "See you in a week or so."

Svend waited at the top, a huge smile on his face. "Welcome aboard. First Mate Henrik, here, will show you to your state-room while I ease the *Baltic Princess* out of the slip."

Annelise recognized the crewman in sailor attire as Charles Bridgeport.

"Wait!" came a shout from the dock.

Annelise's heart thudded to a stop. She and Erik whirled around.

Captain von Rundstedt and two uniformed soldiers started up the gangplank.

Only Erik's arm around her kept her knees from buckling as he took a protective stance between her and the three Germans. *It's over. All our machinations, all for naught. Someone must have informed on us.* She pressed her face against Erik's back, hoping to draw strength from him.

"I forgot to give you my wedding gift," Rundstedt announced. "Extra petrol for your trip." His men held out two gasoline cans.

"Why, thank you so much," Annelise croaked, surprised she had a voice at all as she moved to Erik's side again, a smile pasted on her lips.

"You couldn't have brought anything more timely," Erik added. "We appreciate it."

The Nazi bowed politely, his gaze never leaving Annelise's face, as if the two of them shared some secret. "Think of me when you use them."

Svend moved forward, his bearing confident in his ship's captain's outfit and cap. "We all thank you, Captain, but I'm afraid it's past time for us to be off. Henrik, Jakob, take the petrol these good soldiers have brought us down to the engine room. And, Captain, would you be so kind as to release our mooring rope when you go back down the gangplank?"

Annelise and Erik moved to the railing and waved to their guests as the large craft chugged slowly out of the slip and into the calm waters of the harbor to join the patrol boat. She didn't realize how tense she was until she noticed she had positively mangled Erik's jacket sleeve. She blushed and smoothed out the material.

He merely chuckled as he caught her hand and brought it to his lips for a kiss.

She swallowed. "Let's go below before we reach that German boat. I've used up all my pleasant smiles."

Erik's expression flattened, and he released her hand.

Had he taken her remark personally? "I really doubt I can bear the sight of one more arrogant German," she elaborated.

His face remained unreadable as he turned to Charles Bridgeport and spoke in English. "Annelise is tired. Would you show us to our stateroom now?"

Bridgeport gave a man-to-man wink. "You bet." He led the way into an elegant spacious lounge and down a steep flight of stairs to a hall that bisected the lower level. "This way." He headed toward the bow, hemming Annelise in between himself and Erik.

Bridgeport stopped at a door. "We've put the children in here with you, as requested. I know it's crowded with so many of us on board, but it'd be no trouble at all to make a pallet for the little ones on the floor of the crew's cabin."

It was a ploy to accommodate the newlyweds, Annelise knew. "I'd feel better if they were with me. I guess it's just that maternal instinct we women have."

Erik frowned at Charles. "So many of us. Are there more people than we expected?"

He nodded. "Three. And Axel also brought some ID cards for you to doctor. . .when you have time." His knowing grin evaporated when his gaze switched to Annelise. He opened the door to the stateroom so they could pass. "Herr und Frau Nielsen," he announced in fractured German and closed himself outside.

Annelise barely had time to admire the rich furnishings. The children charged out of the bathroom in street clothes, having switched outfits with other children who'd attended the wedding. Even Rachel's rag doll sported her original calico, none the worse for wear. The money inside would reimburse the new family that provided care for the children.

"You are here! You are here!" Moshe jumped up and down, his huge brown eyes as bright as his sister's. "And the big boat—it is moving!" He dashed to the nearest porthole.

Annelise bolted madly after him and whisked him away

from it. "No. You mustn't look out the window. Not until the German boat is gone. Someone might see you."

"But I want to see," he whined, trying to squirm free.

"You said we'd be safe on this boat," Rachel complained.

Erik took Moshe from Annelise, then reached for Rachel's hand and walked them to the bed, where he sat on the satin coverlet, a child on each knee. "I know it's been hard on you hiding out all the time. But we need you to be patient a little while longer. By tomorrow morning the German patrol boat should be gone, and then you can play on deck as much as you want. How's that?"

But instead of the smiles Annelise expected to see on their impish faces, Rachel's expression contorted into rage as she clutched her dolly tightly to herself. "That is what everyone says. Tomorrow you will be safe. Tomorrow you won't have to hide. Always tomorrow." She shoved at Erik's chest. "Those mean old Nazis always try to catch us and hurt us. I hate them. If I had a gun, I would shoot every single one." Her lower lip pushed out as she buried her nose in her doll's yarn hair.

"Me, too." Scowling, Moshe pointed his fingers like a make-believe gun and squinted. "Pow! Pow! Pow! They are all dead."

Knowing just how the youngsters felt, Annelise began removing pins from her veil.

"Oh, now, none of that," Erik soothed, gathering the pair into his arms again. "It would be easy to hate the Nazis, I know. They've done a lot of cruel things to a lot of innocent people. But God tells us in the Bible that if we love Him, we must forgive our enemies. If we don't, He won't forgive us for the bad things *we* do."

Rachel peered up at him, only slightly placated. "But they

are bad all the time. They never stop."

He nodded. "And one day, if they don't quit doing those hateful things, God will punish them worse than they hurt other people. We need to ask God to help us not to hate them and help us to forgive them. And we can pray they'll stop hurting people before it's too late, because God doesn't want anyone to harm His children." Erik kissed her cheek. "Especially His pretty little flower girls."

"And ring bearers," Moshe added importantly.

"And His big handsome ring bearers." Laughing, Erik gave him a hug and kiss, too.

Giggles erupted as Erik started tickling them.

Removing her veil and jewelry, Annelise wished she could join in on the happy moment. But Erik's words about forgiveness were deeply convicting. She had never forgiven her father. Not once had she been as concerned about his soul as she'd been about her own hurt feelings. Then, even worse, she had transferred her distrust of her father onto Erik. Yet from the very first, he'd thought of her well-being before his own, always shielding her from harm as he'd done earlier today when it appeared they'd been caught. She didn't deserve to be in the same room with a man of his caliber.

Tears stung her eyes. "If you'll excuse me," she murmured, picking up her suitcase, "I'd better change out of this lovely gown before I muss it."

In the bathroom, Annelise undressed, then took a warm shower to muffle her wrenching sobs. She had been so stupid. So heartless. Going to church every Sunday, vowing to God to forgo the love of men for the more holy calling of serving others. Having morning and evening devotions in the privacy of her room. Now she could see how pointless that was without God's love in her heart.

What had her mother cautioned her about before she left America? *Never hold on to bitterness, my child. In the end, it hurts no one more than yourself.* She was right. Annelise understood that now. Her mother had been crushed, but she'd never given up on the Lord. She'd trusted God to see her through, to give her the strength to forgive the husband who had betrayed her in the worst possible way. *Give God your pain,* she had said. *He loves us so much, He wants to take it upon Himself. Trust Him to do this for you.*

Annelise closed her eyes, letting the warm water pour over her, cleansing her body. *Dear Lord, for too long I have held on to the bitterness I feel against my father, and it has paralyzed me. Forgive me for sinning against You and causing You pain. Please give me strength to forgive him for his. . .weaknesses. Fill me with Your love instead.* As she prayed, Annelise felt her unforgiveness spilling from her, flowing down the drain with the water from the shower. For the first time in ages she felt free. . .almost weightless as she turned off the faucets and stepped from the enclosure.

Drying off with a fluffy towel, she gradually became aware of the silence in the next room. Erik and the children must have gone to get a bite to eat. It was dark outside the porthole. They had to be hungry.

She reached for the change of clothes she'd brought in with her and dressed quickly so she could join them. As she brushed her hair, the mirror revealed eyes puffy and red. Not wanting to be the cause of questions or concern, she splashed cold water on them. It helped but didn't completely banish the telltale signs caused by crying. Eventually she gave up and stepped out of the bathroom.

To her surprise, Erik and the children lay in a jumble of legs and arms on the bed, fast asleep. A tenderness enveloped Annelise as she drank in the loving peaceful picture they made. Not wanting to disturb them, she slipped silently from the stateroom and returned above deck.

No one was in the lounge, so she walked out the door opposite the side where the German patrol boat cruised. Anything to prevent the odious reminder of the war from ruining her view or her mood.

The sun was sinking into the western horizon, its bright rays turning the sea into a blaze of glory. As the glowing orb disappeared, she closed her eyes and turned her face into the brisk salty wind, letting the breeze cool the fire in her own face. She breathed deeply. . .the pure freshness was just what she needed.

"You've been crying."

Annelise swung toward Erik's voice. Her fingers rose in reflex to her still puffy face. "Just being a silly girl, I suppose."

"No," he gently disagreed. "It's probably a little more than that, if I'm any judge. Like finding yourself suddenly married—and to such an ordinary guy as me, to boot."

She could tell he was deadly serious. She answered in the same vein. "Oh, Erik, don't you know you are anything but ordinary? You're the kind of man any woman would give her eyeteeth to find. You're everything wonderful that exists in this world."

From the doubtful look on his face, he wasn't buying it. "If I'm all that terrific, why is it you don't want me?"

Annelise had to look away. "I have nothing against you personally. It's—"

"Your father?"

She swung back. "How did you know about him?" As soon as the words left her lips, she rolled her eyes. "Axel, no doubt."

He only smiled. "He does keep himself busy."

Annelise gave a caustic laugh. "Himself and everyone else."

"Getting back to us. . ." Erik collected her hands and searched her face. "Dare I believe you've decided I can be trusted after all?"

She gazed into his eyes, nearly drowning in all they left unsaid. Hoping she wasn't seeing something that wasn't there, she took a breath and risked everything. "I trust you with my life, Erik Nielsen. From now until forever. . .if you're so inclined."

Now it was his turn to search her eyes. "*Inclined?* I've loved you from the first moment I saw you. I know it sounds crazy. You have no idea how many talks I've had with God about it."

"And what did He say?" She couldn't help smiling.

"Oh, seems it was His plan all the time." Erik's own growing smile rivaled the sunset.

He wanted her. He'd even talked to the Lord about her. How unutterably sweet. "I. . .love you, too, Erik. . .but I don't deserve you."

His eyes darkened with pleasure. "That's okay. I'll take you anyway." He drew her into his arms. "From what I hear, I'm perfect enough for both of us."

He thought that, did he? The man's head was getting much too big.

But before she could tell him so, he bent closer. "Welcome aboard my humble abode, Mrs. Nielsen." Then, lowering his head, he covered her mouth with his. . .and showed her just how perfect he truly was.

SALLY LAITY

Sally spent the first twenty years of her life in Dallas, Pennsylvania, and calls her self a small-town girl at heart. She and her husband, Don, have lived in New York, Pennsylvania, Illinois, and Alberta (Canada) and now reside in Bakersfield, California. They are active in a large Baptist church where Don teaches Sunday school and Sally sings in the choir. They have four children and fourteen grandchildren.

Sally has always loved to write, and after her children were grown she took college writing courses and attended Christian writing conferences. She has written both historical and contemporary romances and considers it a joy to know that the Lord can touch others' hearts through her stories.

Having successfully written several novels, including a co-authored series for Tyndale, nine Barbour novellas, and nine **Heartsong Presents,** this author's favorite pastime these days is trying to organize a lifetime of photographs into memory pages.

A Stitch of Faith

by Dianna Crawford

Chapter 1

Copenhagen, Denmark—October 2, 1943

It had been a hard day at the bicycle factory. And eerily unnerving. Sorena Bruhn expelled a weary breath as she unlocked the door to her cramped, one-room apartment. As she stepped inside, the air seemed even damper and colder than it had been on the walk home. Winter was descending faster than usual this year. She carefully removed her hat, trying not to dislodge any of the pins holding up her workday knot of hair.

Turning the light knob on, she pulled her brown tweed coat closer to her throat and quickly moved to the radiator under one of her two stingy windows. She swung the lever that would allow heat to come up from the basement, hoping to feel more comfortable once some warmth filled the plainly furnished room. Afterward she'd be able to shake the uneasiness she'd felt at work all day. . .the whispering among the women that would come to an abrupt stop whenever she stepped anywhere near the assembly line. Even though Sorena told herself they couldn't be talking about her, obviously her coworkers hadn't wanted her to hear what they were saying. Trust was a rare commodity these days.

She'd come to the city only a short time ago, and talking about herself was something she no longer did lightly. She'd divulged only that she'd come from the Isle of Fyn seeking work to help her family. She'd told no one that in the same year she'd become a bride, she'd then become a widow and fatherless. Even seventeen months after the murder of her husband and her father, she couldn't talk about the terrible loss without blurting out her hatred for the Nazis—hatred for the cruel way they'd left her loved ones to drown. Now the despised Germans overran Copenhagen, and even more despicable informers reported every suspicious word or action to the Gestapo. She couldn't risk exposing her own animosity to her fellow workers for fear of getting arrested. And without the money she sent home, her mother and sisters would go hungry.

Still, the women on the assembly line had an important secret they weren't sharing with her. But what?

Unable to shake the feeling that something was dreadfully wrong, she leaned to the side of the radiator and peeked past the blackout curtain to the dark street two floors below. All was quiet. Nothing moved. No trucks, no taxies, no pedestrians. Too quiet for six thirty in the evening. Curfew wouldn't be enforced for more than an hour.

A shiver coursed through her body. She ran her hand over the metal coils of the radiator but felt only the beginnings of warmth—still too cold to remove her overcoat. Perhaps something hot in her stomach would help take away this strange foreboding.

A mere step from the window, her sink counter, stove, and icebox ran along one wall of her narrow room. She reached into a curtained cupboard below to retrieve a pan for yet another lonely meal.

She'd thought leaving the Isle of Fyn would help her forget, but the nightmares had simply followed her. . .Papa and her beloved Curt crying out to her, begging her to save them from the sea they'd been tossed into when they'd refused to hand over their cargo ship. Every day, every time she saw a Nazi strutting up the street in his black uniform and shiny boots, her only desire was to do to him what his comrades had done to her and her family—these killers who pretended friendship as they stripped Denmark of its food and coal while waiting for the moment when Hitler would unleash his full force on their supposed allies.

Pain.

Her hands.

She opened her clenched fists and saw nail indents. Rubbing fingers across her palms, she drew comfort from the fact that not all Danes were being submissive. Every night or so, she was awakened by an explosion somewhere in the city. The underground was resisting the tyranny as best it could until the forces gathering in England came to liberate her small nation. If they ever did. The Germans had been occupying Denmark since 1940.

Perhaps the whispering at the factory today was about the Allied Forces coming. At the mere thought they might invade soon, a thrill spiraled through Sorena. She pushed aside the black cloth again, but this time to search the skies for warplanes.

A sudden pounding on the door shot through her like bullets. No one ever came to her flat.

She whirled around, her heart throbbing as she stared at

the flimsy, paneled barrier.

Nazis? The Gestapo? What did they want with her?

"Open up! Please!" a woman's voice cried.

Sorena nearly sank to the floor with relief. Straightening her shoulders, she started for the entrance.

"Hurry!" came the insistent plea from the other side.

Swinging open the door, Sorena found her neighbor Mrs. Levin standing in the hall. The woman's dark eyes looked as wild as her unkempt hair. Her eight-year-old son was beside her, straining against the two-handed grasp his mother had on his arm.

The woman shoved the boy at Sorena. "Take Shimon. Keep him in there with you. Promise me. Keep him quiet, and no matter what you hear, don't let him out."

"No!" The boy wrenched free.

Mrs. Levin caught hold of his jacket collar and spun him back to Sorena. "Please. I want him safe."

Sorena pulled the rigid boy to her, trapping him within the circle of her arms, then returned her attention to his mother. But before she could question her, the frantic woman pushed Sorena and the boy back into the room and slammed the door in their faces.

"Lock it," came her muffled hiss from the other side.

Shoving the bolt home, Sorena retreated from the entrance, practically dragging the dark-haired boy to the small kitchen table and chairs abutting the space between the two windows. She took hold of his bony shoulders and shoved him into one of the chairs, then pulled the other chair over and sat so she could directly face his rebellious umber eyes. "What's wrong? Tell me."

"The Nazis. They're coming for us tonight."

"I don't understand. Your father's been bedridden since I moved in. What could they possibly want with him?"

"We're Jews. They're coming to take us away tonight. Every Jew in the city. Mama said they won't check your room because you're not a Jew."

"They can't do that. They agreed not to. . ." She didn't finish what would have been an idiotic statement. All summer the Germans had been tightening their grip on the Danes, passing edict after edict, enforcing a curfew. No pretense remained when they disbanded the Danes' small army, confiscating their weapons. And now the Nazis were going to do here what they'd done in every other country they'd occupied: ruthlessly strip all the Jews of their worldly goods and ship them off to some distant slave labor camp.

But Shimon's father was dying of cancer. Surely even the heartless Nazis would see no profit in taking this small family. Yet when it came to the Gestapo, Sorena knew firsthand the evil they were capable of perpetrating.

She took the boy's hands. "Who told you the Gestapo was coming?"

The contortion of fear and hatred made his thin face look years older. "Mr. Goldstein from downstairs warned us a little while ago, but Papa's fever is up again, and he can't be moved. Papa tried to get Mama to take me and go with them, but she wouldn't leave him. She tried to send me." His eyes narrowed. "But I ran down the street and hid until I saw the Goldsteins sneaking away down the alley with their suitcases."

"No wonder your mother is so upset. You should have gone with them."

"I'm not leaving Mama. She needs me to help take care of

Papa. I'm the one who goes out to buy food and fetch the doctor when Papa gets bad and. . ."

The drone of an engine and truck tires rumbling across the cobblestones carried through the window. Then the terrifying sound of screeching brakes.

Gripping Shimon's arm, Sorena moved with him to the window and inched the blackout curtain aside enough to peek.

Nazi soldiers poured off the back of a covered military truck, their rifle barrels reflecting the red of the vehicle's taillights. They charged toward the apartment building's entrance.

Sorena pulled Shimon tight against her.

The clatter and scrape of numerous boots filled the entry hall. The soldiers were inside! Pounding, banging on a door two flights below. Angry shouts echoed up the stairwell.

"They're at the Goldsteins' apartment!" Shimon's voice pitched high with fear.

Sorena covered his mouth with her hand.

His body jerked as they heard wood splintering, the crash of glass, furniture smashed against walls.

More shouts. Boot steps stampeding up the stairs. They were coming.

"Get under the bed," Sorena demanded, trying not to let her fear paralyze her. She pulled Shimon toward the single bed along the side wall.

He balked, struggling to free himself. "No. I have to go. *Mama*."

"No. You're to stay with me." She pinned him against her.

"Ma—" His shout was stopped by Sorena's hand.

She wrestled him down on her bed just as she heard the soldiers crash through the Levins's door.

Shouted demands, some in Danish, some in different German dialects, spilled over each other in a wild jumble.

"When they see how sick your father is," Sorena whispered fast into Shimon's ear, "I'm sure they'll leave them there." *Lord, let it be true,* she added silently. Mr. Levin was much too ill to walk, much less be anyone's slave.

The shrill shouting of Mrs. Levin ripped through the adjoining wall. "He's sick! He's sick! Don't touch him!"

Sorena pulled Shimon to her chest and covered both the boy's ears, wishing she could shield her own against the strident jumble of male shouts, the barrage of smashing furniture, and the shattering of glass.

Then, as quickly as the soldiers stormed in, they left, accompanied by more shouts and loud clomping. Gradually the noise faded away.

Although the boy struggled to free himself, Sorena continued to hold him until she heard the grinding of gears from the street below, then the receding rumble of the truck.

Once she loosed her grip, however, Shimon sprinted for the entrance, wrenching the bolt aside and flinging wide the door. "Mama! Papa!" Before Sorena could reach him, he ran to his apartment.

She followed close on his heels, then almost bumped into him as he stopped, frozen just inside the room.

The apartment resembled a newsreel she'd once seen of the destruction left by an American tornado. Everything was overturned and smashed. Broken glass crunched beneath their feet.

"Mama!" Shimon again shot into action. Frantically he raced around the room, flinging blankets and clothes aside, lifting mattresses in search of his parents. Then with one quick look at the front window, he dashed out of the apartment. "Mama!"

Sorena charged after him.

People living in the rooms across the hall had ventured out as far as their threshold, their expressions mirroring Sorena's own distress.

"Stop him!" she cried out. "Stop that boy!"

But before the neighbors could react, Shimon sped down the first flight.

Sorena went after him, taking two steps at a time. She had to catch him before he reached the bottom.

She didn't. He slammed out the ground-floor entry several yards ahead of her.

Reaching the sidewalk, she knew he'd be following the truck. She stretched out her legs, gaining speed as she'd done in school competitions. But this was a far more important race. The child's very life depended on her winning.

❦

Axel Christiansen rode the brake and clutch pedals of his sedan, slowing to a crawl as he searched for Britta Garbor's home. In the darkness, the crowded townhouses all looked alike. It was vital he and his accomplice get to the party at General von Hanneken's mansion early. Axel turned the steering wheel until his tires hugged the curb, hoping the auto's hooded headlamps would illuminate Britta's green door. Tonight of all nights it was imperative to mingle with the Nazi High Command from the moment the first guests arrived, gleaning every possible scrap of information. Better yet, they needed to keep the Third Reich so amused that the high-ranking officers would neglect to check on the progress of their odious orders.

From behind, Axel heard the sound of running footsteps. He swiveled around and saw a young boy running hard, as if for his very life. The boy had curly black hair, so typical of a Jewish child. The roundup of the Jews must have already begun.

Fully aware of the danger, Axel reached across and opened the passenger door, shoving it wide. "Boy! Get in!"

Too late. The youngster had already shot past.

More rapid footsteps. A woman, her overcoat flapping out behind her, ran with equal fervor several yards behind the boy.

"Quick! Get in!" Axel shouted. He couldn't let the Gestapo seize them. "We'll catch him up ahead."

Her breathing labored, she glanced his way. An instant later, she was beside him. "Go! Fast!" Fiercely she motioned him forward.

Axel tromped on the gas pedal, and within seconds they were gaining on the boy. . . .Axel, dressed in his tailored tuxedo, and this frantic redhead with much of her hair tumbled from its pins.

The boy rounded a corner.

They followed, and a second later the sedan nosed ahead of the fleeing child.

"Get him now." Axel smashed down on the brake and clutch.

The woman leaped out and blocked the boy's path.

He dodged past her.

She was just as quick. Catching him around the waist, she swung him into the auto.

Axel grabbed the youngster's arm and pulled him to the middle as the woman slid onto the seat.

"No!" the boy rasped as he gasped for air. "Mama. . .the truck. See?"

Axel's gaze followed where the boy pointed. A short half-block ahead the red taillights of a German military truck punctured the darkness. In his preoccupation, Axel hadn't noticed the truck.

Two soldiers stood at the back, their rifles aimed toward the interior of the large army transport. Other soldiers disappeared inside a building.

"Climb over the seat," Axel blurted. "Get down low."

The woman didn't have to be told twice. Surprisingly agile in the limited space, she tossed the boy over, then followed, pulling him down to the floorboard with her.

Axel knew that if he turned the sedan around, it would look suspicious, and the driver of the truck would likely give chase. He'd get the numbers off Axel's license plate even if he couldn't catch the much faster auto. Axel also knew that his stopping a half-block short of the truck didn't look much better, but he could easily conjure some plausible excuse. He'd spent the past three years smooth-talking his way around the Germans.

"Cover your heads with your coats," he said over his shoulder to the two on the floorboard. He then pressed down on the gas pedal while easing off the clutch, moving the sedan slowly toward the truck, hoping against hope they would not order him to halt. "If they stop us, don't breathe," he whispered, keeping the movement of his mouth to a minimum.

The woman rose up just behind him. "What did you say?"

Suddenly Axel's back door flew open.

"The kid! Don't let go of—"

The boy dove out onto the street. "Mama!"

The soldiers wheeled around.

Chapter 2

The soldiers' flashlights zeroed in on Axel's face, blinding him.

"Go!" the woman shouted as the car's back door slammed shut. "I've got the boy!"

Axel floor-boarded the sedan, swerving past the beams of light.

"Halt!" a soldier shouted. "Halt, or I will shoot!"

"Get down!" Axel raced through the intersection, then quickly shifted into second gear, striving to reach the next corner and turn before the Nazis fired.

A bullet exploded through the rear window, spraying the interior with glass.

His passengers screamed.

"Are you hurt?"

Another shot pierced the trunk.

The corner.

Axel slammed on the brake and skidded around it.

More screams came from the backseat as the vehicle tilted onto only two wheels. . .tipping. . .tipping. . .

A breathless moment later, the auto righted itself with a

thud, and Axel shifted into high gear, resuming top speed. He glanced in the rearview mirror and beyond the shattered window to see if the military truck still pursued. He'd have to resort to shifting down whenever he needed to reduce speed. His taillights would be a dead giveaway.

Seeing no sign of headlamps, he relaxed slightly. "You never answered. Are either of you injured?"

"Shimon, are you hurt?" the woman asked.

No immediate answer came. Had the boy been killed?

Grabbing hold of Axel's seat back, the boy popped up and screamed into his ear. "No. Let me out! My mama's in that truck!"

The woman wrenched him away. "Your mama told me to keep you safe, and that's what I'm going to do. If she'd wanted you to go with her, she would've taken you."

Through the mirror, Axel made out the shadowy figures of the two as the woman forced the tense child onto her lap and held him tight, speaking in soothing tones.

"I know you're afraid right now, Shimon. But the best thing you can do for your mother and father is to be safe, so they don't have to worry about you. It's very, very important to your parents. Please don't take that away from them."

A pair of headlights suddenly haloed their silhouettes. *The truck?*

"Hold on!" Axel veered to the left and rounded the next corner. He pushed in the headlamp button, sending the street into instant darkness, then turned right.

The next few minutes passed with no sign of another vehicle.

"Watch for a phone booth," he called back to the pair. "It's imperative I call my family. They have to be warned."

"Why? I doubt the soldiers could identify a man inside a car on such a dark night."

"They recognized me, all right. I own one of the few Cadillac sedans in Denmark."

"I see."

Axel detected the same disdain in her voice he'd heard from others who assumed he was a collaborator getting rich off the war.

"Stop!" she blurted. "We just passed a telephone booth."

Axel slammed down on the pedal. "Which side of the street?"

"Left."

He turned around, then threw the gear into neutral and set the emergency brake. "Stay put," he ordered and hurried to the booth. Keeping watch on the unpredictable pair, he fumbled for coins, dropping one before he managed to insert another into the slot.

"Operator."

"Konig 5083, please."

He drummed his fingers on the icy instrument, waiting what seemed ages for someone to answer. He glanced down the street for any vehicle lights.

"Hello," his sister, Annelise, answered in her lilting voice.

"Hi, sis. I need to talk to Erik. Now."

"What's the matter? Something's wrong, isn't it?" As always, she had read the urgency in his voice.

"Just get him, will you? Please."

After a short pause, Annelise's husband spoke. "What's up, Doc?" he asked, carelessly slipping into English, their native tongue.

Axel answered in Danish, always Danish. The Nazis must never know he'd spent most of his life in the United States. "I think I've been exposed. The Gestapo are bound to come search the house. There's no time to waste."

Erik took in a swift breath. Axel knew that as an under-cover agent for the U.S. Army, his brother-in-law understood full well the danger.

"There's a stash of money," Axel continued, "hidden in my leather jacket in the armoire. Take it and head down to the fisherman's dock where the Jews are being taken across to Sweden tonight."

"You'll meet us at the pier?"

"No. I can't chance leading the soldiers to you. I'll lay low somewhere for the next day or so and meet up with you at Grams' cousin's in Lund. Now go. Don't give Grams or Annelise time to think about it. Just tell them they have to put on their coats and walk out the back door. God be with you."

"And with you. Be careful. Don't get yourself killed."

Somewhere in the distance Axel heard shouts and a gun-shot. The Germans were having a busy night.

Fortunately, this street was still dark and quiet as a shroud. But there was no time to lose. He hurried back to the sedan.

The interior light came on when Sorena's good Samaritan opened the driver's door and leaned in, glancing at her and Shimon. Getting the first clear view of her rescuer, she saw he was exceptionally handsome—far more so than a man had a right to be—tall, tanned, blond, and impeccably attired in a rich man's clothes. A white scarf was tossed carelessly around his neck and back over a shoulder, making him look like some silly film star. Sorena hoped he had more brains than one of those vain peacocks.

"The Gestapo is rounding up every Jew in the city tonight," he said, stating the obvious. "Is there anyone you'd like to call and warn? Your family?"

That, at least, was thoughtful. "No, I'm new in the city. Besides, I'm not a Jew. I was just helping a neighbor."

"Oh. Well then, if they don't know who you are, I'll keep the boy with me and return you to whatever building you live in. They won't expect me to show up so soon in that area."

"I wish it were that easy," she countered, "but no one ever misses this flaming red hair of mine. I'm as recognizable as you and your fancy clothes. Besides, I live right next door to Shimon's apartment. Since they've just ransacked it, they'll know exactly where to go back to look for him. . .and me, for helping."

"I want them to catch me," Shimon spewed, trying to squirm free of her hold. "I want them to take me to my mama. She needs me."

"Even if you were able to catch up to them," the gorgeous man said, turning his attention to the boy, "the soldiers wouldn't let you stay with your mother, kid. They'd send you to a different work camp. Wouldn't it be better to be on the outside so you can help us find a way to rescue your parents?"

Shimon's chocolate eyes widened with hope. "You're gonna rescue them?"

The man's features softened. "We'll do everything we can."

But then, Sorena conceded wryly, he could afford to dispense hope lavishly—he'd had no problem seeing to his own people's safety. "I just wish my family on Fyn was rich enough to have a telephone, like yours, so I could warn them."

At the slight crinkling of his brow, she knew her barb had hit its mark. Not that she didn't have good reason to strike out at him and his kind. Many was the night she and her family had gone to bed hungry, while he, no doubt, had been sporting around, going to elegant parties, gorging on extravagant spreads of food. Still, she would need to be more careful. . .at least until he drove them to safety. "From your conversation with your family—"

"You eavesdropped?"

"You weren't exactly whispering," she defended, bristling. "Besides, the window *is* shot out. Which reminds me, is it okay if we join you in the front? It's cold, and we're sitting on a pile of glass." Without waiting for his response, she grabbed Shimon's hand and tugged him outside with her, where she shook loose chunks of safety glass from their clothing before moving to the passenger seat.

The driver, too, got in and slammed his door. Once again they were cast into darkness. Just as well. He'd been wearing quite the scowl.

"As I was saying," she resumed as he shifted into first, "you mentioned your involvement with the Resistance. If you'll drop us within a few blocks of where they're hiding the Jews, I'm sure we can make it the rest of the way on foot without being seen."

"I wouldn't dream of divulging where they are. I've seen how well you two manage on your own. No, I think we'll wind our way out of the city on the back streets until we reach the road to Ballerup, if I can find it. Just before we get to the town, we can cut across the farmland to the north."

"Why? Do you know someone who can help us up there?"

"No."

"You don't? That doesn't sound like much of a plan, if you ask me."

"Plan? A *plan*? Oh, yes, that must be what I left at home in my other coat. So I guess we'll just have to wing it." The man was getting testy. "Keep your eyes peeled for street signs while I try to figure out which way is west."

Either the man really didn't know the direction, or he took great care to elude the Nazis, because he zigzagged through the narrow darkened streets of the old city until Sorena had no idea where they were. Thrice they spotted headlights on a road, and he immediately turned and went in another direction. Because he was forced to drive slowly in the pitch blackness of the overcast night, minutes seemed like hours while he strained to keep the sedan in the center of the winding streets.

At long last, he turned a corner and released a breath. "The paving on this road is different. I'm almost positive it's the one to Ballerup."

"If you'll stop, I can go to the nearest house and ask someone." Pulling her coat tighter around her, she reached for the door handle.

"It's the right road," he declared and gave the car more gas.

Shooting him a disparaging look, she pressed her lips together to hold back her retort. There was no way he could be positive, but obviously he was too full of himself ever to take advice from a mere woman.

For someone he'd just saved from the Gestapo, the redhead

certainly was ungrateful. But Axel knew he couldn't let her rude behavior bother him. Getting young Shimon to safety had to be his primary concern.

It appeared that the Lord was with them. The full moon peeked through the clouds, providing much-needed light. To one side of the road, he spied the rubble of the munitions factory the Resistance supporters had blown up the previous month, which meant this truly was the correct road.

His first instinct was to inform the woman. To gloat. But no, it would be more gratifying to leave her and her doubts dangling for a while. Resting back against his seat, he increased the speed, putting as much distance as possible between him and Copenhagen while the moon illuminated the way.

They'd gone less than five miles when bright points of light, headlamps, reflected in his eyes from the rearview mirror. Others crested a hill about a mile behind him. A convoy of at least three vehicles. Coming fast! With curfew in force by now, the vehicles wouldn't be civilian.

The woman turned and glanced behind her. "Do something! Quick!"

Axel noticed a country lane that crossed the road and headed into the farm fields edging either side. Much too open, but he had no choice.

"Turn right," she ordered. "Looks like the road dips down out of sight."

He took the corner, then upon reaching the slope, let the car coast into the depression. He couldn't afford to use the brakes and have his taillights announce their presence to the approaching vehicles.

As the Cadillac eased to a stop, Axel rolled down his

window to better listen for motors in the stillness of the country night.

The redhead did the same, stretching up.

Suddenly she dropped back down. "Go! They're coming this way!"

"Go! Go!" the boy hollered, bouncing forward.

Judging the distance from the main road, Axel figured he couldn't gain enough speed before the vehicles overtook them. He shifted into low and made a sharp turn, driving into what appeared to be the remains of a cabbage patch.

The ground felt mushy and slick. The back tires began to slide.

He pressed harder on the gas.

The car lurched ahead, then fishtailed to one side and slugged to a stop. With the engine whirring to a high whine, the tires started spinning in place.

"Now what have you done?" the woman accused. "We're caught for sure."

Chapter 3

Axel lifted his foot from the gas pedal. He was only digging the tires more deeply into the mire. The three of them would be trapped, left at the mercy of the pursuers.

An instant later, one of the vehicles he'd spied in the distance—a smaller military truck—barreled past on the road. He exhaled a ragged breath.

Grabbing the woman's hand, Axel placed it over the interior light fixture. "Keep this covered while I open the door. I'll go see if they continue on or turn around. I really don't think they saw us."

He climbed out, closing the door behind him. His shoes squished into the mushy ground as he slogged out onto the road, and bits of mud flew from his feet when he ran up the small rise. At the top, he could make out the truck's lights where it turned off the road a mere few hundred yards ahead.

Pulse racing, Axel was just about to return to the car when the lorry's searchlight came on.

He dropped to the ground and lay motionless while he observed their actions.

The bright beam zeroed in on what turned out to be a farmhouse as the truck slowly pulled into the property. The glaring light swung back and forth, exposing a barn, then moved on to smaller outbuildings before the vehicle finally turned around and headed toward the road.

Axel released a tense breath. Maybe the soldiers were satisfied his Cadillac wasn't at the farm, but he knew better than to let down his guard yet. "Send them north, Lord. Don't let them come back this way."

When the truck complied, he grinned with relief. "Thank you, Jesus."

Picking his way carefully back to the car, he knew the next chore facing him would be to get the sedan out of the mud and onto the road again. . .hopefully without too much criticism from the outspoken woman he'd rescued.

He scoured the deeply shadowed field for something he could place under the rear tires for traction but saw nothing. His nose detected only the rotting remnants of decaying cabbage plants. As he neared his charges, he braced himself for the shrew's remarks.

Then he stopped short. *The dolls!* With the cash hidden inside them, they'd been providing assistance for Jewish children for years. Now they'd furnish a different kind of help.

"The truck drove on," he told his companion, opening the driver's door and reaching in for the keys. "I'll get us unstuck; then we can hide out at the farm up the road. We should be okay there—they've already searched it."

The dim glow of the interior light revealed the redhead's wide-set green eyes. She didn't exactly look convinced. She wasted no time opening her mouth.

He shut the door before she had a chance to utter a censure.

Trudging around to the rear, he opened the trunk. In the pitch blackness, he felt around beside the four crates of dolls, trying to find his crowbar.

The passenger door opened.

He groaned. She couldn't be getting out.

She was. He heard the sucking sound made when her foot sank into the oozy gunk, and he smirked. Even someone as stubborn as she would realize she'd have to get back into the car.

Only she didn't. Just as his fingers closed around the tool, she reached him. "Do you have a shovel in there?"

"No." *Does she think I find myself in this kind of predicament every day?*

"Then how do you expect to get us out? This stuff is. . . *awful*." She raised a foot and banged it against the bumper. Gobs of muck spattered the mushy ground.

Axel was in no mood to enlighten the ingrate—not when he could demonstrate instead. "Can you drive?"

"Yes. But mostly boats."

"Get behind the wheel. Be ready to back up when I tell you." He braced himself for a snide remark, but amazingly, after a slight hesitation, she complied.

"I can help, too," the boy hollered.

"No," Axel countered. "No sense in all of us ruining our shoes." He couldn't squelch a wry grin as the woman slushed around to the driver's side.

After prying the heavy wooden tops off the doll crates, he jammed one lid beneath each rear tire and another right behind it. "Start the motor," he called through the gaping back

284

window. "Put it into reverse, and back up very slowly until I tell you to stop."

The ignition caught, and the engine roared to life. That sound—along with a terrible grinding of gears when the woman shifted into reverse—echoed through the still, dark night.

Axel knew he'd made a big mistake, letting her behind the wheel. Boats didn't have clutches. "Cut the engine!"

His order came too late. The Cadillac jerked and lurched backward, spewing crate lids in all directions. One missed clouting him by a hair. The tires gained the mud again, splattering Axel with rotting cabbage and sludge.

"Stop! Turn it off!"

Shimon echoed the command, as if to make sure she heard it over the engine.

Axel didn't even want to think about the damage to his tuxedo. Seething, he gathered the crate lids and placed them back under the wheels with deliberation. After ordering the culprit to move over, he got into the driver's side. Slowly he eased the car back a couple of feet, then got out and moved the wooden tops under the wheels again, repeating the process over and over until they finally regained the road. All the while, he debated whether or not the woman had deliberately set out to sabotage him. Grudgingly, however, he conceded that it must have been an accident. After all, from the moment she'd proved her inability to assist him, she hadn't offered a single piece of advice. In fact, she'd remained blissfully silent.

Axel guided the car cautiously in the direction of the farm buildings. The clouds were playing peekaboo with the moon, sending the dimly lit road into inky blackness every few seconds. Considering the muddy trail they were leaving in their wake, he regarded the darkness a blessing. "Keep an eye peeled for the lane to the farm," he instructed his companion. "It's no more than half a kilometer ahead."

"Are we gonna stay there?" the boy asked. "I'm tired."

Axel glanced over at Shimon, who was now between them again, snuggled within the woman's arm. Tuckered out, he didn't even resemble the fiercely determined kid of a few hours past. "I'll bet you are."

"There!" the redhead announced. "There's the lane. Turn. Turn!"

Figuring it would be prudent not to further alarm the farm's residents, Axel killed the engine and coasted past the house to the farmyard, bringing the Cadillac to a stop in front of the barn. With any luck, the three of them could sleep the rest of the night undisturbed in the sedan.

A light came on, its glow reaching them from the back porch.

The door swung open, and an older man emerged in rumpled pajamas, one hand shielding his eyes from the glare above, the other grabbing a shovel propped against the wall. "Who's out there?" Coming in floppy slippers toward the car, he raised the shovel and held it poised for attack.

"Go. Go," the redhead pleaded.

"Not yet. Let's give him an opportunity to help us first." Axel rolled down his window. "Hello, my good man."

The thin, sinewy farmer leaned down to look in, the shovel still elevated in readiness. "You the ones those Nazis were looking for?"

Axel decided to risk the truth. He'd found that most Danes hated the occupation as much as he did. "Yes, actually.

286

We figured since they've already searched your place, this would be a good spot to spend the night. If you don't mind our imposing on you, that is."

He peered at Axel, then at his passengers. "Why're they after you?"

"They're rounding up all the Jews tonight. We're trying to save this little boy."

The man finally lowered his weapon and rubbed at a couple days' growth of whiskers. "You'll find no Nazi lovers here. We'd better get you and your car outta sight. I'll open the doors to the milk barn, and you can drive on in. I'll close up behind you." He motioned toward the structure, where a small truck with slatted sides sat parked alongside the entrance, beside a low platform holding milk canisters.

"We appreciate it, sir. Thank you." Axel gave a grateful nod.

The woman leaned past Shimon to speak. "Yes. Thank you. Thank you." Her voice sang with emotion.

The gray-haired farmer tipped his head. "We have more than enough room in the house to put you up for the night."

Axel quickly squelched the offer, not wanting to implicate the kind soul. "We couldn't do that. We'll be fine out here. Really."

"Whatever you say. Don't you folks worry about a thing. I'll fetch you some blankets, and you can bed down in the hayloft."

The sigh that issued from the depths of his passenger's being expressed beyond words all she'd suffered this night.

As Axel drove them into the wide center aisle of a barn stabling milk cows, he felt a twinge of remorse for his part in her angst. But when the farmer turned on a naked light attached to a center post, Axel got a good look at what once had been his custom-tailored tuxedo. He glared at the woman. And to think he'd felt sorry for *her*.

"Looks like you've been out making mud pies." The farmer chuckled as Axel stepped out of his sludge-coated Cadillac.

Axel shot a glance at his mouthy passenger. "Yeah, something like that."

"Mama!"

The scream yanked Sorena out of a sound sleep. She bolted upright and searched wildly about in the thin light of morning. Her gaze landed on Shimon, bracketed between her and their rescuer on the hay, his dark eyes wide, his arms and legs flailing against the layers of blankets.

The man pulled the frantic boy into his arms. "It's all right, son. You're safe. Everything's fine." His voice was low and soothing as he held the child close and spoke against his shaggy curls.

A cow mooed and shuffled below, and Sorena relaxed. The three of them had spent the night up in a hayloft pungent with the particular odor of a dairy. Yet despite the harried events of the previous evening, she'd slept amazingly well. She'd actually felt safe. . .even though a man she barely knew slept a mere few feet away.

"No," Shimon moaned. "Mama's not fine. Neither is Papa. He's sick, and they took them away. I need to find them. I have to be there to help, or Papa will die."

Sorena's heart ached at the sadness of his words. Even if by some miracle Shimon managed to see his family again, she suspected his world would never be the same.

"If you *had* gone with your parents," Axel assured him, "the Nazis wouldn't have let the three of you stay together. Your father will probably be sent to a hospital, your mother to a women's work camp, and you'd go to a different camp with men and boys. You'll be more help to them if you stick with me." He lifted Shimon's chin and looked him in the eye. "I promise you, just as soon as the American and British forces land, we'll join them and go get your parents back, along with all the other people the Nazis stole."

Shimon choked back a sob. "Promise?"

The man, who in the growing light looked more like a clod-buster than a playboy, gave the child a sincere nod. "You bet."

Sorena watched him comfort Shimon. Perhaps she'd mis-judged him. The tuxedo and fancy car could be a ruse to fool the Germans, and he truly might be just an ordinary person. Maybe even a seaman like her husband and father had been. One thing was for sure, though—even with his blond hair going every which way, he was still one good-looking bloke. She blushed at the ridiculous sentiment that had come from out of nowhere.

His gaze drifted her way, his expression unreadable.

Suddenly conscious of her own sorry state, Sorena rose from the hay to make a quick exit. Smoothing down her dress and tweed coat, she glanced around for the shoes she'd removed last night. She spotted what must be her everyday walking shoes, though they were so caked with mud they were unrecognizable.

Would they even be salvageable?

As she slipped her feet into them, the previous evening's fiasco flashed in her memory, renewing her irritation. If her *hero* had driven ahead as she'd suggested, her shoes wouldn't be ruined. But no, he had to do things his way, even if it meant getting them all stuck in that marshy mess.

Then another certainty dawned on her. He'd paid a high price for his choice. The man himself had ended up covered with mud from head to toe. A grin slipped into place as she glanced back to view the evidence in the rays of sunshine slanting through the barn windows.

Alas, his back was now turned away, and he had the blankets pulled up over his shoulders.

But that was all right. His Royal Highness would have to come out into the light of day sometime this morning, and when he did, she'd be right there to revel in the sight.

Chapter 4

Axel stirred in his sleep, and a sharp piece of straw poked through the blanket he lay upon, awakening him. He yawned and glanced around the loft, careful not to disturb the still slumbering Shimon. The high angle of the sun's rays streaming through cracks in the barn, indicated they must have dozed off again after the redhead took her leave earlier this morning. But extra rest was little more than they deserved, considering the harried experiences of the previous night.

And what about his own family? Had Grams, Annelise, and Erik managed to elude the authorities and flee to Sweden? Until he received news of them, Axel could do nothing but leave his worries to the Lord. He breathed a silent prayer for them all.

Reaching over to the boy's sleeping form, he gently roused the youngster awake, then rose to his feet.

Shimon grimaced and stretched his thin, seven- or eight-year-old body, then squinted up at Axel as he rubbed the sleep from his eyes. "Time to get up?"

Axel nodded, brushing dried flakes of mud from his rumpled clothes. "I think we slept a good half the day away already.

And I'll bet that lady friend of yours will make sure we know it." The thought of the wild-eyed redhead brought a grin. That one sure was a handful. Always ready for a fight. Nothing like the women he normally chose to spend time with. "By the way, what's her name?"

"Sorena. That's all I know." Shimon kicked out of the blankets. "She's only been our neighbor for a couple months. She lives in an apartment down the hall from us. And she works all the time."

Sorena. Such a gentle-sounding name for a shrew. Finding his dress shoes, Axel banged them against the floor of the loft, dislodging most of the caked dirt, then slipped them on. "Let's climb down from here and find out what Sorena's up to." Hopefully this day held more promise than yesterday had offered.

Stepping from the last rung of the ladder to the ground, Axel noted that all the stalls that had housed cows the night before were now vacant. Had he actually slept through the milking and feeding, the clanging of bells as the cattle were turned out to pasture? Incredible. Even if the dairyman had seemed wholly trustworthy, Axel couldn't recall having let down his guard so completely since the outbreak of the war. Not good for one's health in today's Denmark.

"Oh, wow! Look at this!" Shimon pointed to a spot on the filthy black Cadillac parked just inside the barn doors. The boy ran a finger across one of the bullet holes marring its once pristine exterior.

The gouges and the shattered rear window attested to last night's narrow escape. "Oh well, we're alive. That's the important thing," Axel replied, calculating the time and expense the repairs would involve—not that he could ever be seen driving the car again. "Let's go up to the house. Maybe we can borrow some soap and a towel."

Shimon eyed him with disdain. "Not me. I don't need to get cleaned up. I was inside the car the whole time. I didn't get dirty like you."

"Maybe not," Axel said, cautiously surveying the uncluttered barnyard and beyond to the road before they stepped into bright sunlight. "But you know how women are. I'm sure the lady of the house will insist on both of us washing up."

The youngster cast him a scathing look.

Something moved off to the side.

Axel spun to face it, then relaxed. A dairyman near his own age came sauntering from the edge of the barn, a pitchfork in hand. Obviously not a Nazi.

"Morning," the wiry, muscular fellow said, a broad grin displaying a mouthful of healthy teeth. He leaned the tool up against the lower stone half of the structure, then hooked a thumb around the strap of his overalls as he studied Axel and the boy with undeniable interest. "Or maybe I should make that *afternoon*. It's lunchtime."

Axel offered the wavy-haired stranger a good-natured shrug.

Shimon surprised Axel by taking his hand as they started toward the square clapboard dwelling a short distance away. Gone was the bravado he'd displayed earlier.

Axel made a mental vow to keep the child safe. "Lunch, eh?" he remarked as they neared the dairyman. "That'll sure hit the spot." His stomach growled at the mere thought of the substantial meal the farmer's wife would likely serve. He'd missed supper last night and guessed that the boy had, too. "I'd introduce myself, but it's probably safer for your kind family if I don't. You understand."

"Don't see how knowing first names could hurt." The young fellow wiped his hand on his pant leg, then offered it. "Name's Knud. I live here with my folks."

Axel liked his open friendliness immediately. "Glad to meet you, Knud. I'm Axel, and my buddy here is Shimon. You have no idea how grateful we were last night to happen on such a welcoming farm right when we needed it most."

Knud nodded, his lopsided smile a bright slash in his sun-reddened complexion. "Oh, I have a pretty fair idea of it. Come on. Let's go see what Ma's cookin' up." He led the way to the house.

After scraping off the remaining dried dirt on a worn scrub brush that had been nailed to the floor near the back door for that purpose, Axel followed Knud and Shimon through the service porch. Loaded shelves held a variety of canned goods, stored items, washtubs, and galvanized pails. But all thought of the practical and functional faded as the aromas of good country cooking met Axel's nostrils.

"You've a bunch of hungry men to feed, Ma," Knud commented as they entered the old roomy kitchen, where an assortment of hanging pots and utensils above a worktable reflected the light from calico-curtained windows. He removed a twill cap from his back pocket and looped it on a wall hook beside the door.

A sturdy woman in a simple gray cotton housedress and floral bib apron glanced up from setting the oblong table in the center of the room. Only the most cursory of smiles appeared on her round, weathered face as she silently resumed her work.

Understandably she was less than thrilled over the danger her husband had invited into their home.

"Good morning, madam," Axel said, his mannerly greeting and friendly tone implying his appreciation of her sacrifice. But all the while, he knew he had to be a ridiculous sight in his irreparably ruined tuxedo. He hoped there were no bits of dirt falling from it onto her shiny varnished floor.

The enticing smell of sizzling potatoes reached him, and he turned.

Sorena stood at the cast-iron stove flipping potato pancakes. The sight of her didn't make things any easier. Having risen hours before he and Shimon, she wore a fresh dress and crisp apron, her long hair brushed into an attractive pageboy. Even her freckles looked somehow at home in this setting with this family. But he knew her superior smirk was for him alone.

Axel cleared his throat and directed his attention to their hostess. "My name is Axel, madam," he said with his best smile, "and my young friend is Shimon. I cannot tell you how much we appreciate your kind hospitality."

The older woman reached up a hand to tuck a stray hair from her bun back into place. She raised her chin a notch and gave a resigned nod as her humorless gaze raked across them. "I suppose a welcome is in order, considering your plight. Let's just hope your trouble doesn't become ours as well." Her attention switched to her son. "Knud, take these two upstairs to wash. Food's about ready."

So his name is Axel. Sorena began removing golden-brown pancakes from the skillet onto a warming plate. *He was certainly*

pleasant and forthcoming with these farm folk. But then, it is to his advantage, after all.

His display of gentlemanly manners began to wear thin, however, after a good fifteen minutes had passed without him or the other two reappearing from upstairs. With nothing left to do but wait, Sorena sat at the table with the older couple. Polite conversation had petered out some time ago, so now she avoided their eyes and gazed about the homey room while the elaborate cuckoo clock on the wall announced a new hour and the delicious-smelling spread of food grew cold. Hands in her lap below the plain linen tablecloth, she tapped her fingertips together in agitation. Part of her felt guilty for ruining their nice meal, even though she knew exactly whose fault it was. Undoubtedly the playboy was upstairs trying to restore himself to his former glory.

"The wife says you work at a bicycle factory in the city," Knud's rawboned father said from the table's head, his words more a query than a statement. Plucking gold-rimmed spectacles off his nose, he swiped the lenses with a kerchief from his overalls pocket.

"Yes." Thankful for the diversion, Sorena elaborated a bit more. "I worked there until yesterday. I don't think I'll be able to go back, though. Not after helping Shimon to escape. It won't be safe to return to my flat, either."

"What will you do?" his wife asked, empathy evident in her tone. "Where will you go?" But before Sorena could answer, the woman's focus shifted to the hall doorway and the sound of approaching footsteps.

Axel strode into the kitchen first, his evenly tanned features and incredibly blond hair making even the cambric work shirt and coarse trousers he wore look stylish.

Sorena deliberately averted her gaze back to the farmer's wife. "Thank you, ma'am, for your concern, but I really can't think about anything else until I know Shimon is safely situated." She glanced at Knud, also in a fresh shirt, his light brown hair neatly combed into a high wave above his forehead, most likely to impress her as he'd tried to do every time he'd come in this morning.

She centered on the boy, and her mood lightened. She couldn't help smiling at the effort that had gone into slicking down those unruly curls. "Come sit by me." She patted the wooden chair next to her—the only empty one on her side of the table. Far more comforting to have Shimon there than either rude Axel or the over-solicitous Knud.

The youngster, seeming to appreciate the invitation, ran to join her and scooted into his seat. He grabbed his fork and grinned up at her, exposing a missing eyetooth. "Sure smells good."

"I agree," the gray-headed man of the house said, wagging his own fork at the boy. "How about we all sit down so I can ask the good Lord to bless the food."

Sorena bowed her head but barely heard the rumble of the lanky dairyman's prayer as the two young men took their places directly across from her. Even with a wave from her side-parted hair falling across her brow and shielding her a little, she felt their gazes burning her cheek.

Shame on them. They should be respectfully listening to the man.

Shame on me. I'm the one who should be listening instead of judging others.

Amens sounded from around the table, proving Axel had

been paying more attention to the prayer than she had.

Heat sprang to Sorena's face when she raised her head and found both men still staring at her. She snatched the nearest serving bowl and spooned some sauerkraut onto Shimon's plate, then passed it on and accepted the platter of potato pancakes from her host.

"Shimon," their hostess began, her stern features softening. "I brought the sausage up from the cellar just this morning. It was made from ground goose, not pork, so I do believe everything on the table is kosher."

"Thank you," he said, diving in. "I'm very hungry."

"And you, Mr. Axel," the older woman said, a jovial smile lighting her face, "I must say, your appearance has improved considerably from when you first walked in."

Axel matched her smile with an easy one of his own. "I do apologize if I tracked any dried mud onto your spotless floor."

Sorena tuned out the woman's next gushing remarks. Apparently Axel's practiced charm had completely won the old gal over. Instead, Sorena kept filling her own plate and Shimon's. But once the food had made the rounds, she was obliged to politely chew and swallow her meal across from the two entirely too attractive younger men. . .who seemed to be sharing some private joke. She made a point of concentrating only on her eating.

"Knud and I were talking upstairs," Axel said out of the blue, directing his comment to her.

Knowing she'd started at the sound of his voice, Sorena gathered her composure and settled back in her chair. "And?"

"He's agreed to take the crates of rag dolls I have in the trunk of my car into Copenhagen this afternoon along with his milk deliveries."

"Dolls?" Axel certainly didn't look like a doll vendor. She arched her brows. "Don't you think we have more important matters to attend than selling your merchandise?"

He studied her a moment, then glanced around the table, his expression sober. "What I'm about to say cannot leave this room. That *merchandise*, as you call it, happens to be dolls that were smuggled into this country from America. They're stuffed with money and occasional donated valuables to help finance the escape of Jewish refugees. Considering the events of last night, even you can see they're needed now more than ever. And since I can no longer deliver them personally. . ."

Sorena flinched. He'd put her in her place. Royally. Perhaps she deserved it, always thinking the worst of him when in reality she knew next to nothing about the man. What had he done since she'd crossed his path except try to help her and Shimon, endangering himself in the process? Being rich and heart-stoppingly gorgeous didn't automatically make him callous and superficial. She cringed just thinking of her judgmental attitude.

The farmer's wife leaned forward. "What about the risk to our son? He goes through checkpoints on his way in and out of the city, you know. The last thing we need is to draw undue attention from the Gestapo."

"We thought about that," Axel answered earnestly. "We'll remove the funds from several dolls on top of the lot. Give the empty ones to the guards if they're interested. Knud will tell them you've been working on them in your spare time to sell during the Christmas holidays."

Her rail-thin husband kneaded his whiskered chin. "Sounds believable to me."

"Yes," his son said from beside Axel, taking on a self-important air. "And when I hand the dolls over to Axel's contact, I'll have the fellow arrange transport for our three guests across the sound to Sweden." His gaze reached past the table and held Sorena's, and he hiked a brow as if she were on the menu. "Unless you'd like to stay behind. I'm sure we could keep you busy and out of harm's way right here on the farm." An unmistakable gleam sparked in his blue eyes.

"That's true," Axel said thoughtfully. "There's no reason for the young lady to make that journey. I'd be happy to escort Shimon the rest of the way. Right, buddy?"

The comment stung Sorena. He wasn't missing his chance to rid himself of her.

"Of course," Axel went on, giving the boy a playful wink, "you'll need to carry a doll or two along."

Shimon stiffened. "Who, me? I'm not carrying a sissy doll."

"And I'm not deserting Shimon," Sorena announced, glowering at Axel. She then turned to the farmer's son. "I thank you and your family for that most generous offer, but I promised Shimon's mother I'd keep him safe, and I cannot and will not renege on something so vital."

The farmer's wife placed a hand over hers and gave it a squeeze. "You're a decent, hardworking girl. No one can fault you for standing by your promise."

Kind words for sure. But Sorena had a strong suspicion that the woman would be more than grateful to see the last of the three fugitives. Life would be much safer for this farm family without any strange faces around.

And Axel? He'd be far happier if she stayed.

Chapter 5

Soon after the noon meal, Knud left for Copenhagen, his old gray farm truck loaded with canisters of rich milk. Axel immediately made himself useful by volunteering to do chores around the dairy. As the afternoon dwindled, his latest task consisted of raking out cow stalls and laying fresh straw. . .anything to stay busy and keep away from Sorena. For some reason, he felt a strong attraction to her—freckles, sassy mouth, and all. Aware of a strong personal tendency toward competitiveness, he was pretty sure Knud's interest in her was what had piqued his own.

"That has to be it," he muttered as he leaned the pitchfork against the wall and strode out of the barn, brushing straw from his borrowed work clothes. He glanced down the road toward the city and stretched a kink out of his back. It was nearing dusk, and the farmer's son had yet to return. So many things could have gone wrong. Or, he surmised, Knud may have been delayed merely by waiting for underground resistance contact Johann Zahle to organize an escape plan for Axel and his charges.

Cowbells clanged across a deep stretch of pasture, and Axel saw the seasoned dairy farmer and Shimon bringing in the herd for milking. He grimaced. More work to be done. Peering toward the road again, he hoped to discover the man's strapping son and his two toughened hands coming to help.

But the chore of milking a score of cows was almost finished before Axel detected the rumble of the truck and the clatter of empty galvanized cans bouncing in its bed. As he'd been instructed earlier, he stripped the last of the creamy liquid from a brown Jersey he'd been milking and hurried out to hear how the young man had fared.

Uneven light from the house and barn blended with the truck's headlamps as Knud hopped down from the running board, a pleased expression on his ruddy face.

Axel exhaled a breath of pent-up worry and went to intercept him.

"I have good—" Knud stopped talking mid-sentence when the back door squeaked shut, revealing Sorena.

She appeared almost mysterious, even beautiful, the way the light and shadow played across her feminine features as she approached them warily. "Yes? Finish what you were saying." Her tone had lost last night's demanding quality and now sounded merely eager.

Knud grinned. "The dolls are delivered." He moved closer to her like a moth drawn to flame, then stopped and looked back at Axel. "You were right about the sentries. When I told them my mother makes dolls to sell for the Christmas season, they weren't the least suspicious. Of the eight we emptied of money before I left, only one remains. The guards bought the others to send home to Germany for their own children."

"And Johann?" Axel asked. "Did you find him okay? Talk to him?"

"That I did, and I gave him the dolls and the leftover money." The dairyman glanced again at Sorena and visibly sighed. "I'll tell you all the details. But first I have to hose out the cans for tomorrow's milk."

"I'll help," Axel blurted. After the hour he'd just spent in the barn with those smelly bovines, perhaps the spray would wash off some of the stench.

As he and Knud unloaded the large-handled cans and set them on the slatted platform, Shimon banged out the back door, munching on a spicy muffin. He ran after Sorena coming across the barnyard. "We're not leaving before supper, are we?"

Axel chuckled. The growing boy had not lost his appetite. Mercifully, Shimon didn't comprehend the kinds of senseless horrors his parents faced.

Knud looked much too athletic, muscling off a can in each hand as if he were lifting weights—plainly for Sorena's benefit. "No. You'll be needing a good hot meal in you first."

Sorena looked up from a length of hose she was uncoiling next to the barn. "Why is that?"

Her voice, Axel noticed, had a pleasing huskiness to it, sounding nothing like the shrew she'd first seemed to be. Maybe that shrill tone hadn't been a normal part of her nature. He shouldn't have judged her so harshly during last night's extreme threat.

"You'll be crossing the sound tonight in a rubber raft." Knud set down his cans and regarded her.

Axel frowned. He couldn't have heard right. *A rubber raft?* "That's the best Johann could do?"

"Yes." Knud continued to study Sorena as he spoke. "Your friend said you're lucky to get even that. Everything that floats has been put into service to take the Jews across." He finally averted his gaze from the redheaded beauty. "You'll be happy to hear, though, that the Germans weren't as successful as they might have hoped. They managed to round up only a few folks. Thousands of Jews have already made it to safety."

"Not my mama and papa," Shimon lamented, his young voice full of hurt.

Bringing the hose to the men, Sorena detoured and came up behind the boy. She wrapped a motherly arm around his shoulders. "I know. And we won't forget them. Will we, Axel?"

"Absolutely not." Placing a can on the platform, he mustered a smile for the youngster. "Shimon, would you run in and find out when supper will be ready? I'm so hungry I could eat one of those cows I just milked."

Axel waited until Shimon sprinted away before resuming the earlier subject with Knud. "What about transportation to the coast? It would be too risky to take my car."

"True. Tell you what. If you'll permit me to siphon the petrol out of it, I'll drive you there. We're only allotted enough for milk deliveries." Knud turned to Sorena and straightened to a rather impressive stance. "I'll take you also, if you still feel you must go. I'm sure that with Axel's experience in the Resistance, he's more than capable of seeing Shimon to safety. If they did happen to get caught, what help could you be if you were imprisoned, too?"

"He's right, Sorena," Axel agreed. No longer all that interested in ridding himself of the spirited redhead, Axel's concern was solely for her safety. Her staying behind would be best. . .even if Knud's offer had an underlying motive.

Sorena, dressed in dungarees and a heavy coat, sat scrunched between Knud and Axel on the truck seat, her knee knocking against the gearshift every time the tires hit a bump. As the vehicle sped through the night, the roar of the engine precluded all hope of conversation. For that she was grateful, considering neither man wanted her along on the forty-kilometer ride north to Helsinger.

Shimon had fallen asleep in Axel's lap, with one leg draped across hers, shortly after they began the trip. She hoped he wouldn't awaken until they reached their destination—the home of the Resistance worker who would take them to the raft.

Trying to keep her mind off the dangerous journey at sea awaiting them, Sorena toyed with the yarn hair of the rag doll she held and gazed out the window, counting the thinly scattered lights of the farmhouses they passed. Knud had been careful to slow down as they drove through the town of Hillerod, and it seemed the Lord had been looking after them, because they hadn't had to detour around any roadblocks.

"I see some lights up ahead," she said, pointing. "Is that Helsinger?"

"What?" Knud leaned closer.

"Helsinger," she repeated more loudly in his ear.

"Yes. Axel!" he shouted, rousing Shimon in the bargain. "Give your little friend to Sorena. You get down on the floorboard."

Sorena's heart started pounding as she stared hard, trying to figure out what exactly Knud saw.

Axel, too, hesitated a moment, then did as he was told.

Knud reached into the crack behind the seat and pulled out

a smelly dark tarp. "Sorena, cover Axel up. Then drape your legs across him and rest against the window as if you're relaxing. Shimon, pull that cap down over your curls, grab hold of the doll Sorena is holding, and lean against her. Pretend to be asleep."

After checking her own beret for stray hairs, Sorena tugged the boy close as she cut a glance over at Knud. "You didn't have us do this at Hillerod."

"Hillerod isn't sitting next to the narrowest spot between us and Sweden, either. The Nazis keep a tight lock on this place."

"The road. It'll be blocked?"

"Most likely."

"And you plan to go right up to it."

He shrugged. "Don't worry. Leave it to me."

Don't worry! "Isn't there some way we can drive around it?"

"No. Besides, that's what they expect from folks who have something to hide."

It sounded plausible, especially since Knud seemed composed and sure of himself. But Sorena felt as if they were driving right into the barrel of a loaded cannon.

Axel, on the floorboard, squeezed her ankle. "Relax. Play it cool."

Easier said than done. Within seconds, a bright spotlight zeroed in on them as a military truck edged out, blocking the road.

"I'll do the talking," Knud said, shifting into a lower gear.

"But we don't have any papers!"

Shielding his eyes from the glare, he ignored her and slowed to a gradual stop just short of the Nazis. He rolled down his window, the motor idling.

A German soldier with a flashlight in one hand and a rifle in the other came up to the driver's side of the farm truck. Another walked around to the rear.

The closest one hopped up onto the running board and searched the cab's interior with his light.

Half frozen with fright, Sorena silently pleaded with God to help her appear calm and to blind the man to the bulky tarp concealing Axel.

The guard aimed his torch at Knud's face. "What are you doing out on the road after curfew?" he demanded in his heavy German accent.

"Some of my friend Einar Klipping's cows have come down with a fever. He asked if I could help him out. I'm delivering some milk to make up for his shortfall."

The casual tone of his voice eased Sorena's panic, but only slightly. She felt the truck dip as the other soldier climbed up into the bed. She had to stay calm, but with Axel beneath her feet and a Jewish boy clutching her waist, her every instinct spurred her to run for her life.

"Give me your papers." Slinging his rifle strap over his shoulder, the guard stuck out a gloved hand.

"Sweetheart," Knud said, offering Sorena a nonchalant smile, "get my authorization out of the glove compartment, would you?"

Noticing the tremor in her hand as she reached to comply, she quickly used the other to still it, then opened the glove box and retrieved the forms. "Here you are, dear."

While the soldier scanned the documents with his light, the other German hopped off the back and joined his comrade. "Is only milk in back. Nothing more."

His cohort gave a nod. "Good. And these papers seem to be in order." He handed them back. "Now give me the woman's."

Sorena swallowed a gasp, her every sense on edge. Slowly sneaking a hand to the side, she wrapped her fingers around the door handle.

"Sweetheart, did you bring your identification?"

Her mouth dropped open. He was the one who was supposed to have all the answers. "No," she shot back, outrage choking off her voice. "You said you'd get it."

Knud turned back to the guard and winced. "She's right. I did say that. I reckon we'll have to turn around and go back for it."

The guard looked from Knud to Sorena, then frowned and rolled his eyes. "I will let you through this time. But do not let me catch either of you without them again. Do you understand?"

"That I do. Thank you, sir." Shifting into gear once again, Knud pulled slowly away.

Sorena heard some muffled huffing at her feet. Axel. Was he crying?

"You can get up now," Knud announced. "It's safe."

Axel eased up from the cramped position. And he wasn't crying but laughing. He scooted onto the seat, still chuckling. "Good job, Knud. Be sure to wait for the changing of the guard before you come back through here."

His mirth obviously was infectious, because Knud joined him, then Shimon.

Sorena supposed that was as good a way as any to release the tension, though she'd prefer to cry. Or better yet, faint.

Finally the laughter tapered off, and Axel did something most unexpected. He pulled her and Shimon close, as if he truly cared. "Knud, I'd like to introduce you to my secret weapon. Miss Smart Mouth. No man can stand against it."

❦

Once the truck reached the outer edge of Helsinger, caught in the fingers of a wispy fog, Knud took a cobbled side road leading toward the sound. He stopped at a small cottage, whose address he said he'd been instructed to keep to himself.

"You're to knock three times," he told Axel. "Then two. When the door opens, ask for Peter."

As soon as Axel piled out of the crowded cab with Sorena and Shimon, he checked up and down the street just to be sure no one was about. Then, after Knud drove away into the night, he followed the instructions. Fortunately, the person who answered the summons claimed to be Peter. The small trim man ushered Axel and his charges inside.

Axel had to duck to go through the low entrance. The smell of burning coal oil assaulted his nose, but the simple, dimly lit parlor was quite warm, considering the coastal dampness outside.

A woman of medium build in a faded pink chenille robe sat in a rocker near the gray stove. She looked up from her knitting and scoured the heavily dressed threesome as Shimon quickly hid the hated rag doll behind his back.

"Emma," the man said, addressing his wife, "I'll be gone a little while. You needn't wait up for me."

"Another of your midnight trysts?" the woman asked, her brows arched high in skepticism.

Her husband headed toward the back of the house without replying. His only words were for Axel and company as he gestured for them to follow. "Out this way."

Wherever they were headed in the foggy darkness, the man didn't waste time. He set a swift pace.

Axel hefted Shimon up onto his shoulders and hurried after Peter, trusting that Sorena would be able to keep up on her own. Would she call out if she couldn't? She hadn't uttered a word since he'd termed her *Miss Smart Mouth*. Knowing her, he'd probably hear plenty about it before this night was over. Still, he felt a niggling guilt for being so insensitive.

After a fast walk of about ten minutes, they started down a sandy slope toward the gentle sound of lapping water. Where the ground leveled out, the sand was damp, and tall reeds crowded the path on either side.

Peter slowed to a stop. "We'll be leaving the trail here," he said under his breath.

Axel stepped off into mush and reeds. He couldn't imagine who could possibly hear them so far out in the marsh, but he appreciated the fellow's caution nonetheless.

Behind him, Sorena gasped.

He knew she didn't enjoy experiencing a second night of sloshing in mud.

As if understanding her plight, a muffled giggle came from Shimon as he nuzzled within the warmth of the woolen scarf Knud's mother had insisted he wear.

Moments later, the man stopped. "We're here. I've put some blankets in the raft. It'll be bitter cold out there on the water."

Axel strained his eyes but couldn't see anything for the sea grass. He lowered Shimon to the soggy ground. "I'll help our friend haul the boat down to the water. You stay back with

Sorena and hang on to that doll. Could be we'll need the money."

When he joined their guide, the man had one end of the raft above the reeds, a rounded black silhouette against a horizon almost as dark.

Running his hand along the smooth rubber skin, Axel felt along for the opposite end. He found it much too soon. Grabbing the handle, he lifted it up and gauged the distance between him and Peter. "This isn't more than six feet long."

The man shrugged. "Best I could come up with on such short notice. The Germans are watching every craft they know about. Besides," he added as he led the way toward the water, "this is less likely to be spotted. You can launch in water half a meter deep. The patrol boats won't expect to find anyone crossing from here." He paused. "Watch that you don't drift toward the docks, though. The tide's going in that direction. Fix your position on one of the stars and keep going straight."

Trudging along behind him, Axel looked up into a sky of mostly clouds with a lone star peeking out here or there. He had limited experience at this sort of thing and didn't relish having to row across the sound in such a dinky raft with only the illusive stars to guide them.

"I know the stars," Sorena said quietly.

Her voice surprised Axel. He'd been unaware of her presence right behind them.

She touched his arm. "I'll see we maintain a true course."

"Once you get out in the sea lane," Peter said, "there's more than patrol boats to watch out for."

More good news.

The man continued. "From what we hear, the Nazi wolf

packs have been taking a real beating the last few months. Scores of their subs have been sunk or crippled. Something about the Allies having improved sonar. To keep us from observing the extent of their losses, they no longer come sailing in during broad daylight. Now they sneak in by night with no running lights. Watch for them, too. Even if they don't see you, their wake could swamp the raft."

"Right." Axel caught his breath as he stepped ankle deep into bone-chilling water, then recovered. "On my shortwave radio, I heard they'd taken major losses back in May. I'm glad to have it verified. We're winning this war, you know."

"Yes. We have to." The man stopped and set down his end of the raft. "This is far enough. But before you set off, sir, I need a private word with you."

"Sure." Maybe the fellow had some word of Annelise and Grams. "Sorena, you and Shimon climb into the raft while I speak to our friend."

Once they slogged the several yards to a drier surface, Axel was first to speak. "When you were contacted to help us, were you by any chance given word of my family? Did they reach Sweden safely?"

Peter shook his head. "No mention of anyone in particular, but my contact reported a miraculously successful night, and they hope to get the remaining people across in the next couple of evenings. I did hear some rather disturbing news, though. Remember all those Danish soldiers the Germans shipped off to work camps in August? A few of our boys escaped and made it back to Copenhagen. They said the Nazis were working the boys eighteen, twenty hours a day on starvation rations. Some have already died, and it won't be much longer before the rest go, too. They're faring no better than the Jews."

Axel clenched his teeth. He couldn't help but think of the Danish mothers and fathers, and what it must feel like to lose those sons who were the promise of the future. Then there was Shimon and all the other Jewish children he and his family had sheltered over the past three years. Every day that passed, the Germans turned more of them into orphans. "Yes, the Allies have to invade soon. With all the losses the Germans are taking on the Russian front, they're getting frantic. And more vicious wherever they still have control."

"Keep that in mind while you're out on the water. No matter what, don't let them take you alive. You *or* your wife and son."

Peter started back toward the raft before Axel could correct his misconception. But then, what did it matter? They'd probably never meet this fellow patriot again.

When the two of them reached the water, Axel saw that his two charges had settled into the small craft with Sorena holding it in place by grounding an oar. They looked impossibly vulnerable. Too vulnerable. This whole plan was insane. "Get out. Between the patrol boats, the subs, and the possibility of springing a leak in icy water, I can't risk taking you two out there. We'll hide out in Helsinger until a motor boat is available."

Sorena swung to face him in the darkness. "Every minute we remain in Denmark we're in danger. But even if we take our time, we can be across in four hours. It's only seven kilometers across at this spot."

"How would you know that?" The woman always had to argue.

"Because I've traveled these narrows transporting cargo hundreds of times. I'm the oldest of five daughters. There were no boys in the family, so I started going to sea with my father by the time I was eight."

Shimon piped up. "You did? Really? When you were my age?"

"That's right." She focused her attention on the boy. "Taking my turn at the wheel and everything. Of course," she added, her voice becoming testy, "I wasn't required to dig out of the mud."

She never missed a shot.

Sorena turned back to Axel. "Have a little faith. I know these waters. I can get us safely across. Besides, I need to get someplace where I can earn some money as soon as possible. Now that my father and my husband are. . ." She swallowed. "The funds I send my family are all they have to live on. The authorities sank our freighter."

Husband? Dead? And her father? The Germans had taken so much from her, and he'd been angry and upset about losing a few possessions. "Don't worry about your family. I'll see they're provided for. But this is much too dangerous. God entrusted you to me, and I won't risk your lives like this."

"If it was just you, you'd take the risk."

"That's different, and you know it."

"Do I?" She jerked the oar out of the mud and hooked it into its slot. "Shimon and I have already decided. We're going. With or without you."

Chapter 6

Sorena couldn't make out Axel's features in the darkness, and she preferred it that way. She'd openly defied him and knew he would be furious. She could hardly blame the man. For some reason, he brought out the worst in her.

He stood there, unmoving in the shallow, chilly water, facing her and Shimon for several minutes. Finally he spoke. "Shimon, this is very dangerous. If we're sighted out on the water, there's no place for us to run and hide."

"The night will hide us," her little trooper replied confidently. "And so will God." With a resolute nod, he adjusted the woolen scarf Knud's mother had given him more snugly about his neck.

Sorena loved his mettle. Seated behind him on one of the strips of canvas stretched between the raft's sides, she reached forward and squeezed his shoulder.

"Very well," Axel muttered, stepping into the raft between the two. "But this is on your head, lady."

He was angry.

"I shouldn't have said that."

An apology?

"Move up to the seat with Shimon. I'll paddle. You keep

315

your eyes on the stars."

Although Sorena figured she knew more about rowing than he did, she decided it was best not to argue. She handed Axel the oar she'd been using to steady the raft, then grabbed hold of one side and edged past him to join the boy.

"I'll help you, Sorena," Shimon said. "You just point out the star we're going to follow."

His words brought to mind the nativity story and the wise men being led by a star. She patted the child's knees. "I'll do that. The fog seems to be breaking up."

"Well, Peter," Axel said to the man who'd led them there, "I guess we're off. *Mange tak.* A thousand thanks. We appreciate your help."

He gave a somber nod. "God be with you." He gave the little raft a shove, sending it out of the reeds toward the inky expanse of the channel.

Axel slotted the oars into the rings, then maneuvered the clumsy inflated boat around until his back was to the sound.

Sorena appreciated his knowing enough to do that. Perhaps he wasn't a total novice. She swung her legs over to face forward—and to face him.

Shimon did the same.

"God in heaven," Axel said quietly, "our lives are in Your hands. Keep a tight hold."

"And thank You, Father," Sorena added, placing an arm around Shimon as Axel leaned into the oars, "for sending a godly man to watch over Shimon and me."

As soon as the words were out, she realized she'd placed herself in a vulnerable position where Axel was concerned, admitting that she needed him. Truth was, she did. Who knew what might have happened to her and the neighbor boy if it hadn't been for Axel? What other individual would have come to their aid with no thought regarding his own safety? She busied herself by unfolding one of the blankets their latest benefactor had supplied and wrapping it around Shimon. "If we see a boat, duck your face into the folds and get down low."

She shook out another. Then, despite her hesitancy to be too close to Axel, she stood cautiously on the unsteady floor and wrapped the second blanket around his shoulders while he continued to row. She could actually feel the warmth of his breath on her hands as she drew the wool beneath his chin. Trying to keep her gaze occupied with her task, she caught a flash of his white teeth when he grinned.

It had a strange effect on her insides. Heat rushed to her cheeks. She sat back down and gathered a blanket for herself. Knowing how red her freckled face could become, she was grateful for the darkness.

"I see some stars over there," Shimon said, jutting his chin in their direction.

Sorena looked up. The light fog seemed to be drifting toward the west. She spotted a bright star near the northern horizon along with a cluster of smaller ones. Lyra. "Shimon, look just above the hills across the sound. Do you see the star peeking over? That's the one we're heading for. Keep us going straight for it, okay?"

"I will." His words sounded confident, even though his teeth had begun to chatter.

Sorena picked up the last blanket and bundled his legs.

When the splash of rowing slowed to an even pace, she became aware of Axel again.

He leaned forward and spoke quietly. "You're good with children. Do you have any of your own?"

"No. But I helped raise my younger sisters. What about you?" she ventured. "Do you have a wife and children home waiting for you, worrying over your return?"

He put his back into rowing again. "Nope. I've been too busy fighting the war." He hesitated for a heartbeat. "I. . .was sorry to hear about your losses. I hope they didn't suffer."

His kind comment brought a flood of memories. Sorena closed her eyes against the pain and struggled to find her voice. "The North Sea is even colder than this. I don't imagine they suffered very long."

"I see." He started rowing with more fervor.

She was glad he did. That was hard to talk about, hard to think about. And she didn't want to go into detail, especially in front of the boy. "When you get tired, I'll row awhile."

Axel, with Shimon snuggled against him, silently thanked the Lord for keeping them safe. They'd been on the water close to three hours, and not a single vessel had passed. He watched with admiration as Sorena rowed with the efficiency of an old salt. Just a little longer. Sweden's shore couldn't be much farther.

A rumble carried from off in the distance.

The noise came from the east, but a mist hugged the water. Axel could see only a muted glow. He removed his arm from around the boy and stood.

About half a kilometer away, more defined light slowly scanned the water.

"What is it?" Sorena asked urgently.

"A patrol boat. Coming in our direction."

"Straight for us?"

"No. As long as it doesn't change course, it won't run us over. But to be sure, stop and row the opposite way for a few seconds." Axel tried to sound calm for their sakes. Taking his seat once more, he regretted having agreed to bring them out here. Sorena had already been through so much, and so had Shimon. The possibility of failure weighed heavily on Axel's shoulders.

The searchlight popped out of the mist.

"Cover yourselves and get down in the bottom," Axel ordered.

Sorena lifted the oars out of the water and laid them aside as Axel pulled Shimon down with him and covered them both with a blanket. "I'm sure a black raft this small will be hard to make out, even with a searchlight."

He felt Sorena crowd in beside Shimon.

The boy started shivering again, and Axel rubbed his back. "It's okay. They won't see us."

The patrol boat roared closer.

Listening to the approaching motor, Axel worried that his earlier assumption had been off the mark. It sounded like it was heading directly for them! He raised the edge of his blanket enough to peek over the side.

"Are they near?" Sorena asked anxiously, her voice no more than a whisper.

"If it stays on course, it should pass about ten meters away."

He heard her swift intake of breath. "We'll be caught in its wake for sure."

Seconds later, the vibrating roar became deafening.

Axel reached across Shimon and put a protective arm

around Sorena, pulling her closer. If anything happened to them—to her—he would never forgive himself.

Light pierced the blanket covering Axel. The searchlight! His pulse throbbed.

The glare lasted less than a second as it moved across them.

He held his breath, waiting for the beam to zero in on them again. . .for the *rat-tat-tat* of a machine gun. But he heard no shouts, no change in the engine's rhythm. Still, his heart pounded so hard he thought it would burst. "I think we're—"

A powerful wave cut off his statement. Paralyzingly cold water sloshed over the bow. The little boat emerged and rode down, only to be hit by a second surge not quite as strong, sending in more water.

Sorena rose and threw off her drenched covering. "Quick. Soak up as much as you can with your blankets. Axel, you're stronger than I am—wring them out while I row. We've got to keep Shimon warm, get him to shore before hypothermia sets in."

The woman did have a way of taking over. But Axel couldn't deny she made good sense. Far better to have a woman with pluck than some helpless female prone to tears and fainting spells. His admiration for her went up a notch, and he wondered what other hidden qualities she possessed. He plucked up a dripping blanket and wrung it out. Then he reached for Shimon's. The shivering boy's teeth were chattering audibly as he clutched the soggy doll to his chest as if trying to shield it. Axel took the doll and squeezed the water out of it, then returned it to Shimon and began rubbing the boy's arms and back through the blanket to increase circulation. The worst of the crisis was over.

Axel had just relieved Sorena at the oars when he noticed a faint light in the east. The sun would be up within the hour.

"Look." Facing him in the dimness, Sorena gestured straight ahead. "I see the shore. We're almost there." She grabbed hold of the shivering boy and hugged him close. "Just a few minutes more, and we'll get to a nice dry place, find some good hot food."

Axel felt like laughing with relief. Digging the oars in deeper, he put all his remaining muscle into getting them there as fast as possible. They were going to make it to Sweden's neutral ground.

By the time they were within a hundred meters of shore, the predawn light brought glorious color back to the wisps of damp hair that had escaped Sorena's beret. Axel was stunned by her beauty. With the way she cradled Shimon, he would have sworn she could've posed for a painting of the Madonna. But as lovely as she was on the outside, her appearance couldn't hold a candle to the glow of beauty that came from within her. He couldn't help staring.

At that moment, she lifted her gaze up at him and kept it there. Her expression did not change, but a subtle warmth came from her eyes to his. Approval. . .and maybe admiration. Maybe even more.

When she finally looked away, he felt bereft, as if something precious had been taken from him.

Suddenly she turned to him, her eyes wide. "The patrol boat! It's back!"

He swung around. It was heading right for them at full speed. A man in the conning tower had his attention trained on them. Where was the fog when they needed it?

Axel rowed as hard as he could.

Sorena stumbled past him.

He felt the raft dip as she leaned over the front, frantically scooping water away with her hands. Any second now they'd be in range of the mounted machine gun.

※

Sorena glanced over her shoulder as she madly swept her hands through the water. She cringed at the sight of the uniformed soldier at the bow, the machine gun aimed at them. They weren't going to make it. The three of them would die right here, within fifty meters of the beach. Even the innocent child Shimon.

"Dive!"

Before she had a chance to react to Axel's command, he shoved her over the side. She and Shimon plunged into the icy, breath-stealing waves beneath Axel. He shoved them down farther.

Bullets pierced the water, but she couldn't go any deeper. She'd struck bottom. It was no more than a meter deep.

On top of her, Axel buckled. Sorena knew instinctively that he'd been hit. His grip on her grew slack.

Seconds later, the firing ceased abruptly.

Beside her, Shimon flailed about in a frenzy. Had he taken a breath, swallowed water?

Sorena grabbed his arm and gathered him to herself. Planting her feet on the sandy bottom, she broke the surface enough for them both to gasp for air while she searched for the enemy.

The speed of the chase had taken the Nazi boat past them. But now, out in deeper water, it was reversing its engines to slow while circling. In less than a minute the machine gun would be in position to fire again. As long as the three of them remained in the water, the Germans would consider them fair game.

She looked around for Axel and found him facedown in the icy shallows, drifting away from them!

"Shimon! Grab my neck. I need to help Axel." Reaching for him, she used all the strength she possessed to flip his big frame over. Then she clutched his collar and slogged on numb legs toward shore. Shimon's stranglehold nearly pulled her under.

A faint cough let her know Axel was still alive. She nearly cried out with relief.

"Kick your feet out behind you, honey. Help me!"

The roar of the patrol boat's engines grew louder in her ears, but she couldn't spare the time or energy to look back. She made for some tall reeds hugging the shore.

The boat's engines shifted into forward, plowing straight for them.

Sorena feared the reeds would not provide a good enough hiding place. The gunner would surely strafe the shoreline.

Driftwood lay scattered across the beach. And nearly covered by accumulated sand sat a log! "Thank You, Father," she breathed aloud. "Shimon, you can let go now. It's not deep here. Take one of Axel's arms and help me drag him up onto the beach."

The boy's entire body was shaking, but he didn't hesitate. With God's help and precious few seconds, they managed to position Axel's lifeless weight behind the log.

"Stay down," she commanded, ducking out of sight of the patrol boat.

As Sorena moved to check Axel for wounds, the machine gun shattered the air, splintering driftwood in a steady stream of blasts.

Bullets ricocheted in every direction.

A line of shots raced across the log.

Sorena shielded Axel's body with her own as flying sand peppered her hands and the back of her neck.

Then, as suddenly as it had begun, the firing stilled.

The enemy's engines continued to throb at idle as the boat hovered beyond the shallows.

Would the Nazis challenge Sweden's neutrality by coming ashore?

For eternal moments, she strained her ears to listen for their movements above the sound of her labored breathing. At last the patrol boat revved its engines and chugged away.

Weak with relief, and beginning to shake uncontrollably, Sorena raised up to make sure the vessel was gone.

"Look at all the blood."

Shimon's statement jolted Sorena. She moved off Axel and peered down at him. On one side of his head, his blond hair and the sand beneath it were crimson. He was bleeding profusely.

She pressed her hand over the source. "Shimon, your scarf. Give me your scarf."

When he thrust it at her, she wrapped it around Axel's head as quickly as her numb, trembling fingers would allow. "Run up the bank, honey. Go to the first house you see and get help. Fast. Go!"

Wide-eyed, his teeth chattering, the boy took off, scrambling up the crumbling bluff with amazing speed.

Sorena looked down at her fallen hero, this man who had shielded the two of them with his own body. That's when she saw another red stain seeping into the sand—from his leg.

He's been shot twice!

Her fingers stiff from the cold, she unbuckled the belt at her waist for a tourniquet. "Please, Lord, don't let him die!"

Chapter 7

anic and anguish gripped Sorena as she knelt beside Axel, pulling the belt from her borrowed dungarees. His lifeblood was seeping from him. . .because of her stubbornness. With freezing hands she threaded the leather strip beneath his leg, then tugged it tight across the wound and buckled it.

Was he still breathing? Her hands shook as she saw the nearly imperceptible rise and fall of his chest. She touched his arm. His skin felt so cold. She glanced around for something to use to cover him. Nothing. Heaven help her, she had to keep him warm. She lay beside him, spreading her soggy coat over them both. Thoroughly wet and cold herself, she doubted she'd be much more than a windbreak, but she didn't know what else to do.

"Please, God, help Shimon to find help quickly," she pleaded through chattering teeth. "I've already lost two loved ones to the Nazis. I don't think I could bear to lose Axel, too." She felt him take a deeper breath beneath her, and hoped that was God's way of saying He'd heard and cared.

"Down there!" The young voice sounded like Shimon's.

Already? He'd left only an instant ago. Struggling to her feet, Sorena scanned the top of the low bluff.

One fellow, then another popped into sight. They charged down the bank with the energy of men not yet thirty. Close on their heels, Shimon followed, swaddled from neck to ankle in one of their coats.

Sorena had never felt such relief. She blinked back pooling tears.

"How bad was he hit?" the first yelled in a Swedish lilt.

"He's unconscious," she called, "but still alive. You got here so fast!"

"We heard the gunfire," the coatless man offered as he neared, "and were coming to investigate."

His companion dropped down to examine Axel. "Good. You've stemmed the bleeding." He glanced up at the other fellow, sturdy and muscular as himself. "Olaf, help me lift him. We must get these folks inside before they freeze."

Moving to assist, Olaf eyed Sorena, then nodded in the direction of the shore. "You came across in that rubber boat?"

She peered toward the water.

The bullet-flattened raft was being dragged along on the swell of a gentle wave. *And the rag doll!* Surely God's work. Caught in a fold of the collapsed rubber, it bobbed listlessly in time with the raft's movements.

"Yes," she answered past numb lips as she went to fetch the money-stuffed toy. "It was our only choice. Everything else was being used to ferry the Jews across."

"Don't we know it." The one called Olaf grunted as he and the other man hoisted Axel's dead weight. "For two nights now they've been landing all up and down the coast from Hoganas to

Falsterbo. So many folks needing shelter and food."

"But we'll manage to find places for them and for you, too," his friend added as Sorena hurried to catch up to them, the doll in her hand. "We always do."

The men carried Axel to one of a cluster of small homes set back from a boatyard and marina cluttered with nets and buoys.

When Sorena opened the door to make way for the group, a blast of heated air hit her face like a thousand needles. She couldn't remember the last time she'd been this cold.

But no colder than Axel, she surmised as his limp body was carried past her.

Or Shimon. She caught the skinny boy's hand and hurried him inside, monumentally grateful that one of their rescuers, the man called Olaf, had loaned the child his coat.

"Sven," he directed, "we'll put him in the front bedroom."

Watching after the pair attired in the sturdy rubberized boots and knit caps of fishermen, Sorena concluded the home must belong to Olaf since he knew its layout.

A petite blond woman with a pleasant face stood in an archway leading from the tidy front parlor to the low-ceilinged kitchen. Drying her hands on her apron, she motioned to Sorena. "I am Greta Lagerlof. Come. Bring the boy in here. It's warmer by the cookstove."

"Thank you, Greta. I'm Sorena, and this is Shimon."

Shimon balked, planting his feet. "What about Axel?" he asked, oblivious to his own chattering teeth. "I need to stay with him. He's hurt bad."

With her thumb, Sorena smoothed the worry lines pinching his brow and attempted a confident smile. "We wouldn't want to be in the way just now, sweetheart. And you're very cold. As soon as you're warm again, we'll see if it's okay for you to go sit with him. In the meantime, we'll both pray very hard that God will make him better. Is that a deal?"

"I guess," he said grudgingly. "He has to stay alive, you know. Me and him have important things to do."

"I know. So you have to be well and strong, too, not sick in bed."

He nodded and went with her to the kitchen, where their hostess was pouring a kettle of hot water into a large pan.

"Greta," Sorena began, "I'd really appreciate it if you would help Shimon out of his wet clothes and into something dry."

"Of course. And you, too." A kind smile deepened the fine lines on the woman's attractive face as she nodded toward the stove. "I've also made some cocoa."

"That sounds wonderful. But I need to check on Axel first." She gave Shimon a nudge toward Greta. "I'll only be a little while, I promise."

As she started through the homey confines of the house for the door to the bedroom, Sven came out, his sharp blue eyes halting her in her tracks. "I am going for the doctor. I'll have him here in a few minutes." Adjusting the knit cap he'd pushed back on his head, he left.

Sorena's heart contracted in alarm. Hurrying to Axel, she joined Olaf, who was bent over the bed. The man had unconscious Axel lying on his side while he worked off the soggy wool coat.

Still holding the equally limp rag doll, Sorena dropped it on a nightstand. "I'll help you," she told the brawny Swede, and together they eased the jacket off, then Axel's shoes and socks.

His feet, she noted, were even colder than her hands. She began rubbing them brusquely to create some warmth.

"That'll help, madam," Olaf said, "but I think we can do better. Go ask my wife to fill a hot water bottle for his feet. And have her put some flannel sheets in the oven to warm."

When she returned a short time later with the rubber bottle, she noticed Axel's clothing on the floor. The blankets had been pulled up to his neck. She moved to the foot of the bed and lifted the covers just enough to place the hot water container at his feet. "How does Axel's leg look?" she asked Olaf. "Is it very bad? When you took off the belt, was it still bleeding a lot?"

"Ah, so Axel's his name. Good to know. As for the bleeding, with him being so cold, that probably helped keep it to a minimum. And your name is?"

"Sorena Bruhn. The boy in the kitchen is Shimon." She noticed a bloody white cloth beneath the scarf at Axel's head, and all effort at making polite conversation fled.

Olaf saved her the trouble. "Yes, the head wound is still seeping a bit. That's natural. Those are always the worst for bleeding. But his breathing is steady, and your man looks to be in good shape."

Sorena was more than ready to latch on to any scrap of hope. "Do you really think so? Oh, yes, Greta said it'll be a few minutes more for the flannel sheets."

"Fine. Now how about going and getting out of your own wet clothes while I wait for Dr. Heidenstam to get here?"

"I'd rather not leave Axel in case he wakes."

"And I'd just as soon not have two invalids on my hands. Go

on, now, before you come down with pneumonia." He gestured toward the door with a nod of his head.

The man spoke logically. After all, she'd said nearly the same thing to Shimon moments ago. But. . .

Her gaze was drawn to Axel again. He looked so pale, so. . .

The sturdy fisherman took her by the arm. "Go. Now."

Momentarily, Sorena found herself seated next to Shimon in front of the open oven door, both of them wrapped in blankets, with their feet soaking in pans of heated water. Mrs. Lagerlof had been a godsend, and Sorena had never felt more coddled in her life—especially when the lady handed them cups of hot cocoa. She was beginning to believe that becoming warm again was possible. She sipped the sweetened drink and let it trickle down to the cold reaches of her insides. "You have no idea how wonderful this is," she said, hoping to express her thankfulness.

Greta smiled. "This is hardly the first time someone's come in freezing. My Olaf's gotten drenched a time or two himself."

"I know what you mean." Sorena chuckled at her own memories. "I come from a seafaring family, too. Our home port is on the Isle of Fyn." The smile faded. "Or was before the war."

The blond woman placed a hand on her shoulder. "And it will be again. Soon. Our government wouldn't have had the nerve to stop the Nazis from using our railroads to cart their troops across to Norway if they thought Germany was still capable of doing something about it."

"That's encouraging. But the Nazis still rule the Baltic Sea. I can attest to that."

"Not for long. I truly believe God is on our side."

"Yes. He has to be." Sorena glanced at Shimon, a child of

God's covenant with Abraham. His eyelids had drooped along with his curly top. Poor little tyke. He'd been through so much in the last few days and hadn't slept much, yet he'd been amazing throughout the whole ordeal. She reached over and deftly lifted the cocoa from his hands.

Greta came forward and took the cup from her. After placing it on the table, she stooped and removed the sleeping child's feet from the pan, then dried them. "I'll take him into Hildy's room. It's time for her to get up for school anyway."

School? It was hard for Sorena to digest such an everyday happening. "You have a daughter?"

"Yes. Hildy's seven," she whispered, reaching down for Shimon. "This is her first year, and she's very excited about going."

As the hostess carried Shimon through a door adjoining the kitchen, Sorena wondered how long it would be before he, too, would be returning to a classroom. At least that could now be a reality for him.

But had it cost Axel his life?

Urgency overtook her again. She lifted her feet out of the water. Bending to dry them with the provided towel, she heard a quick knock at the door and turned toward the entrance.

The man called Sven burst in, his cheeks flushed.

Right behind him came a distinguished older man in faded black, carrying a worn leather satchel.

"This way," Sven directed.

Before Sorena could get up and secure the blanket around herself properly, the two men had disappeared into the front bedroom.

Hiking the edge of the blanket off the floor, she flew after them. She had to be there when the doctor examined Axel. Had to know if he would live.

He has to.

For Shimon's sake. . .and for hers. There was so much she needed to say to Axel, so much to take the blame for. She was the very reason he lay at death's door. She and her stubborn determination.

Chapter 8

"G ood evening, Sorena." Still wearing fishy work clothes, Olaf Lagerlof strode into Axel's antiseptic hospital room. "Thought I'd stop by on my way home and see how you're doing. Maybe talk you into coming along for supper."

Sorena appreciated the many kindnesses the Lagerlofs had extended to her and Shimon over the past week while she'd waited, hoped, and prayed for Axel to awaken. She rose from the bedside chair. "Thank you. But he's had some eye movement recently. I don't want to leave him yet."

"He's come to?" Olaf glanced at Axel, who lay as still as the day they'd brought him to Helsingborg's only hospital.

"No, his eyes were closed. But the nurse said the movement was a good sign."

"I see." Though he appeared unconvinced, Olaf's demeanor brightened. "I do have some good news for you. I received a radio message from the *Herring Hound* a few hours ago. Your mother got the money you sent. Captain Perrson said they were faring well."

"Oh, thank you. That is such a relief."

"I'll tell you who else would be relieved. Shimon—if you'd come to the house with me. You didn't leave here at all yesterday. Greta enrolled the boy in school with Hildy this morning, hoping to get his mind on something besides you and. . ." He nodded toward Axel.

Sorena gave a defeated sigh. "I suppose that's best. Dr. Heidenstam isn't handing out any promises. But Axel must wake up. He has to. There's so much I need to say to him."

"Maybe. But what *you* need is to get out of this room. Breathe some fresh air. Have a good, home-cooked meal. Even if he should come around while you're gone, he'll still be here when you get back. Think of your own health. If he wakes up—"

"You mean *when*. . ."

"*When* he wakes up, you don't want to be sick in bed yourself." The big man grasped her shoulders. "Take a look at those dark circles under your eyes. If it was me lying there and you were my wife, I'd want you to get your rest."

Her face warmed at the intimate reference, and she smiled. "I will, Olaf. I promise. Tell Shimon I'll be there before bedtime to say good night."

"We'll hold you to that," he said with a mock frown. "Greta will keep a plate of food in the oven for you."

Greta. Olaf. Axel couldn't wrap his mind around those names. If only he could get his eyes to open.

"An hour more. Two at the most," came the familiar voice. "Tell Shimon I'll be home soon."

"Will do. See you then."

Footsteps faded away. The man Olaf had left. But the woman was still here. He could hear her moving closer, hear her breathing.

She'd mentioned another name. Shimon. . .a Jewish name. *Shimon!* Clarity returned. Axel's lashes sprang open, and he lurched up. "Shimon!" Pain exploded in his head. He fell back to his pillow and closed his eyes.

"Axel?"

Slowly raising his eyelids, he focused on the flame-haired woman leaning over him.

"You're awake! Thank God." Tears flooded her wide-set green eyes. She took his hand. "You're awake."

He recognized her. Sorena. She didn't appear to be injured, but what about Shimon? "Is the boy all right?" The words came out hoarse.

Tears rolled unchecked down her pale cheeks as she nodded. "Yes. Shimon is fine. Terribly worried about you, but otherwise. . ." She took a shuddering breath. "Just fine."

Axel raised his free hand to check the source of his head pain. "How long have I been out?"

"Eight days. You were shot. One bullet grazed your skull; another went through your leg." She swiped at her flooded eyes. "I'm so relieved. We didn't know if you'd ever. . . I'll get the nurse." She squeezed his hand and gifted him with a heart-stealing smile. "I'll only be a moment."

Pausing at the door, she looked back. Fresh tears streamed past the radiance of her smile. "You're with us again." Filling her lungs, she disappeared into the corridor.

Axel gazed after the redhead. She sure was emotional about his regaining consciousness. Had she somehow come to care for him while he was asleep and unable to talk back? He marveled as he explored the thick bandage along the left side of his head. Sorena.

He preferred to think she'd started to care before he'd been shot. He'd sensed her softening during that long night in the raft. Even before that, he'd begun to see her with—he hated to admit it—a tenderness. But then after sharing a life-threatening experience, being thrown together night and day, all pretense had been stripped away. They'd come to know each other in a short span of time.

Now that he thought back, there wasn't anything about her he hadn't grown to love. Not even her mouth. She'd seen right through his most devastating smile, just like Grams always had. . .and he dearly loved that old gal for it. Grams knew him for the spoiled, reckless guy he was and loved him anyway. From the look on Sorena's face, she did, too. Possibly.

As his head cleared more fully, other disturbing memories surfaced. Grams. Erik and Annelise. He had to get to a telephone. Find out if they'd made it safely across the sound.

A large-boned woman in crisp white marched in ahead of Sorena. "Splendid, Mr. Bruhn. You've decided to rejoin the world of the living." She came brusquely to his bedside and shoved a thermometer into his mouth, then caught his wrist to take his pulse.

Mr. Bruhn? Puzzled at the address, Axel refrained from speaking around the glass tube. Sorena must have had a good reason for giving the attendant that name.

"Good. Good." The nurse released his wrist. After checking his bandage and fussing with his blanket, she removed the thermometer and read it. "Better. It's coming down. I'll fetch your doctor. He'll want to examine you now." With an efficient smile, she left, leaving him alone with Sorena.

For the first time, he noticed the dark circles beneath her eyes. She couldn't have slept much in days. She had to care!

She pulled a chair close and sat. "You're probably wondering why Nurse Almquist called you by my last name, Bruhn. I don't know yours. Everything happened so fast," she said with a slight smile, "we never really introduced ourselves."

"Ah." Axel's mouth began to curl. "I'm Axel Christiansen, at your service, milady."

"Another thing," she added, pinkening, her lashes lowering. "I've let them think I'm your wife. Otherwise, they wouldn't have allowed me to stay here through the night."

Axel blinked in surprise. "You've been here day and night for over a week?"

She shrugged. "I did go to check on Shimon every day to bolster his spirits. He's been so worried about you. The doctor wouldn't let him visit while you were unconscious. But now that you're awake, there shouldn't be a problem."

"Yeah, I'd like to see the little guy myself. He really grows on you, doesn't he?"

Sorena met his gaze again. "He does. The people we're staying with, the Lagerlofs, have offered to keep him till the end of the war. They're nice people with a daughter a year younger than he is. But I'm not ready to let him go." Her exquisite features softened. "And he keeps reminding me you two have plans."

"I did promise we'd go after his parents once the Allies march into Germany. I know it's farfetched, but I'd like to keep my word if there's any way possible."

"Then you agree," she breathed on a sigh. "We won't leave

Shimon with the Lagerlofs."

She was discussing the boy's fate as if he were their child. *Fascinating!* Axel decided to test the waters even further. "Then for the time being, we'll just keep him with us at my great-aunt's manor house in Lund. It's big enough to billet a regiment."

"We'll live with you? At a manor house?" Her sea-green eyes reflected a mixture of emotions.

He knew if he wasn't careful, he'd scare her off. "Don't worry. It's old and drafty with separate wings. We might not see each other for days on end. And since the economy was so bad before the war, it's desperately short of servants. You won't be living in any more luxury than before."

"I didn't say—"

"You didn't have to. Those beautiful, expressive eyes said it for you."

Her cheeks grew rosy, and she turned away.

This woman would never be able to lie to him.

"What's keeping the doctor?" She checked the wall clock. "He said he wouldn't leave for home until six."

As if by command, a dignified, gray-haired gentleman appeared at the door, a stethoscope draped about his neck.

Axel watched Sorena quietly withdraw and turn her back to them while the physician poked and probed him for what seemed a quarter hour.

"No signs of paralysis or loss of eyesight or hearing," the man commented as he worked. After he recorded his findings on the chart at the foot of Axel's bed, he turned to Sorena. "Mrs. Bruhn?"

She turned back to face them. "Yes?"

"I'll release your husband to your care in a day or two, once the swelling on the brain is gone and he no longer has a headache. Of course, he'll be on crutches for a few weeks, but his leg is healing nicely. There seems to be no permanent damage."

"Oh, thank you. That's great news." The sincerity of her words warmed her expressive eyes. . .and his heart.

"I would imagine. Just one more thing, madam. I suggest you have a serious talk with your man about taking such risks. You could've both been killed—and the boy as well." Finishing in a stern tone, he started for the door.

"But it wasn't. . ." Sorena gave up as he hurried away. She turned to Axel. "I don't know what to say. Dr. Heidenstam shouldn't blame you. It was me. Me. You almost died because I forced you to go."

"No." Axel caught her hand. "I wanted to make the crossing. It was taking you and Shimon I objected to. I couldn't bear the thought of anything happening to you. Or him."

"And nothing did." Her lower lip quivered. "You took the bullets for all of us." Her eyes glistened with renewed moisture.

"Hey." He squeezed her hand. "Didn't you just hear the doctor? I'll be good as new in a couple weeks."

The statement didn't seem to help. "Why must you act so noble?" she practically wailed. "Offering me a place to stay—and after all the mean things I said to you. . ." Her words lost power as she drew a ragged breath.

She looked absolutely stricken. Axel couldn't abide having her feel so down. Not his spunky Sorena. He raised up on his elbow, ignoring the pounding in his head, and quirked a grin. "You know, I'm really starting to like this, you all contrite and apologizing. I'll have to get shot more often."

That did the trick. Her jaw dropped, and she started sputtering, but no sound came out.

Axel's grin broadened. He'd rendered his mouthy redhead speechless. . .at least for the moment.

With bewilderment written across her freckles, she tugged free of his grip and back-stepped toward the door. "I promised Shimon I'd go get him the instant you woke up. I'll have him here in a little while."

"I'll be waiting," he called after her.

When Axel lay back on the pillow, he noticed a buzzer and pushed it. He needed to learn of his family's fate.

Shortly, he was being wheeled along the gray linoleum floor to the front desk, where a phone awaited his use. Once the local operator transferred his call to Lund, he heard ringing on the other end and imagined the sound echoing off the ancient stone walls of the manor.

On the eighth ring, his chest tightened with concern. Someone should have answered by now.

"*Hejsan?*" came his sister's voice in Swedish.

Thank You, God. He released his breath and responded in their customary Danish. "Annelise. You're there. For a minute I thought. . ."

"Axel? *Axel!*" Her shout pierced his eardrum. "Grams! Erik! Come quick. Axel's alive! Where are you?" she asked only slightly calmer. "Why haven't you called before? We've been sick with worry."

"It's okay, sis. I've been taking a little nap, but the doctor says I'll be just fine."

"Doctor! Where are you?"

"At the hospital in Helsingborg."

"Hospital? In Helsingborg?"

"The phone, give it to me," Grams demanded in her gruff voice. "Axel?"

"I'm fine, Grams," he avowed. "I'm supposed to be released in a day or two."

"You are sure? I need to see for myself. We'll take Hannah's Rolls and be there in. . . How far away is that?"

"About sixty kilometers. But I'd rather you wait, Grams. I'll be out in a couple days, and you can come get me then. No sense wasting precious petrol. Oh, by the way, I've invited a couple of people to come stay with us."

"Axel, Axel," she said in exasperation. "You always manage to find someone, don't you? Who is it this time? Jews passing through or airmen or sailors you found out in the sound?"

"Actually, I'm hoping these two won't be just passing through. I want them to stay."

"Oh? Why is that?"

He could just picture the arch in those silver brows. "You'll understand when you meet her. I mean *them*."

"Her? Did I hear right?" Annelise obviously had been listening along with Grams. "Don't tell me your bachelor days are finally coming to an end, brother of mine!"

Axel had to think about that one. But not for long. "If I have my way about it."

"I can't believe it!" she exclaimed. "The Axel has fallen!"

The second Sorena pointed out Axel's hospital room, Shimon forgot her instructions regarding being quiet. He bolted for it, his leather soles slapping loudly on the linoleum, the water-stained rag doll he'd insisted on bringing dangling haphazardly from his hand.

Reaching the doorway, she saw the surprising sight of Axel sitting in a wheelchair, his head still bandaged and his leg propped. He'd already engulfed Shimon in a bear hug and was grinning so broadly his azure eyes crinkled.

So did her heart. She could see he truly loved the boy.

"I knew you'd wake up," Shimon declared, not quite releasing his hero's neck as he remained beside the wheelchair. "Me and Sorena been praying and praying." He eased away slightly, focusing a direct look at Axel. "Besides, me and you still have a job to do, saving Mama and Papa. And God knows that. That's why He didn't let you die."

Out of the mouths of babes and sucklings hast thou ordained strength because of thine enemies. Awe filled Sorena as she pondered the familiar scripture verse. For Shimon to have such faith in the face of so much evil bolstered her own.

Axel must have been affected, too. He shot a glance to her, then took Shimon's slim cheeks in his hands and kissed the top of his curly head. "You bet. Just as soon as the Allies come."

Reluctant to intrude on their man-to-man moment, Sorena didn't venture forward. Watching the two of them together was so touching, she could've cried. But she'd already done too much of that this evening.

"And look!" Shimon shoved the moldy, smelly doll in Axel's face. "I still have this. We didn't lose it, no matter what."

"I'm real proud of you." Axel took the weathered toy and looked up at Sorena. "Both of you."

"But Sorena already took some of the money out and sent it to her mother."

She cringed. She'd wanted to divulge that news a bit later.

"Good," Axel said. "That's what it's for, to help refugees. And that's us."

"Yes, sir," Shimon agreed. "For sure. But not for long." He flicked a glance at her. "Sorena says when you get out of here, we're gonna go live in a great big house with your family. With plenty of food—like at Knud's house. You and me and Sorena."

Axel looked over the child's head and met her gaze. "That's right. Until the Nazis are run out of our country and we can go back home. You, me, and Sorena—if she's willing to put up with us, of course."

"Sure she is," he announced. "She's been taking care of you and praying for you, just like Mama does Papa. And she won't leave you now just when you're better, cause my mama would never leave my papa." He turned to her. "Right?"

The child was making too many assumptions. *What must Axel think?* She felt the blood drain from her face.

"I think we're rushing the lady, Shimon," Axel said gently. He flashed her one of his most charming grins. "She's already promised to come with us to Lund. That's enough for now. Once she's all settled in and feeling at home, we'll show her what a fine couple of chaps we really are."

Axel sported his bandages like badges of honor, and his hopeful grin was almost comical. So was Shimon's gap-toothed giggle. Sorena couldn't help smiling herself. "It doesn't look to me like you're waiting."

Still grinning, Axel reached back for the metal water pitcher on his bedside table and handed it to Shimon. "Be my buddy and go have the nurse fill this for me?"

Obviously proud to do his hero's bidding, Shimon scampered off.

"Come closer, Sorena," Axel coaxed, his tone husky. "We don't have much time, and there are some things I really need to tell you."

When she stepped to the side of his chair, he took her hand, and before she realized what he was doing, he put it to his cheek.

The gesture made her heart skip like a schoolgirl's.

"I know we got off to a rough start. And I know it's sudden, but this experience has changed me forever. It's as if I've spent my whole life standing outside myself looking in. I never took anything seriously. . .until now. The way I feel about you I'm taking very seriously. You're the first woman I've ever met who's seen me at my worst. And by jingle, you're still here."

Hesitating only a second, Sorena knelt down beside him. "I think we've both seen each other at our worst. But don't forget, I've seen you at your best, too."

He leaned nearer. "And did you like what you saw?"

She could barely speak. "I. . .yes."

His gaze gentled. "Did you know I love every one of your freckles?" he asked softly, his breath feathering her face, he was so close. "Especially this one." His lips brushed her cheek.

Sorena's pulse missed a beat.

"And this one." He kissed her nose. Releasing her hand, he cupped the back of her head, and his mouth claimed hers.

Unbelievably, her playboy was kissing her. And it was fine. Perfect. Even exhilarating. With awakening love, she slipped her arms around his neck and returned his kiss. After endless months of grinding sorrow, joy was filling her again. To the brim, and overflowing. . .

From somewhere in the distant swirl, she heard a child's thin voice. "Wait here, nurse, 'til they're done kissing. Kisses make everything better, you know."

Sorena couldn't argue with that.

DIANNA CRAWFORD

Dianna Crawford, a best-selling author with two RITA nominations, has penned seventeen novels and seven novellas. She and her husband have four grown daughters and now reside in the Sierra Nevada Mountains of California. Aside from writing, Dianna is active in children's ministries.

A Letter to Our Readers

Dear Readers:

In order that we might better contribute to your reading enjoyment, we would appreciate your taking a few minutes to respond to the following questions. When completed, please return to the following: Fiction Editor, Barbour Publishing, Inc., P.O. Box 719, Uhrichsville, OH 44683.

1. Did you enjoy reading *The Stuff of Love*?
   ❑ Very much—I would like to see more books like this.
   ❑ Moderately—I would have enjoyed it more if _____
   _____
   _____

2. What influenced your decision to purchase this book?
   (Check those that apply.)
   ❑ Cover   ❑ Back cover copy   ❑ Title   ❑ Price
   ❑ Friends   ❑ Publicity   ❑ Other

3. Which story was your favorite?
   ❑ *A Living Doll*   ❑ *A Thread of Trust*
   ❑ *Filled with Joy*   ❑ *A Stitch of Faith*

4. Please check your age range:
   ❑ Under 18   ❑ 18–24   ❑ 25–34
   ❑ 35–45   ❑ 46–55   ❑ Over 55

5. How many hours per week do you read? _____

Name _____

Occupation _____

Address _____

City _____ State _____ Zip _____

E-mail _____